RIMROCK

•••••

"I'll have that gun you're so proud of, Blanton!"

Reno stood at least two hundred feet from Blanton, and his voice floated on the air with a hollow, ghostly ring. He stood there as if carved in stone, the long-barreled Navy Colt in his holster and his face drawn into angular planes that threw his dark eyes into relief.

"Reno, you'll never take my gun!" Blanton turned to face Reno. "I knew you'd try to be a hero. Well, you just came to your own funeral!"

He started to walk toward the still figure in front of him, but Reno cried out sharply, "Hold it right there, Blanton! Drop your gun in the street right now—or else go for it!"

GILBERT MORRIS

RIMROCK

Tyndale House Publishers, Inc.
Wheaton, Illinois

Library of Congress Cataloging-in-Publication Data

Morris, Gilbert.
　[Deputy]
　Rimrock / Gilbert Morris.
　　　p.　cm. — (Reno western saga) (Jim Reno westerns series ;
　#2)
　Originally published as: The deputy. c1986.
　ISBN 0-8423-1059-2
　I. Title.　II. Series: Morris, Gilbert. Reno western saga.
III. Series: Morris, Gilbert. Jim Reno westerns series ; no. 2.
PS3563.O8742D46　1992
813'.54—dc20　　　　　　　　　　　　　　　　　　　　92-9439

Printed in the United States of America

98　97　96　95　94　93　92
8　7　6　5　4　3　2　1

ONE

Stage to Rimrock

There was no escape from the fine dust that seemed to surround the rolling stage like a dense cloud. Ada Lindsey dabbed at her face, stared at the grimy results, then forced herself to maintain the ramrod posture she had maintained ever since the stage had left Dallas.

Three nights spent in wretched stage stations with greasy meals and dirty beds crawling with insects had etched fine lines in her face, but at the age of fifty-five she had endured the discomfort better than might be expected. She was a small woman, the delicate bone structure of her face and hands revealing her patrician heritage. Small ears almost hidden beneath the brown hair lost nothing by the silver sheen that tipped the ends. Her arched nose above firm lips betrayed the iron will that lay beneath the surface. Dark blue eyes deep-set over high cheekbones made no attempt to avoid direct contact with the men who sat across from her on the hard leather seat.

"Have a little water, Mother." The tall, lean young man who sat next to her pulled a limp leather flask from a space beneath his feet, but before he could remove the brass cap, Ada shook her head and straightened her back a fraction.

"No." Nothing other than this, but there was a studied rebuke in the word which stung the young man. He hesitated, then flung the water bottle behind his feet with more violence than was necessary.

The whale-fat whiskey drummer who sat directly across from him grinned broadly. He almost said, "Mama spanked the baby!" but something about the lean chin and a restless look in the eyes of the young man restrained him. *A dude, all right, but looks like he might be a handful if he ever cut the apron strings,* he thought.

They were mother and son; both had the same sharp facial planes which were somehow not Western. The young man's jaw and cheekbones were pronounced as were the woman's, but in the man they were sculptured into an intense masculinity, augmented by the craggy brows that shaded dark blue eyes. He was lean, but the wiry cast of his torso gave promise of considerable strength which would increase with age.

The drummer, whose name was Smith, searched for a flaw in the young man. It was his theory that every man had one, and usually he prided himself on being astute enough to discover a trace of it in the face. As the stage rocked and swayed across the monotonous Kansas landscape, he studied the young man who had leaned back and closed his eyes. Finally he had it: *The mouth—that's it! Despite all them fine looks and high-falutin' ways, he's got a pout like a kid who's had his candy took away from him!* There was a pronounced fullness to the mouth, especially the lower lip, which gave the face a vulnerable look despite the masculine good looks. But it was not youth, Smith decided. He had seen the knife-edged lips of Billy Bonny when the Kid was younger than this one.

He jist ain't pulled away from Mama's apron string yet. Smith grinned, and diagnosing the young man's character made him feel so good he pulled a full bottle of whiskey from a black leather bag beneath his feet, uncapped it, and almost took a drink. A wicked light appeared in his eye, and he leaned forward and held the bottle out to the woman.

"Have a snort, ma'am?"

As he had expected, the woman looked at him as if he had crawled out from under a rock, her blue eyes icy with contempt. It was what he wanted, and he thought, *Reckon you're one of them purse-poor Southern gals whose feet never touched the ground before the war. Expect you'll git a leetle of that pride rubbed off after you hit Abilene.* But he said only, "No? Well, here's to you then, ma'am. The ladies—God bless 'em!"

The young man straightened up and for one brief instant the drummer thought that he saw enough fire flicker in his face to bring a start of fear. These Southern fools would just as soon kill a man as spit where a woman was concerned. But the moment passed, and Smith breathed again. *Nope—not with that baby pout!* He handed the bottle to the man next to him, a burly cowboy. "Have a snort and pass it on, brother."

The cowboy's eyes lit up and his throat worked compulsively as he swallowed. He gasped as he lowered the bottle and whispered, "Wow!" then passed the bottle to the man beside him.

"Thankee kindly." He was a mountain man, wearing worn, fringed buckskins, and he drank the whiskey smoothly as if it were lemonade. "Mighty fine panther spit." He grinned agreeably. "Yep, some whiskey would draw blisters on a rawhide boot—but now *this,* wal, it's so good you can taste the feet of the gal what hoed the corn it was made of!" He passed the bottle on, considerably depleted, and the two older passengers took their turns. They looked like clerks, with the sallow skin of men who seldom saw the sun.

Finally the bottle passed from a rawboned farmer wearing new overalls to Jeff Lindsey, who handed it on with a shake of his head. *Reckon his mama won't let him drink with the men,* Smith thought. The last passenger, a thin man dressed in a gambler's showy clothing, smiled through thin lips and took a pull, then handed the bottle back to Smith.

"Thanks." The gambler's voice was reedy and coarsened by a thousand nights of breathing harsh tobacco smoke and sipping raw whiskey. "How much farther to Rimrock?"

"Dunno," Smith said. He put the bottle away. "My first trip on this line. I usually take the Shawnee run."

"Not too fur," the mountain man said.

"How far *exactly?*" Jeff asked in the manner of one who liked his information in specific terms.

The eyes of the mountain man swung in his direction, taking in the black broadcloth coat, the string tie, and the patent leather shoes. He was silent so long that the young man's face began to burn, and finally he answered lazily: "Oh, it ain't but about two curves and a cuss fight, I reckon." He appeared not to see the anger in Lindsey's face as he added, "Jest a mite further than you can chunk a tater."

The stage gave a lurch, dipping so sharply to starboard that all the passengers were thrown in that direction. Jeff Lindsey attempted to catch himself, but the weight of the men to his right drove him against the slight form of his mother, crushing her against the varnished oak.

"Mother, are you all right?"

She fixed him with a steady stare. "Jeff, I haven't been all right since we left Dallas. And I don't expect to get better until you get this fool notion out of your head."

She had spoken in a low voice intended for his ears only, but Smith the drummer missed none of it—including the wince that the woman's sharp words drew from the young man. He shrugged and took out a cigar. Soon the fine dust that boiled in through the window mixed with the strong stench of the weed, but nobody protested.

For the next hour the coach jolted along, a crawling speck that moved slowly across the flat Kansas prairie. The fiery July sun seemed to penetrate the interior of the coach, so hot that all the passengers lay back in their seats gasping for breath. Twice they passed large herds headed north. The rolling dust gathered into clouds that rose high in the summer sky, then descended, coating the world with a coat of gritty gray film.

Finally the guard called out, "Stop ahead. One hour to redd up."

The weary horses managed a final burst of speed, which the driver halted with a squeal of brakes that pulled the stage to a halt beside a dreary building made of sawmill slabs and covered with sod. A rusty pipe rose through the dry grass, sending a faint trickle of greasy smoke listlessly across the sky, as if uncertain whether to rise or fall.

As the passengers stumbled out of the stage on legs grown numb, a fat, red-faced individual with a dirty red bandana covering his head came out. He counted the passengers, said in a sullen tone, "Grub's inside. Privy's over there."

"Let's walk a little," young Lindsey said. Taking his

mother's arm, he led her past a barn and across a stretch of bare earth cluttered with rusty tin cans, chicken feathers, and several piles of decaying garbage.

"I suppose this is the garden spot of Kansas," Mrs. Lindsey said with a mirthless laugh.

"Oh, Mother, we've been through this a hundred times! You *agreed* to come!"

Her face softened, and the traces of a former beauty were caught in her smile. She touched his arm, saying in a gentle tone, "I'm sorry, Jeff. You're right. I did agree to come."

"It'll be better when we get to Rimrock."

"No, it'll be the same." She took a fine lace handkerchief from her pocket, wiped the dust from his cheek, then replaced the handkerchief with a frown. "When your father and I were first married, we lived in a series of towns like this one. They were all the same, Jeff. The most desolate places on the face of the earth!"

"That was over twenty-five years ago."

"Frontier towns never change. But I didn't leave your father and take you to civilization because life was boring. No, it was the utter contempt for human life, Jeff, that I couldn't bear!"

"Maybe if Dad hadn't been a peace officer—," he suggested, but she shook her head suddenly at the thought.

"That was part of it. I couldn't live every day of my life waiting for a deputy to come with the message that Jesse was dead on some barroom floor!"

They walked on slowly, and Jeff tried to think of a way to make his mother understand what he felt. He knew from bitter experience that the years his mother had spent as the wife of a small-town Texas lawman had marked her so deeply that nothing could ever change her. Finally he said heavily, "I wish you'd stayed in Dallas."

She stopped and held his arm with a surprising strength. "No! You—you're all I have, Jeff!" She bit her lip, shook her head, and made herself smile at him. "I won't complain again. I know this means everything to you. But I still say you would have been better off with Creasy's law office in Dallas."

"I guess we better get back." He turned her back toward the station and tried again to explain why he had left the security of a law office in a big city.

"You saw those big herds headed toward Rimrock, Mother? They're going to change this country! All during the war Texas sold no cattle to speak of. Now that the war is over, the East is hungry for beef. That's why all these trails headed to Kansas are running over with trail herds. And the action will be at little places nobody ever heard of—little towns like Dodge City, Hays, Abilene. All those trail towns have one thing going—they're on the railroad leading to Chicago and the East."

"I know all that, Jeff, but. . . ."

"Mother, if I'd stayed in Dallas at Creasy's, I'd have been one clerk out of twenty or a hundred. But if I go to Rimrock, I'll be one of a few lawyers, maybe even the *only* one. And how many times have we dreamed about my getting into office, Mother? I can do it at Rimrock! You know I can."

She brightened at that. "If you could do *that*, Jeff, it would be worth it all."

"We'll do it, Mother, you'll see! It'll be just like you always said it would be." He had the power to raise her spirits, and when they got back to the station she took her place and managed to eat some of the greasy beef and drink some of the strong black coffee.

Jeff smiled as he ate, pleased that he had finally found a key for keeping his mother happy. She had resisted his notion to go to Rimrock, especially since his father was there serving as marshal. He had never been able to gauge her feeling for the father he had seen only once on a brief trip to Oklahoma when he had been only fifteen. At times he suspected that although she had divorced Jesse Lindsey she still had strong feelings for him. Not that she ever said so, but she had never remarried and never shown more than a casual interest in another man.

Just as Jeff finished his meal, a door to the back of the room opened to what was obviously the station keeper's quarters. Jeff could see by the light of a single window a sagging bed and a washstand. The door was suddenly filled by a man who stood there looking out at them.

"Oh, yeah, I 'most forgot, Rainey," the station keeper grunted as he began collecting the dishes. "This here feller's horse up and died on him yestiddy. He's paid up to Rimrock."

The driver sopped the white gravy from his plate with a piece of cornbread, popped it into his mouth, and then swallowed it. He belched explosively, shoved his chair back, and pressed his hat down firmly on his head. "All who's goin' better git movin'."

He led the way to the stage where the guard held six fresh horses. They stamped and tossed their heads as the passengers mounted and were routinely cursed by the driver who snatched the reins.

The passengers all waited until Jeff handed his mother up and got in to sit beside her. Then they hauled themselves aboard and waited for the new passenger to get in.

Jeff caught a view of the man as he picked up a saddle

from the porch, moved across the yard, and stood just beneath the window waiting to toss it up to the guard.

He moved so slowly, almost painfully so, that Jeff assumed he was an elderly man, but as a slanting beam of sunlight illuminated the features, he saw his mistake.

The face beneath the low-crowned hat was wedge-shaped, tapering from a broad forehead to a chin which sloped forward aggressively and was punctuated by a shallow cleft. Heavy black brows shaded deep-set eyes, very dark and almost hidden by the shelter of the high cheekbones, and the same shade of raven black glistened in the hair that ran raggedly from beneath the hat. A dull pallor tinged the man's skin except for two red spots on his cheeks.

"Toss it up." As the guard spoke, the square hands holding the saddle tightened, and a ripple of muscle flexed, sending the heavy weight upward. There was an ease in the motion that hinted at power in the rather trim body, but suddenly the man swayed back and only by grabbing at the shoulder-high wheel did he save himself from falling to the ground.

"Dead drunk!" Ada said in disgust. "Jeff, we can't have him in here with us!"

Jeff nodded, but the mountain man said wryly, "Guess iffen you kept drinkin' men off stages, they'd all go bust."

"I'm afraid that's right, lady," the gambler said. "He can sit by us, though. Won't be any trouble to you."

"He'll have to behave," Jeff said sternly. But as he watched the painful progress the passenger made getting aboard, he saw that there would be no trouble. Grasping the edges of the door with both hands, he paused as if gathering his strength. He pulled himself through the door and spotted the space between the drummer and the gambler. He fell into

9

it with a gust of spent breath. His hands, they all saw, were trembling, and the whites of his eyes gleamed until he closed them and leaned back against the cushion without a word.

"Hyupp!" The driver sang out, and with a lurch the stage rolled out onto the road.

"Just a couple of hours to Rimrock," the farmer said. He was watching the face of the new passenger, as were the rest of them. "Ort to be in before dark."

The gambler moved slightly away, leaning back so that he could study the man's face carefully. His brow furrowed into deep lines. Finally he asked quietly, "Don't I know you, mister?"

The rolling of the stage moved the man's loose body from side to side, and it was obviously an effort for him to open his eyes and focus on the face of the gambler. "My name's Rossiter," the gambler added. "I think we must have met somewhere."

Slowly the man's lips moved, as if he were coming out of a deep sleep. When he did answer, the voice was slurred, the words running together. "Dunnoyou." Then the eyes closed and only the pressure of the bodies of the men on either side of him kept him from slumping to the floor.

"Dead drunk!" Ada snapped. "Shouldn't be allowed to ride with decent people!"

"Hope he don't puke," the drummer said. "If he starts gaggin', we better holler to the driver to stop."

Nothing like that happened, however, and soon all except the gambler Rossiter ignored the man. It was nearly an hour later and the sun was beginning to touch the flat horizon with streaks of crimson when Rossiter broke the silence.

"This man isn't drunk—he's sick!"

They all looked and it was obvious that the dark-haired man was ill. His face was flushed, and when the gambler touched his brow, he said, "He's burning up!"

"Fever." The mountain man leaned around to look at the lolling body of the man. He leaned across and pulled an eyelid up; there was no response as the white of the eye shone dully. "Got somethin' for sure."

"What!" Jeff was fully alarmed now. He leaned out the window and shouted, "Driver! Stop the coach!"

"Whut fer?"

"We have a sick man in here!"

"Wal, hold yer taters—they's an old shack down the road 'bout a quarter, and we need to water the hosses."

In less than five minutes the stage rolled to a stop and the driver peered in. Rolling a massive cud from one cheek to the other, he asked, "Whut's his trouble?"

"I think he's got scarlet fever," one of the pallid men answered. "There's been lots of it around."

"Does it look like this?" Mrs. Lindsey asked fearfully. She had seen that disease wipe out a large segment of a small Texas town once, and she knew that there was no defense, nothing a doctor could do for such a thing.

"Could be jest the flu," the pallid man said. "All them things look alike at the early stage. Could be cholera or diphtheria."

"Get him out of here!" Mrs. Lindsey said in a tight voice. She was not a flighty woman, but the fear of contagious disease was too much for her. "I will not ride with that man!"

"Ah, we're only 'bout an hour from Rimrock," the driver complained.

"I *insist* that you get him out of this stage!"

The driver stared at her, then spat out his wad of tobacco. He saw that the woman was verging on hysteria, so he said, "Wal, I guess we kin leave him here."

"Leave him here!" Rossiter said at once, anger in his voice. "Alone in this place?"

"Won't be fer no more than a couple hours," the driver snapped. He had had some experience with sickness himself, and it made sense to keep the man out of town if he really did have typhoid.

"Git him down!" The man's body was limp as they handed him down, his head bumping the floor of the stage. "Watch out! Don't brain the pore feller!"

Rossiter said, "Throw down his saddle." When it hit the ground, he pulled it into the shack, took the bedroll off, and made the unconscious man as comfortable as possible.

"This is wrong!" he exclaimed bitterly. "I wouldn't leave a dog out here alone like this!"

The driver cursed, spat, and said, "I ain't gonna argue with you. Everybody back inside!"

Jeff turned, avoiding the glance in Rossiter's eyes, and walked hurriedly back to the stage. Getting in, he said in a low voice, "I don't like this."

"What else can we do?" Ada asked. "You heard the driver—they'll send a doctor out right away."

Inside, Rossiter was staring down at the man, watching the chest rising and falling in a very shallow way. The others filed out quickly, and the driver said angrily, "You comin' or not?"

The slender back of the gambler was turned to the door, and he said in a low voice, "I'm staying. Put my bag off."

The driver stared at him, then called out, "Throw the

man's bag down, Earl." Climbing back to his seat, he took the whip, cracked it over the head of the off horse, and the coach shot out into the falling dusk.

Inside, nobody said anything for ten minutes, then Smith said defensively, "Well, *I* can't hang around and play nurse-maid!"

"Me neither," one of the sallow-faced men said, and the other nodded in agreement.

The burly cowboy said with a truculent edge to his voice, "Aw, that tinhorn ain't got nothing else to do!"

"Shet your filthy mouth!" The mountain man moved so quick the movement of his hand was like a snake striking. Grabbing the husky puncher by the collar, he said, "You ain't got no call to be proud—so jest you open your face once more an' I'll be happy to redecorate it fer yuh!"

The cowboy was obviously a pretty tough hand, but some-thing in the face of the older man, or perhaps the Arkansas Toothpick stuck in the fringed belt, made him speak softly. "Well, what about *you!* I didn't notice you stickin' around!"

The lean face of the mountaineer changed, and he dropped his hand, muttering, "Yeah, that's plumb right. I reckon none of us air anything to write home about." He leaned back, and there was not another word said as the stage rolled toward Rimrock.

Al Rossiter moved the saddle and his worn suitcase into the shack. He found an oil lamp half-full and a rusty cookstove with three legs. The nights were cold, and he knew that the fever would probably turn to chills, so he made a sweep around the shack finding plenty of dead wood. Going through the saddlebags of the sick man, he ran across a blackened cof-fee pot, some coffee in a leather bag, and a chunk of bacon. He dredged up a bent frying pan from a corner of the shack, and went outside again with a tin pan that hung over a peg in the wall. A small creek not a hundred feet away offered plenty of fresh water. As the darkness closed in, he went back inside and sat down beside the sick man.

Lighting a slender cheroot, he stared down at the pale face now drenched with sweat, wondering what made him stay.

"Not my style," he said half to himself in the falling darkness. "Never was one to give up much for anybody." He saw that the man was beginning to shiver, so he got up, started a fire in the stove, and put water on to heat.

The man's eyes opened, and Rossiter asked, "You awake?"

There was no answer, and the eyes were unfixed. Rossiter took some water in a cup, lifted the man up, and put it to his lips. He drank thirstily and then began to shake so violently that Al thought he was dying. He wrapped him tightly in the blanket and sat back, smoking, thinking, and wondering about his actions again.

The chills got worse, then began to modify as the fever took over two hours later. This time the eyes opened, and there was recognition in them.

"Feel pretty bad?" Rossiter asked.

The man said weakly, "They put me off?"

"Well—"

The dark eyes regarded him intently, and there was a trace of a smile on the broad lips. He said in a painful whisper, "You make a living taking care of sick cowboys?"

Rossiter grinned and said, "Maybe it's the beginning of a new career for me. You want a drink of water?"

"Yeah." He drank slowly and lay back exhausted. But his eyes were still intently fixed on Rossiter. He lay watching him for a long time, then said, "You sure are a funny sort of gambler."

The remark seemed to irritate Rossiter. He shrugged angrily, and there was no contentment in his thin face. He threw the cigar out the door and said, "Well, I ain't been a roaring success at *that,* to tell the truth." He had sharp features, like a hawk, with light blue eyes that moved restlessly, and his mouth was thin, almost a knife edge. He said, "I still think we must have met somewhere. My name's Al Rossiter."

He waited for the sick man to give his own name, but weariness struck him like a blow, pulling the lids down heavily. He managed to open them again, saying in a whisper, "Much obliged." Then he dropped into a heavy sleep that soon turned into a fever so fierce that it frightened Al. Once he had to hold the man down by force as delirium took him. He was yelling something about the round top and screaming for somebody to bring some guns up.

Finally he wore himself out, and Al took a pull from a silver flask he carried in his suitcase. He stared down at the face bathed in sweat and murmured softly, "With the kind of luck I been having, that driver and those sorry passengers will forget to send a doctor."

There was a dark streak of fatalism in the man, and he sat there staring through the single window, wondering what the lacy network of stars that decorated the sky had to do with Al Rossiter and his problems.

TWO
Echoes from the Past

"You go on down to the store and do your shopping, girl. I have to go get bawled out by the town council."

"Why don't you just shoot the whole bunch of them, Dad?" Rachel Lindsey's gray eyes sparkled at the thought, and she added, "Well, maybe just in the foot, just to scare the daylights out of the whole sorry bunch!"

Jesse Lindsey, marshal of Rimrock, smiled at the girl, thinking again how she had put color and interest into his life. She had deep yellow hair like her mother, and the same ivory tint to her skin. The gray eyes must have come from her father, whom Jesse had never met. After his wife had divorced him, Jesse had married Louise Duncan, not out of love, but in order to provide a home for the woman and her child. She had been a widow in Broken Bow when Jesse had served as a deputy, and although she had known that Jesse had married her for no romantic reasons, she had been a good wife. She had lived only five years. Jesse had legally adopted the girl and brought her up as best he could alone.

He shook his head at her suggestion, saying, "Can't do it. They pay my salary."

"Well, don't you put up with anything from any of them, you hear me? After all, you're the one that keeps this two-bit town from getting swallowed by the trail hands." She patted his cheek as she had done since early childhood.

"Run along now. Buy yourself a new bonnet. Maybe you can get a fellow to come courting. Lots of single men around."

"Lots of gophers and hoot owls, too!" she said with a laugh. She sobered and there was a hesitancy in her manner as she asked, "What time does the stage get in, Dad?"

"About dark, I reckon. Get along. I'll buy your supper after the council meeting."

"All right."

He watched her move along the boardwalk toward Tyler's General Store, slightly surprised as always at the beautiful young woman who had developed from the awkward, knobby-jointed child.

When she turned the corner, Lindsey turned toward the bank where the town council met. The bank was set in the apex of a triangular group of frame buildings, nudging out into the middle of a large square now half-filled with buggies, wagons, and horses.

Most of the people he passed as he made his way to the side door greeted him by name, and he answered in the same measured tone and the same courteous nod to all of them.

He was sixty years old, and the burden of wearing a star in a long series of raw frontier towns, as well as the strain of commanding troops in the terrible battles of the war, had stooped his once erect shoulders. His step was slower, he knew, but he accepted that as he had accepted all losses. One of his aides had said to another in the thick of battle at Gettysburg: "You can't tell *nothin'* about how we're doin' from watchin' Major Lindsey! He allus looks the same, whether we're whuppin' Yanks or they're whuppin' us!"

A reporter who was doing a story on Western lawmen had said, "Jesse Lindsey looks like what a Western lawman *ought* to look like—but usually doesn't."

He had been six feet tall once, but now fell somewhat below that. His once muscular frame had shrunk, the lost weight showing in the loose flesh around the neck and in the hollows of his face. The once dark hair was now almost white, as was the drooping moustache that hid the firm mouth. Liver spots were evident on his hands, and he moved carefully, like one who has a pain that he has to nurse along and learn to live with. Yet there was still the fearless direct stare of cobalt blue eyes—the predatory hook of the nose lending a hawkish daring to the craggy features.

He reached the side door, knocked, and it opened at once. Odell Bracy, the president of the bank, let him in saying, "You're late."

Bracy was a handsome man of forty. He looked more like a gambler than a banker, with his ruffled shirt, brocade vest, and string tie. Married to a woman who had brought him enough money to satisfy his greed—but not enough beauty to satisfy his lust—he spent much time in long trips away from home, wallowing in the fleshpots.

"You're gonna be held up, sooner or later, Odell," Jesse remarked as they went upstairs to the banker's office. "Wonder you ain't been hit already. It'd be a piece of cake."

Bracy did not answer. He hated to spend money and refused to put in a vault and strengthen the security of his bank. He did not like to be corrected by anyone, especially by Jesse Lindsey.

"I'll take care of my business, Marshal." He led the way into the office, where he sat down behind an oak desk. "Let's get this meeting under way. We have a quorum, I think."

"You'd have a quorum if you was here all by yourself, Odell." The speaker was Bones Morehouse, owner of the local feed store and several thousand acres of farm land. He had little use for Bracy and always voted against any measure the banker proposed. It may have been envy, for Morehouse was as ugly as Odell Bracy was handsome. Tall, gangling, with a lantern jaw and a mouth like a catfish, he dressed like a pauper and had the manners of a field hand.

"What's the business?" Ernest Faulkner asked. He was the mild-mannered owner of the livery stable and hardware store, and he wore what appeared to be the same suit month in and month out—a heavy navy blue coat with sleeves too long and trousers too short. He tried to keep the peace at the infrequent council meetings, but it was too big a job for him.

"You ought to know *that,* Ernest!" Bracy snapped. "We've talked about it the last three meetings."

R. G. Tyler sat in a cane-bottom chair, his head tilted back against the wall. The owner of the general store, Tyler was a big man with a florid complexion. He opened his eyes and brought the legs of his chair down with a loud thump. "We've been over that so often I'm sick of it." He was a shrewd businessman and said what was on his mind bluntly. "Let's talk about this new ordinance on building."

"Later." The banker leaned back and let his heavy gaze fall on Marshal Lindsey, who stood looking out the window at the busy square below. "Marshal, I've tried to tell you this before, and this is the last time. You have got to do something about these wild trail outfits! They are a menace to our community! I don't propose to put up with it any longer, so you take the proper action."

"You want me to shut Dance Street down?" Lindsey shot back at once. He turned and his hawklike gaze fell on Bracy like a blow.

"Well—I don't think—that is, we have to be wise about this!"

Bones Morehouse had a laugh like a hyena, and it rasped out now as he said, "You'd scream like a Sioux if Jesse did that, wouldn't you, Bracy? You couldn't stand to lose all the money those outfits bring into town!"

"That's not the issue!" Bracy said. A flush colored his forehead, and he added, "I think it's the job of the marshal to keep the town safe without . . ." He hesitated and waved his hand. " . . . without closing down some of the local businesses."

"What you mean, Bracy, is that you want to keep the whorehouses and the saloons going full blast, but you don't want any of the trouble that goes with them!" Bones rasped out his laugh again, and added, "You sure are a prize hypocrite, Odell!"

Jesse stepped back to stare down at the street, ignoring the argument which he had heard many times. They would shout and argue, but in the end they'd shift the burden onto his shoulders—the way town councils always did.

He looked toward the end of Grant Street, where the stage would arrive, wondering how it would be to see Ada and the boy again. He longed to see once again the woman he'd loved with the fierce heat of a young man's passion. Now, after the barren years, she was coming back into his world. He had known so many disappointments he knew better than to build any hope on this new thing. But lately he had found himself having strange thoughts about what might come of it.

Finally he heard Bracy say, "Jesse, you will have to do a little more to keep the citizens safe. We can't have any more tragedies like we had last week."

A drunken cowboy had fired off a burst of shots, killing an elderly man two blocks away. Jesse had taken the cowboy's gun—at some risk, but the judge had ruled it a case of accidental homicide and let the man go with a stiff fine.

Jesse agreed with Bracy that the town was getting too wild. "How about another deputy?" he asked.

"We don't have the money, Jesse." The banker shook his head firmly. "You'll just have to make do."

"Do the best you can, Jesse," Tyler said. "Nobody is expecting any miracles."

The marshal stared at the council members, a cynical smile on his thin lips. "Anything else?" he asked, and when there was no answer, he turned and left the room.

As he made his way down the street toward the jail, he felt the rhythm of the town picking up. Even though it was only a little after four in the afternoon, and Dance Street with its raw music and elemental pull at the flesh would not be in full swing until much later, there was a stirring which he had learned over the years to gauge.

There was a heartbeat to a town, a tide which ebbed and flowed, and he felt it as a wild animal felt the pressures of its world. Had he not had that instinct, he would have been lying in an obscure grave long ago. He thought, with a sudden sense of pride, that though his draw might be slower, his mind and his sense of the movements inside his town were as sharp and keen as ever.

Zane Williams, the night deputy, looked up as he entered the jail, his thin sandy hair sticking up in all directions as if he had just gotten out of bed. Williams, skinny and disjointed, had big ears and fair skin that stayed sunburned and refused to tan. But he had a sense of loyalty to Jesse Lindsey that was not bought by the meager salary he received.

"You ought to be asleep," Jesse said. He picked up the mail and after glancing at it, threw most of it in the battered trash can.

"Too hot to sleep," Zane murmured. He got up, stretched, then put on the heavy gun belt that looked too big for his small frame. "You et yet?"

"Going down to get Rachel now. Come on, I'll buy you a steak at Rudy's."

"All right." His light blue eyes lit up, as Jesse had known they would, at the invitation. It was no secret to the marshal that Williams was hopelessly in love with his daughter, and it gave him a heavy feeling, as it always did when he thought of it, to realize that nothing would ever come of it. Rachel was fond of the skinny young man, but it was obvious to Jesse as well as to Williams that there was no hope for the deputy. More than once Jesse had tried to get Zane to quit and get a job with a future, but like the moth that couldn't pull away from the candle, the sad-eyed deputy stayed on, feeding on his bitter desire.

Jesse locked the office, and the two men ambled down the street, crossed the square, and met Rachel as she was coming out of Tyler's store with several bundles in her arms.

"Looks like you bought out the place," Jesse said smiling. "You get that bonnet?"

"No, I got some material to make you some new shirts.

You could throw a cat through the tears in some of your old ones. Hello, Zane."

"Hello. Your dad's threatened to buy my supper. You hungry?"

"Starving!" She walked with them toward Rudy's Café and they found the place surprisingly crowded for such an early hour.

Rudy Gatlin, the owner, was helping the single waitress. He glanced up and, seeing Lindsey, called out, "Set down here, Marshal." He was a short, fat man with a frightful scar pulling his right eye downward and distorting his mouth into a continual leer, the result of a Confederate bayonet charge at Shiloh.

The three sat down and Rudy asked, "What'll you have?"

"The usual—except Mack Stevens butchered one of his sows today. Ought to be some pretty good fresh pork chops."

Pork in the summer was rare, since most butchering took place in the fall or winter. "Be a change from that stringy beef you been foistin' off on your innocent customers," Zane growled.

"Reckon you lost your innocence before you ever ate any of my food," Rudy said grinning. "The same for you two? Got some fresh greens and okra from the Chinaman."

"Sounds good," Jesse agreed. "All right with you, Rachel?"

"Fine."

They sat there speaking idly as they waited for their food, and both Rachel and Zane noticed that Jesse had little to say. He was not much of a talker in any case, but there was a far-off look in his eye, and he stirred himself only when the food came and they began to eat.

Even then he merely picked at his food, and finally Rachel asked, "Not hungry, Dad?"

"Not very." He put his fork down and picked up the cup of thick black coffee. "I guess I'm a little worried about Jeff. Maybe I did the wrong thing, getting him set up here."

"Don't see why you'd think that," Zane said. "Young lawyer could do real well around here."

"He might do better in the big city."

"He wants to come, Dad." Rachel gave him a smile and patted his arm. "I think he'd have come anyway, even if you hadn't encouraged him."

"I guess so." He started to say something, but the couple that entered through the front door seemed to stop him.

There was only one empty table in the place—next to the one they were occupying, and the pair made their way to it.

"Afternoon, Marshal," the man said. He was a massively built individual, the deep arch of his chest swelling the starched shirtfront, and his neck sloping down to massive shoulders. He had a broad face, heavy in the jaw and wide across the brow. A streak of light in his slate-colored eyes was hidden by the heavy lids, and there was a smile of amusement on his meaty lips.

"Hello, Burdick. Afternoon, Lola." Lindsey gave his customary even greeting to the pair, and Zane and Rachel nodded.

"Hello, Rachel," the woman said with a smile. "Haven't seen you much lately."

It was unlikely that she would, for Lola Fremont moved in different circles. She was the widow of Milt Fremont, a saloon owner who'd left her the Nugget, one of the many saloons in Rimrock.

Lola had the same high color and bold good looks she'd had when she'd been a dance hall girl that Milt had fallen for. She was tall and full-bodied, and her rich auburn hair fell in profusion around her creamy shoulders. She had broad cheek bones, light green eyes, and lips that would have tempted a saint.

Rachel said, "Been pretty busy, Lola."

Neal Burdick touched the woman's arm possessively, guided her into a chair, then sat down across from her. He gave the order for both of them to the waitress and then turned to face the marshal with a sly look on his heavy face.

"Hear law and order is coming to Rimrock, Marshal."

That Burdick would know of Jeff's arrival came as no surprise to the marshal. Burdick was a power in the town, owning the biggest saloon, the Palace, and having a finger in the rowdiness, the gambling, and the liquor that made Dance Street the biggest industry in town.

"Guess the town can stand a little law," Jesse said idly. He glanced at Neal Burdick and added, "Any objection, Neal?"

"Me?" A mock astonishment masked the big man's face and he said lightly, "I'm all for law and order every time, Jesse. Just have to keep a balance, don't we now? Even the city fathers want an open town."

Zane said tightly, "Someday the town will get enough of you and Dance Street, Burdick. I hope I'm the one to hang a padlock on your door."

Burdick's mask slipped, and Jesse saw instantly that beneath the jovial surface lurked a carnivore. A deadly and implacable force flowed through the man.

The marshal got to his feet and put a bill on the table. "Let's go meet the stage."

As they left, Burdick called out, "Bring the counselor by to meet me, Jesse. Maybe I can throw some business his way." He laughed suddenly and turned to face Lola, who had been watching the scene with a cynical smile.

"What's all this, Neal?"

"Lindsey's son is fresh out of law school, and he's coming to Rimrock to save all of us sinners from sin and degradation." Burdick grinned widely and then added, "Way I hear it, the kid thinks he's some kind of a knight on a white horse."

"Better mend your ways, brother," Lola said with a smile. "Sounds like you might be his prime target."

The broad fingers of Burdick laced together as he considered the idea, then he shrugged. "He'll be a pest for a while, I expect. But he'll come down to earth soon enough."

"Like his father?" Lola mocked gently. "I haven't noticed Jesse Lindsey doing anything like that."

"Different. The boy's mama raised him in the East." The huge fingers flexed and the raw power of the man flashed out of the hooded eyes as he said in a different tone, "He'll fall in line—or get rubbed out. I'm a little tired of all this Southern pride Jesse Lindsey puts on display."

There was a thoughtful look in Lola's eyes as she ate her meal, and despite his tough words, Burdick seemed to be lost in some hidden thoughts.

The dying lights of the sky had been augmented by the pale yellow glow of lanterns strung along Dance Street as the marshal and Rachel made their way through the jostling crowd toward the Wells Fargo office where the stage stopped.

Already a steady grinding roar of tinny piano music and loud voices emerged from the saloons and hurdy-gurdies, and the boardwalks were crowded with punchers fresh off the trail. Most of them were freshly shaved, bright-eyed with liquor and anticipation, ready to wash away the boredom and monotony of the trail with a night of action.

None of them were drunk enough to give trouble so

early, but as Jesse walked steadily through the midst of the stream of humanity, he knew that by midnight tempers would be raw, and the jail would, in all probability, be packed the next morning.

"Stage isn't in yet," Rachel said as they passed from Dance Street and walked toward the station.

"May be a little late."

They found a couple of cane-bottomed chairs, and for over an hour sat listening to the roar of Dance Street increase in volume. Once there was some sort of disturbance which drew Lindsey's instant notice. Zane crossed the street, disappeared for a brief time, then headed toward the jail with a battered puncher in tow.

"Zane's a good man," Jesse observed. "Ought to get out of this business and get a better job."

Rachel didn't answer. She had been quiet for a long time, thinking about Jeff and his mother and how their coming would change her father. She had known for as long as she could remember that Jesse had never gotten over his first wife, and she knew also that he had longed for a son desperately. She was afraid, somehow, of the coming of Ada and Jeff, for she sensed that Jeff was not the man that Jesse Lindsey wanted for a son, and she saw nothing to indicate that Ada had any feeling at all for him.

"I expect Jeff has changed a great deal," she said tentatively.

"Sure. I haven't seen him since he was fifteen." He paused and added with an odd note in his voice, "I don't reckon his mother will have changed though. She never did."

Rachel shot a quick glance at him; it was the most personal comment she'd ever heard him make about Ada, and it told her a great deal.

"There's the stage," Jesse said, and they got to their feet as the coach rolled in out of the darkness into the yellow glare of the lanterns on the sidewalks.

The door opened, and even though Rachel had never seen Jeff Lindsey, she knew at once that this was Jesse Lindsey's son. He had the same craggy good looks, the same sloping shoulders and ease of movement. His mother appeared in the door of the coach, and Jesse helped her down.

Rachel stared curiously at the woman who had haunted Jesse for twenty years. *She's beautiful!* was the thought that flashed into her mind, and it caught her off guard. She had expected a certain degree of handsomeness, but the classic face of Ada Lindsey lost nothing by age. The years had mellowed what must have been a spectacular prettiness into a sculptured, almost Grecian, perfection.

Rachel stood back as the three pulled off to one side allowing the rest of the passengers to get out. Jesse was the first to speak. He stared at the face of his son for a long time, then he smiled and said, "Jeff, you're a man!"

"Good to see you, Dad," Jeff said warmly, and the eagerness with which he took the hand that was offered him, as well as the light in his eyes, warmed Rachel's heart, for she saw that it was something that might be good for Jesse.

Then Jesse turned squarely to face Ada, and the two seemed alone on the street. There was a moment when Rachel thought she saw a breaking of Ada's iron control, a trace of warmth in the fine eyes, and perhaps a hint of a smile on her generous lips. But then it passed, and she put out her hand, saying in a level voice, "It's been a long time, Jesse."

He took the hand carefully, took his hat off, and finally said, "You're just the same, Ada."

They stood there studying each other, and Rachel saw the curious stares that caught at them from several who gathered around the stage. "Jeff, I'm your new sister, Rachel. Welcome to Rimrock."

Jeff took the hand she thrust at him, swept his hat off, and said, "Good to be here, Rachel. I haven't had much practice being a brother, so you'll have to help me out." He smiled at her, and his face was so much like his father's that Rachel returned it. "Anybody you want licked?" he asked, then shot a glance at his father. "But I guess you don't have that trouble, being a lawman's daughter. I don't think you've met my mother."

"No." For one brief instant Rachel had the impulse to embrace Ada Lindsey, but there was a reserve in the older woman that told her that it would not be received well.

She nodded and said, "You must be tired. Let's get your luggage and get you settled."

"That would be nice, Rachel," Ada said, and permitted herself a small smile. "How pretty you are!"

Jeff was staring at the girl, taken off guard by the warm gray eyes and the fire of womanliness that stirred his senses.

"I'll get your small bag now, Mother. Maybe you can get someone to bring the trunk, Dad?"

Jesse spoke to a tall man, "Bring the trunk and the other bags to the hotel, will you, Thad?"

They moved away from the stage, but before they left, the driver said, "Marshal, we left a gent over at the old station in pretty bad shape. You need to see he gets a doctor."

"Accident?" Jesse said, pausing to get the story.

"Naw, jest sick. They wuz a gambler stayed to take keer of him, but I said somebody would come. You take keer of it?"

"I'll see to it, Henry."

"The fellow is in pretty bad shape, I'm afraid," Jeff said as they made their way toward the hotel. "He may have typhoid or something like that."

"You know the man?"

"Oh, no. He got on at the station run by the fat man."

"Have to roust Doc Mitchell out of his poker game."

"He's not playing poker tonight, Dad," Rachel said. "Mrs. Shultz is having her baby, and Doc had to go this morning."

"Oh, well, I'll have Zane go after him soon as we get you settled, Jeff."

They entered the hotel and the clerk got up with a smile. "Howdy. I reckon this is Miz Lindsey—and Mister Jeff Lindsey?"

"This is my boy, Chet—" There was an awkward pause, then Jesse finished by saying, "—and this is his mother."

Ada flashed him a quick look, a smile touching the corners of her lips. "You've gotten a little more tactful, Jesse," she said quietly.

Jesse flushed, took the key, and said, "Sorry the house I found for you ain't ready, but it'll only be two or three days."

"This will be fine, Jesse," Ada said. She took the key he handed her and looked to Jeff. "I suspect you're hungry, but all I want to do is lie down."

"You've done well. It's been a tough trip," Jeff said. He hugged her and said, "Sleep until noon, then we'll have a late breakfast."

"I will." She started up the stairs, paused and looked back with a break in the reserve that she wore. "Maybe you and Rachel will join us, Jesse?"

He nodded and said, "We'll see you in the morning."

After she had left them, he turned to Jeff and said, "I've got to see about that sick man. You want to wait—or you want to hit the sack?"

"Oh, I'd like some good coffee and some good cooking!"

Jesse laughed and said, "Rachel, you take him to the café. Tell Rudy to give him some good grub or I'll close his place down!"

He left them, and Rachel slipped her arm into Jeff's with an easy natural motion that pleased him. "Come on, Jeff. I could eat again myself. As you'll find out soon enough, I eat like a pig! I'll be fat as a squaw if I keep it up!"

She took him to Rudy's and by the time they had waded through a platter of eggs and three chops apiece, they were completely at ease.

He was, she decided, bound to be a success as a lawyer. He had an easy flow of words and the air of one who could hold his own in any company. His wide grin and affability were a good combination.

"How come you're not married, Jeff?" she asked suddenly, and he was taken aback by her direct question. It was not the way young women behaved in his circles, but it was refreshing.

"Why, guess I'm not through sowing my wild oats," he admitted grinning. "How come you're not?"

"Oh, I'm just the old maid type," she answered with a smile that belied her words. "But I know all the eligible females in a hundred mile radius. They'll have to do anything I want in return for an introduction to my handsome brother. Won't I make them lick dirt though!"

He laughed, then suddenly a shot rang out and he gave a start. "Was that a shot?"

"Probably some puncher letting off steam," she answered indifferently. "If he gets out of line, one of the night men will collar him."

A frown creased Jeff's brow and he said, "It's a pretty wild town, isn't it?"

She shrugged. "About like all the rest, I suppose. I grew up in towns just like it, so I suppose I've gotten hardened."

Jeff pulled at his collar, then worried the handkerchief in his pocket. "I'd like to do something to make the place better." He looked out at the dark street, then added, "That's really why I—why we came to Rimrock, Rachel. I guess it sounds stuffy, but I'd like to use my training to help make places like this better."

She stared a him, then smiled, the warmth of her gray eyes catching the reflections of the lamps. "That's not stuffy, Jeff. It's what your father has done all his life."

Jeff shifted and appeared to be a little uncomfortable. Finally he said, "Rachel, my father is a great man—but things are changing. I mean, there was a time when the only way to tame a town was to pull a gun quicker than anyone else."

"But now?" Rachel asked quietly, her eyes fixed on his lean face. She felt that she had to know this man, for somehow she knew that Jesse Lindsey would find grief or joy in him.

"Oh, you know," Jeff said uncertainly. "I mean, the West is going to have to give way to law, Rachel. That's what I want to do—bring law to Rimrock."

She watched his face carefully, then said only, "Your father can use all the help he can get—but remember one thing, Jeff."

"What's that, Rachel?" he asked when she paused.

She reached out and put her hand on his arm to soften the impact of her answer.

"You can't stop a crazy gunman by quoting from a law book."

He took it well, grinning ruefully, and his boyish charm warmed her faith. "Sure, I know. But I intend to try. Maybe with Dad's gun and my law book we can do something."

Just at that moment Jesse entered the café, and the sight of Rachel and Jeff sitting there brought a smile to his face. Then he sobered and walked over to them, saying, "Got a problem here. Doc Mitchell did go to birth that baby, but after that he went on his way to Hays City for some kind of medical meeting. Won't be back for three days."

"What are you going to do, Dad?" Rachel asked.

"Going to try to get some of the deacons from the church to do something. Maybe Ed Loudermilk will get his woman to go. She's a pretty good nurse."

"I don't think that will do. Edna's been sick herself," Rachel said.

"I'll have to do something. The bishop won't be here for a week. He'd know what to do."

"We shouldn't have left him there," Jeff said. "I didn't feel good about it."

"I'll just have to build a fire under those deacons," Jesse said with a grim smile. "They're always testifying about how it's the Christian way to help the helpless. This'll give them some good practice."

Rachel shrugged and said, "I know how it will be. They'll have some excuse and it will all fall on you."

"Judge not, girl," Jesse said. "Jeff, you better sack in. I'll see you in the morning."

He turned and left them abruptly. Jeff said thoughtfully, "Does he get stuck with things like this often?"

Rachel said, "It goes with the territory, Jeff—for a man like Jesse Lindsey."

THREE
Law by the Book

The abrupt sound of a wagon creaking to a halt outside the shack brought Al Rossiter out of a fitful sleep. He had spent most of the night keeping a close watch on the sick man, keeping him wrapped in the scanty blanket and giving him sips of water.

Sometime before dawn he had catnapped in the rickety kitchen chair, and as he got up to go stiffly to the door, he rubbed his aching neck with his left hand and with his right fished a pepperbox derringer out of his inside coat pocket.

With a characteristic caution he stood just to the left of the door and waited until there was a knock from outside.

"Who's there?" he asked.

"Marshal Lindsey from Rimrock."

Pocketing the gun, Rossiter opened the door. He stepped back to admit the lawman followed by a young woman.

"No doctor?" the gambler asked.

"Out of town," Jesse grunted. He walked over to look down at the sick man. "Let's have some light here."

"He's got the worst fever I ever saw," Rossiter said. The

young woman picked up the lamp, then held it so that its feeble light illuminated the face of the man on the floor.

"Looks pretty bad," the marshal said. The girl knelt and placed her free hand on the man's face. "I shouldn't have let you come, Rachel," he added, shaking his head.

She gave no sign that she heard, but finally looked up at the gambler. "I'm Rachel Lindsey, the marshal's daughter. What's your name?"

"Al Rossiter."

She got up and gave him a steady look, then said, "It was good of you to stay."

The statement seemed to trouble the gambler, as if she had pointed out a weakness.

"Know this man?" the marshal asked.

"No." He almost mentioned the feeling of having met him somewhere, but it was not his habit to volunteer information, so he let the moment go. "I went through his possessions, Marshal, but there's nothing with his name on it." Rossiter allowed himself a thin smile, adding, "He has two dollars and thirty-two cents in cash—no money for a doctor."

"Dad, we can't leave him here," Rachel said. "We'll have to take him to town."

A bitter light appeared in Lindsey's eyes, and he struck his thigh suddenly in anger. "No sense asking those church folks to help. I asked three of the deacons, and they all said no."

"If he's got scarlet fever or something like that, I can't blame them much," Rossiter said. "It can spread pretty fast."

Rachel put the lamp back on the table, glanced back at the sick man, then said quietly, "Some of the church people may help, but we'll just have to take care of him at our place for now."

"You sure?" Jesse asked. He had no fear for himself, but the thought of Rachel coming down with a fatal disease shook him.

She knew his thinking, and a smile broke the sober cast of her face, and the sudden beauty caught at Rossiter. He had not known many good women—had almost come to doubt their existence. It warmed him to see the woman pat her father's arm and say, "I'll be all right. Remember that verse you made me memorize once: 'No evil shall befall thee; no plague shall come nigh thy dwelling'?"

Jesse grinned and shook his head. "You always manage to back me into a corner with one of them Scriptures!" Then he looked at the gambler, a light of approval in his direct gaze. "You must be a God-fearing man, Rossiter. Not many would've stayed to help a sick man like this."

Rossiter allowed a brief smile to touch this thin lips and answered, "Don't guess I've ever been tagged with that label, Marshal Lindsey. But it was pretty raw, the way they put this fellow off the stage."

Jesse nodded, then said, "I got a wagon outside. Reckon the two of us can handle him."

Handling the unconscious man was difficult, but they got him into the wagon. Rachel sat down beside him saying, "I'll see he keeps wrapped up, Dad. He doesn't need all this cool morning air." There was, Rossiter saw, a quiet efficiency in the way she managed the cover. As she took the sick man's head into her lap to keep it from banging against the floor, there was a broad maternal cast to her full lips.

Rossiter tossed his bag and the saddle into the wagon, climbed up to sit beside Lindsey, and said, "Not sorry to be leaving here."

"You headed for any place special?"

Al Rossiter considered the question, and there was a fine thread of sadness in his answer.

"No." He seemed to feel the need to add a moment later as the wagon creaked along, "No, I'm not headed any place special."

Jesse Lindsey looked at the red rays of dawn beginning to streak the horizon eastward, then glanced at the thin face of the gambler. He spoke to the horses, then said gently, "Well, I guess most folks ain't really goin' no place special."

Sometimes he was falling down into a black hole, and he would tense his muscles, getting braced for the terrible moment when he would strike the bottom. A roaring at those times would fill his ears like the rush of a tornado, and when he opened his mouth to speak, to call out, the wind filled his lungs, stifling him like a massive blanket.

But there was never any end to that, and that terrible fall often faded into a strange quietness, so hollow that tiny sounds seemed to echo deep down in his brain. At those times, there would often be a bright light, never harsh, but soft and gentle, that bathed him in warmth, driving away the bone-cracking chill that racked him.

Worst of all was the dream that he was on fire. His whole body seemed to be laced with a searing heat that blistered him to the bone. His skin seemed parched, so dry that it seemed to crackle like paper, and his eyes were fried with the intense pain.

But always, when that heat became unbearable, there would be a coolness that began with his face, a touch so light that it was like a bird's wing brushing his skin. Then the cool moisture bathed the rest of his body, washing away the pain and the fear that always came.

More than anything else, there was the feeling that he was drowning, trapped beneath a weight that he struggled to break through. Sometimes he would be so far beneath the surface that there was only a faint sense of some sort of light far overhead. At other times he was so close to the surface that he could see movement and hear the voices of those who were outside. And it was at those times that he often cried out, trying to make himself heard.

More than once, he almost broke through, and he learned to distinguish those outside. One voice was rough, as rough as the hands that touched him when it came. He learned to withdraw when that happened, dropping down into the dark hole.

But there was another voice, and the hands that went with it were gentle. Often he could almost make out the words, which seemed to be calling him to come, to follow, to leave his place. And he attempted to break through, often hearing his own voice saying words he couldn't understand, or sometimes crying out in fear as an old nightmare reached out to fill his mind. Then he struggled to break through, to leave the darkness of the pit and enter the world of light and meaning.

Then came a dream that was worse than all the rest, so terrible that panic cut through him like a knife. He thought that he was being shoved down into the dark pit by a host of men who wore blue and had no faces. He knew that if they didn't stop he would fall into that ugly pit, and he knew that he would never rise again but fall forever into the darkness. So he began to claw and fight against the men, and he heard himself crying out: "Mac! Mac! Bring up the guns! They're forming for a counter-charge, Mac! Hurry—bring the guns!"

But he felt himself falling, being shoved into a dark pit by the faceless men, and just as he felt himself slipping into it, he gave a great cry and a mighty lunge—and he broke into the world of light.

"It's all right—you're all right!"

His eyes opened and closed abruptly as the light hit them, but he tried again and there was a face in front of him. He blinked, and his vision cleared to reveal a woman with a pair of soft gray eyes and a broad mouth. She was holding him firmly by the shoulders.

He stared at her, licked his lips, and tried to think. The room swirled as he lay there, then steadied. He was in a room that was dark except for a low-burning lamp on a pine chest, and the shadows flickered over the woman's face, outlining the high planes of her cheeks and making dark hollows in her eyes and throat.

He opened his lips and tried to speak, but they were too dry, and his only utterance was a croaking sound.

"Drink this," the woman said. She held him upright with one hand, picked up a glass of water with the other and held it steadily as he gulped thirstily.

"You're all right now," she said, replacing the glass. "How do you feel?"

He cleared his throat and managed to say rustily, "I'm . . . all right." He stared around the room and asked, "How long have I . . . been here?"

"Three days. You've been very sick."

He stared at her, trying to collect his thoughts, but weakness pulled at him.

She saw his eyes flickering and said quickly, "Do you think you could eat some soup? It would make you stronger." Without waiting for an answer, she pushed him gently until he lay flat, and keeping her hand on his chest, she added, "Try to stay awake."

Then she was gone, and his head whirled. He felt the familiar pull of darkness, but forced himself to keep his eyes open, slapping his hands together to resist that pull. She came back after what seemed like a long time, a bowl of steaming food in her hand.

"You'll have to sit up." She pulled him up, then put a towel under his chin and started spooning hot broth into his mouth. Hunger took him almost like a blow, and he ignored the scalding nature of the broth, swallowing it greedily until it was all gone.

"No more for now," she said firmly. She put a cool hand on his brow and said with a smile, "Your fever's broken."

He stared at her, his dark eyes made cavernous by the fever, but no longer dull. "Is this a hospital?"

"No. I'm Rachel Lindsey. This is my home."

He wanted to ask questions, but weakness hit him like a blow. She caught it and said, "You can sleep now. I'll be here."

He drifted off, but it was a natural rest, not the nightmarish coma of fever. She paused long enough to see his face relaxed, then smiled and left the room.

He awoke five hours later to find the room flooded with bright sunlight and a man sitting by his bedside looking into his face. He felt helpless, and a sudden caution showed in his face as he sat up in bed.

"I'm Jesse Lindsey. How you doing?"

The dark eyes lowered to the star Lindsey wore, then he said huskily, "Pretty well." He looked around the room and asked, "You bring me here, Marshal?"

"With a little help. How long you been sick?"

"What day is this?"

"Friday morning."

"Let's see, I started feeling pretty puny last Sunday, then my horse got snakebit and died the next day. I was lost for a while." A grim smile touched the drawn face as he added, "If I hadn't found that coach stop about when I did, reckon I'd be real peaceable by this time."

"You nearly was, anyhow," Lindsey said with a nod. "Doc said he thought at first you had typhoid, then later he changed it to scarlet fever. Then he said he didn't have any idea *what* it was."

"I think it was rabbit fever. I ran out of grub and ate a wild rabbit a few days ago. Think I may have got some of the blood in a cut on my hands."

"Yeah, that could be. You want something to eat?"

"I ate some soup last night—I think."

"Sure you did. That was my daughter, Rachel, who fed it to you. She's gettin' a little sleep. She ain't had much for a fact since she took to nursing you."

He got up and left the room, and while he was gone, the patient saw his clothes on a chair by the wall. Moving slowly he swung his feet out over the side of the bed and held to the bed as the room spun around. He took a deep breath and got to his feet.

Jesse was pouring some hot soup out of a big saucepan into a bowl when Rachel came in sleepy-eyed.

"What you doing up?"

"Can't sleep in the daytime, Dad." She took the bowl away from him, picked up a spoon and napkin and asked, "He's awake?"

"Just woke up."

"Find out anything about him?"

"Not yet. Maybe he'll feel like talking after he eats again."

They went down the hall and found the man sitting on the chair. He was wearing the butternut-colored trousers and was weaving slightly in the chair attempting to pull on one of his boots. There was a determined look on his pale wedge-shaped face as he doggedly stabbed at the boot with his foot.

"What do you think you're doing?" Rachel asked sharply. She put the soup down and went to stand over him with a frowning expression. "If you think I'm going to let you kill yourself after all this, you can just think again!"

A smile touched the lips of the man in the chair, and he said, "You sound like a sergeant I had once who used to peel me pretty regular."

"She's used to having her own way," Jesse said with a straight face. "What's your name, son?"

There was a slight hesitancy in giving his name which neither Jesse nor Rachel missed.

"Reno. Jim Reno."

"Well, Reno, I got a town to look after. You just take it easy until you get your strength back."

"I guess you know I'm broke."

Jesse snorted and turned to go. "You don't worry about that, Reno."

"Marshal, . . ." Jesse turned to see Reno get to his feet with a steady light in his dark eyes. " . . . I won't forget this."

Jesse shrugged uneasily and said, "That gambler who stayed with you at the shack, he's the one you got to thank—and Rachel." He left without a backward look, slamming the outside door with a bang.

"Here, eat this soup before it gets cold—and get some socks on," Rachel said.

He sat down and put the socks on, then began to eat the soup. She watched him quietly, going back into the kitchen once to refill the bowl and add two biscuits and some butter on a plate.

When he had finished, she took the dishes and looked down at him with a smile. "I think you're going to live, Mr. Reno."

She left then, and for a long time Reno sat there looking at the door and thinking. Finally he grinned and said, "Well, if I have to owe my life to somebody, I guess I couldn't have picked better folks."

"Guess you've all met Jeff Lindsey," Odell Bracy said expansively. He waved his hand toward the young man, then went on to add, "I think he's just what we've been needing around Rimrock, so I've asked him to explain a few ideas that we've cooked up."

All seven of the town council were crowded into Bracy's office, in addition to Jesse and Jeff, and there was a look of uncertainty as Bracy said, "Jeff here is a fine young lawyer, and I guess with a father like he's got, there's no question about his grasp of problems that face a town like ours. Jeff, why don't you tell the council some of the ideas we talked about yesterday?"

Jeff got to his feet, a little flustered. He had met the banker only the day before and was just in the process of meeting the other leaders of Rimrock. He had mentioned a few ideas rather generally, and when Bracy had invited him to come to a meeting of the town council, he had no idea of addressing the group. He felt awkward also in that he had not had time to share his ideas with his father. But he took the opportunity, deciding that he could talk things over with him afterward.

"I appreciate this chance to meet you gentlemen," he said easily, "but I want to assure you that I really am in the process of learning. The ink's not dry on my degree yet, and I must ask you men to inform me about the problems of Rimrock."

It struck a good note. Even Bones Morehouse seemed to approve, which rarely happened. Jeff talked for about fifteen minutes, outlining his views, mostly dwelling on measures that had been successful in other towns. Finally he said, "Well, I realize that you men have thought of these things, but I would like to thank you for the opportunity of letting me bring them to your attention."

He would have sat down, but R. G. Tyler said suddenly, "I like all you've said, young man, but I have one question."

"Yes?"

"How you reckon to carry them out? Rimrock isn't as tame as most of those places you've mentioned."

It was the crux of the problem, and a murmur of agreement went around the room. Jeff took a deep breath and plunged into the idea that he'd intended to keep under cover.

"Well, you are right, Mr. Tyler. And I have only one suggestion that I think will bring about permanent changes in the town. You need a special prosecutor."

"What for? Ain't we got a marshal?" Bones snapped. "I'll bet it'll cost a mint!"

Jeff turned with a smile toward his father and said, "Nobody here knows how vital a role Jesse Lindsey plays in this town—and will continue to play. But you all know he's worked to death trying to keep the lid on. What we need here is a man who will put the town first, a man with new ideas." Then Jeff smiled and added almost in passing, "We also need a man who will work for nothing until there is enough money in the till to pay him."

"You refer to yourself, I presume?" Tyler asked. He looked hard at the young man and shook his head. "I don't want to sound skeptical, but I never got anything worth having for nothing."

Jeff laughed and his ease was apparent to every one of them. "I believe that's correct, Mr. Tyler, and I warn you right at the beginning, that I will make a mint out of this sooner or later."

"Now *that* sounds like lawyer talk!" Bones said with a grin. "I'm for it if you can do it and stick somebody else for your fee. What's your plan?"

Jeff looked at them and said in a steady voice, "We've got to tame the town. But we can't call in a town-tamer. You all know the worst side of that—the answer is worse than the original problem."

"You're right there, Lindsey," Ernest Faulkner nodded. "Over in Hays they called in Ben Thompson, and he killed more people than any five hard cases!"

"How do you intend to get this job, and what do you intend to do after you get it?" Jesse spoke for the first time, and there was a mixture of pride and doubt on his seamed face.

"The first is simple," Jeff said carefully. "There's a county election in three weeks. All we have to do is announce that the office of special prosecutor will be filled. Then I'll have to beat anyone who runs."

"Won't be no mad stampede if it don't pay nothin'," Bones said.

"What will your platform be, Jeff?" the banker asked.

"We stick to the book!" Jeff said, and there was an intensity on his thin face as he leaned toward them. "We'll pass a no-gun ordinance and make it stick. We'll make the law so tough that the gunmen will know that there's no *if* about it—they go to jail immediately!"

"Won't that keep the trail herds from stopping here?" Bracy asked.

"Wild Bill made it stick at Abilene," Jeff shot right back. "The herds are still stopping there."

"What do you think, Jesse?" Odell Bracy asked smoothly. He knew that the plan would never work unless the marshal did his share. That was why he had arranged the meeting. Bracy loved to pull strings, and he saw himself as the prime mover of Rimrock.

Jesse stared at Jeff, then said slowly, "No. It won't work."

Jeff bit his lip, then asked quietly, "Why not?"

"Because you can't have your cake and eat it, too. You can either let the town have its wild element—keep a limit on it— or you can run them out. But you can't have Eastern sort of peace in a raw trail town like this."

"Now, Jesse, I think we ought to talk about it," Bracy said, and for the next thirty minutes there was a heated discussion that did exactly what the banker expected. They agreed to table it, but Bracy knew that with the election so close, they would have to decide soon. He smiled at Jeff, thinking how much easier it would be to run the town from behind the scenes with this boy as a figurehead.

Jeff fell in step with Jesse after the meeting broke up, saying, "Mind if I go a way with you, Dad?"

"Come on home for a cup of coffee, son. I think Rachel's got a fresh peach pie."

They talked idly of unimportant things, neither wishing to bring up the council meeting. They were strangers, both of them eager to move into a closer relationship, but aware of the dangerous differences between them.

"Come on in," Jesse said. He led Jeff to the kitchen, saying, "Feller followed me home, Rachel. You got any handouts for a hungry lawyer?"

"Hello, Jeff," Rachel's eyes lighted up and she put her hand out. "Why didn't you bring Ada?"

"She's having tea with some of the ladies," Jeff answered. He turned to face the man sitting on the high stool, peeling potatoes. "We meet again," he said, and there was a distressed look in his thin face as he added, "Might as well take my medicine. I was one of those on the stage . . . that put you out. Take a sock at me. I'd feel better."

"This here is my boy, Jeff, Reno," Jesse said quickly. "Jim Reno."

There was a smile on the face of Reno as he said, "Forget it, Jeff."

"Not likely!" Jeff slapped the table, saying harshly, "I don't know what in the world I was thinking about! I never pulled a stunt like that in my life!"

"I have," Reno said smiling. "Lots of times."

"Don't believe it!" Jesse said. "Anyway, it's all over. How about that pie?"

They all sat down, and Rachel put pie and coffee on the table, then asked almost at once, "What was the meeting about this time, Dad? Trying to cut your budget again?"

Jesse swallowed a bite of pie and said, "Actually, I think it was the other way around this time. Bracy thought he was foolin' me, but what he actually done was to try to sneak Jeff here into my job."

Jeff turned red, stuttering, "Ah, now . . . th—that's . . ."

Jesse laughed and waved his hand. "Just kidding, son. Not that some of it ain't so. Odell Bracy is a puredee operator, and I guess you seen that."

Jeff grinned. "Sure, but we'll fox him. No fancy dan of a banker is a match for a set of Lindseys!"

Jesse went on to tell about the meeting, making light of it, but there was a worried look on his drawn face that Rachel knew well.

Jeff seemed a little uncomfortable also, and soon he got up saying, "I'll have to run."

"I'll see you to the door," Rachel said quickly. They left Reno and Lindsey talking at the table, and she stepped outside with him.

"Jeff, be careful. Odell Bracy is honest enough, but he'll use anyone he can."

"Sure, Rachel." He smiled down at her. "I'll be careful."

She reached up and touched his cheek, then smiled and said, "It's good to have a big brother, Jeff."

Her face was framed in an oval light, and he could smell the fragrance of her hair. She was suddenly desirable, and he said in a different tone, "Well, not *quite* a brother, Rachel."

Her eyes widened and she bit her lip, then said, "Good night, Jeff."

She left him quickly, returning to the kitchen. She picked up the dishes, thinking about the attractive face of Jeff Lindsey, so much like his father. Then she looked at Jesse and thought, *He must not be hurt.*

Reno was listening intently as Jesse described the meeting, and when he finished he looked at the older man thoughtfully.

"Well, it looks like a little law by the book, doesn't it, Marshal?"

There was a sadness on Lindsey's face as he nodded and said, "Jeff's got good ideas. Too bad some of them just won't work around here." He got up and went heavily out of the room but paused at the door long enough to remark, "It would be nice if everything ended like in the storybooks, wouldn't it, Jim? But it never does."

As the two sat there listening to him walk heavily away, Rachel asked quietly, "Sometimes it ends like the books, doesn't it, Jim?"

He turned to gaze into her eyes, and there was a plea in her face, a pain so sharp that he wanted to reach out and comfort her. But he only said, "I guess it depends on who's writing the story, Rachel."

FOUR
Trouble on
Dance Street

Except for those nights when cowhands packed the streets, Rimrock was no more active than any other frontier town, and as Jim Reno walked along Grant Street he saw nothing that he had not seen in a hundred other towns. Even the shape seemed vaguely familiar. The bank, the hardware store, a dressmaker's shop, and a gun shop flanked one side of the main street. Across the broad street was a line of false fronts, including the jail where a sleepy-eyed deputy leaned back in his chair, dozing in the early morning sun.

Reno's progress did not go unnoticed as he made his way to the intersection where the only other broad street crossed Grant. He noted, without appearing to do so, the glances given by shopkeepers and clerks engaged in the ritual of opening up, and gauged that his story was as well recorded as if it had been written in the county newspaper. A smile touched his lips and he thought, *Guess I'm the local celebrity.* It was the way of small towns—to be curious of any stranger—and he did not resent it.

Although he had never seen the town, he could have

described the section which ran at right angles to Grant Street. Dance Street ran east and west, and to the south of it Reno spotted the stock pens and the railroad station. It was the railroad that breathed life into Rimrock, taking the cattle far away from flat Texas plains and shifting them to the bawling stockyards in Chicago. If it had not been for those narrow bands of steel, the town would have remained a barren spot in the Kansas plain.

Dance Street ran counter to Grant in more ways than direction. Reno glanced at the line of saloons punctuated by rudely painted signs and found the one he was seeking. Many of the squalid dens he passed were no more than single rooms with rough-hewn bars and a few battered chairs around low tables, but the Nugget was far above most gambling halls he had seen.

He noted the clean windows and the freshly painted sign that swung above the batwing double doors. He was forced to step aside to avoid the dust which a one-armed sweeper raised as he cleared off the wooden walk. Stepping inside, he saw that the floor was clean, the cuspidors were gleaming, and a bartender with a clean apron was idly polishing a line of shot glasses. Although it was not yet noon, two rough-looking punchers were already sitting at one of the highly polished tables playing cards with a bottle and two glasses in front of them.

Reno walked to the bar. Catching the eye of the man polishing the glasses, he asked, "Al Rossiter around?"

"Probably not up yet." The bartender had been a pug at one time. His broad Irish features had been flattened and scarred by many blows, but the small eyes that gleamed under the bushy red eyebrows were shrewd and alert. He was at

least six-four and must have weighed over 220. The years had
thickened his middle, but Reno noted he had huge forearms
and his fingers looked like bananas wrapped around the
glasses.

He was watching Reno steadily, filing information, and
finally he suggested with a voice roughened by whiskey but
musical with the accent of Ireland: "Al's got a room upstairs.
He usually comes down for breakfast about this time."

"Guess I'll wait."

"Sure. Something for you?"

"No thanks."

"You must be the fellow Marshal Lindsey's been keeping."

"That's right. Jim Reno."

"Rosy Tucker." The bartender gave him a huge paw that
seemed a foot wide, then with a small smile said, "Help yourself to the coffee."

"Sure." Reno walked over to the potbellied stove, took a
cup from a shelf fastened to the wall, and poured himself a cup
of steaming black coffee. He sat down, his back to the wall. He
was not surprised that the big barkeep knew about him, and
he observed that the two men playing cards threw him a
glance from time to time.

One of them, a skinny man with one eye cast and two
guns slung on his thighs, got up and walked past Reno's table,
giving him a searching glance, as if trying to catalog him.

What he saw was not impressive, for Reno had spent the
cool early morning chopping wood for Rachel's cook stove. His
faded overalls were patched in several places, the grey cham-
bray shirt was thin and had no collar, and the shapeless bro-
gans he used for heavy work had passed the stage of repair.
He wore the slouch hat—favored by Confederate foot sol-

diers—pulled down over his eyes. Leaving the house earlier, he had said wryly to Rachel, "I'm taking a turn around town. If I don't come back by noon, I'll probably be in jail—arrested on the charge of being a bum."

Reno looked up and caught the contemptuous gaze of the skinny puncher, who dismissed him and walked back to his table. He said something that made the other man laugh, and they went back to their cards.

Five minutes later Rossiter came down the steps and the barkeep said, "Fellow looking for you." He nodded toward Reno, who had seen the gambler enter. The two met at the bar.

"Rossiter?"

"Yes. You're looking a little better than when I first saw you."

"Guess I have you to thank for that."

Rossiter shifted uncomfortably. "I didn't do much."

"Don't see it that way," Reno said. There was a steadiness in his dark eyes that impressed the gambler, and although his words were mild, Rossiter felt the underlying strength of the man. He looked like a bum, and there was still a pallor which the sickness had left on his olive skin, but there was no mistaking the quality that lay beneath the surface of the man.

"Name is Al. How about some breakfast?"

"Had a bite already," Reno said. He shrugged and added, "I'm in your debt, Al. Feel free to call."

The two men at the table had taken this in, and now the one with the cast eye spoke up. "Better write that down, Rossiter. This yahoo may be a millionaire in disguise!"

The other man laughed loudly. "Yeah, he looks like a pig farmer, don't he?"

The two got up and wandered over to stand in front of Reno and Al, and the gambler said, "Take it easy, Riley."

"I always take it easy, don't I, Jack?" He was a little drunk, early as it was, and the mismatched eyes gave him a sinister air. He teetered back on his heels and drawled, "You startin' to take care of wanderin' tramps, Al? Looks like this one is about to cave in on you."

"What's your name, pig farmer?" his companion asked. He was one of those wiry men, laced with tough sinew and muscled. He had high cheekbones, like an Indian, and his black eyes glittered as he stared at Reno. There was a stark cruelty on his face, and his smile did not touch his black eyes.

"Take it easy, Jack," Al said quickly.

"I take it any way I find it, Al. You know that." He ran his eyes up and down, looking at Reno with a wide grin, then added with a sneer, "I just don't like pigs. What you think about that, pig farmer?"

Reno regarded the puncher steadily, then shrugged. "Your privilege," he said, and turned to lean on the bar.

His action irritated the puncher. He pulled at Reno's shoulder, turning him around, and said in a harsh voice, "Easy won't do it, pig farmer. Don't turn your back on me."

The quiet air of the saloon suddenly changed and there was a wicked light in the eyes of the two punchers. They had been idly engaged in some sort of game, but now there was tension in the air.

Reno had turned away, but now he looked right into the eyes of the man who stood in front of him, and although he wore no gun, something Jack saw in the face caused him to step back and put his hand on the .45 strapped to his thigh.

Rosy Tucker, the barkeep, spoke softly, but he put his hand beneath the bar and his eyes glinted with a strange light. "I guess you ought to get back to your card playing, Jack. You, too, Riley."

Both men turned to Tucker, hard-eyed and alert, but something in the big barkeep's face gave them pause, and Riley said, "Come on, Jack. It ain't worth the trouble."

The other tried to bluff it out, but finally dropped his eyes and with a curse went back to the table, where the two men sullenly began drinking from the bottle and playing cards.

"Riley Doucett and Jack Canby," Rosy said. "They think they've got to prove how tough they are to every stranger who hits town."

"Seen a few like that," Reno said. "Most of them end up in Boot Hill."

"Yeah, but don't mess with them, Reno," Al warned. "They're scum, but they have teeth."

Reno did not seem worried, and he said only, "Just came by to say thanks, Rossiter. The marshal told me what you did." He stared at the gambler and put his hand out. "I owe you something. Put it on my tab, will you?"

Rossiter took the hand, stared at the face of Reno, then grinned and said, "Sure."

Reno nodded to him, then said, "Thanks for the coffee, Rosy," and left the saloon, aware that he was being watched by Doucett and Canby.

"Seems like a pretty nice fellow, Al," Rosy said.

Rossiter nodded and answered, "I think you're right, Rosy." He threw a contemptuous glance at the two at the table. "If those two don't like him, he can't be all bad!"

As he made his way back down Dance Street, then turned off on Grant, Reno dismissed the incident. The two gunmen had not disturbed him; he had proved his courage often enough that he felt no need to answer the challenge of every two-bit tough that wandered by. A smile touched his lips as he suddenly thought of how he would have behaved in his youth. *Guess I'd have strapped on a hog leg and shot it out till somebody was past arguing. Good to have gotten past that stage.*

Marshal Lindsey's white frame bungalow was located on what was called Morgan's Lane, and when Reno went inside he found he had company.

A large man wearing a black frock coat got up as he entered, and Rachel nodded to him. "This is our preacher, Jim—Bishop Joe Sheridan. He's preacher for our church, but he's a traveling bishop in this area, too."

Joseph Sheridan got up and gave Reno a quick look, then put out a hamlike hand. "Glad to meet you, Reno."

"How are you, Reverend?"

"Better than I deserve!" The preacher was a massive man, well over six feet, and most of his two hundred pounds was packed in solid muscle. He had a round face decorated with muttonchop whiskers, and his eyes gleamed with humor as he added, "Hear you cheated me out of a good funeral service."

Reno grinned and nodded. "Sorry about that, Reverend, but you'll have to blame Al Rossiter and Rachel for the whole thing."

"So I heard. Well, I'm sorry that I didn't get here in time to help, but maybe I can do a little something now. You need a job?"

"Sure."

"Well, I know of one—but it's not much."

"I'll take it."

"Without knowing what it is?" The preacher chuckled softly, then went on. "One of my flock, Ralph Pitts, has a problem. He's a drunk. Keeps the livery stable for Ernie Faulkner, but he's not reliable. Think you could handle it?"

"Sure. When do I start?"

The bright black eyes of the preacher searched Reno's face, and he said, "You don't mince words, do you, son? Which outfit was you with?"

Reno smiled and answered, "Third Arkansas. Which was you with, Reverend?"

"Third Michigan," Sheridan said with a grin. "I think you and me might have been shootin' at each other at one time or another, son."

"Glad we both missed," Reno drawled.

"Me too. Well, you ready?" The preacher turned to Rachel who had watched this exchange with a smile. "I'll see you in church, Rachel. I want you to have a solo or two ready."

"All right. Will you be home for dinner, Jim?"

"Keep the pot warm," Reno said, and followed the bishop out. They turned toward Grant and the bishop said, "Not much of a job, Reno."

"I'm in your debt, Reverend." He added, "Seems like I'm in everybody's debt."

Bishop Sheridan gave Reno a swift glance and asked gently, "That bother you, Reno?"

"Some."

"Pride—we all have too much of it. Got to learn that no man lives to himself and no man dies to himself."

Reno thought about that as they turned down toward the stable and finally said gently, "I don't know about that, Brother Sheridan. I guess both of us have seen a lot of good boys go down—and it seems to me like they were pretty well alone."

"That's the way it looks, but I decided it couldn't be that simple. You were at Gettysburg, Jim?"

Reno nodded. "I was there."

"I was at Little Round Top. Just a few of us, and it looked like the whole rebel army was coming to get us." There was a faraway look in Sheridan's eyes as he recounted the story. "My two best friends dropped beside me, shot through." He shook his head and the hand that wiped his brow trembled. "I don't know how any of us made it, the way you fellows charged up that hill!"

"Not many of us got there," Reno said softly.

"No, I guess not." They were almost to the stable and the preacher shrugged and said, "Jim, I'd been to many a revival meeting as a young man, but religion never rubbed off on me. I can't explain it—never have been able to—but as I lay there in that hail of bullets, I found God. Never have been able to get away from him. If you don't know about that, you will someday. Well, this is it."

Faulkner's Livery Stable was housed in a large barnlike structure past Race Street, just opposite a blacksmith shop. The bishop greeted a short man wearing a navy blue suit and a black hat. "Jim, this is Ernest Faulkner, the owner. Ernest, Jim Reno. I think he'll do you a good job."

"You known him long, Brother Sheridan? I got to have a steady man."

"We met up a few years ago, Ernest." The bishop gave Reno a sly glance and said, "His organization made quite an impression on me. I'll stand for him."

"All right, if you say so."

"I'll expect to see you in church Sunday, Jim." He turned and walked away, his back as straight as a ramrod.

Faulkner was in a hurry, and he gave a few instructions to Reno, ending with: "Not much to it, Reno. If you run into any problems, I'll be down at my hardware store."

He hurried off, and Reno spent an hour cleaning the place up. No one had done much of that, apparently, and he had just finished cleaning out the stalls on one side of the roomy barn when a small boy came running through the doorway, running into Reno's legs. He would have fallen, but Reno caught him and held him up. "Watch out there, young fellow."

The boy was skinny as a snake, and the large blue eyes were undershadowed with dark circles. He had a mop of thick cotton-colored hair, and Reno saw at once that no one had taken much care with him. He was wearing a faded pair of trousers made for a much larger boy, so large that the legs had been hacked off and the waist was gathered around the boy's middle with a piece of cotton plow line. His shirt was too small, and he was barefoot.

"My name's Jim," Reno said, seeing the boy stare at him suspiciously. "I'm the new man."

"Where's Ralph?" the boy asked, and there was an angry light in his eyes as he stared at Reno.

Reno realized that Ralph must have been the one who drank too much. "I guess I'm his replacement."

"He was doing all right!" the boy said sullenly. "Wasn't no need for old man Faulkner to can him just because he took a snort now and then!"

"He a friend of yours, son?"

"I ain't your son!" the boy snapped at once, and Reno realized he had touched on a sore spot. "My name is Lee Morgan."

He turned to go, and Reno asked quickly, "Is Ralph any kin to you, Lee?"

"Naw, I ain't got no kin. I . . . I worked for him sometimes."

Reno nodded, and he snapped his fingers as if he had just thought of something. "Son of a gun! I was just about to go out and try to hire *me* some help!"

"Really!"

"Sure, I was—but maybe you can keep on working here for me like you did for Ralph. I sure would appreciate it. Why, I don't even know where things are around here."

The boy's thin face lit up, and he said in a rush, "Yeah, I can work for you, mister. I can do anything around here! Why, sometimes when Ralph was—" The boy stopped and his face reddened, as he went on. "I mean, he let me take care of the horses and clean out the stalls and sweep. And he paid me a dollar a week—sometimes."

"A dollar?" Reno seemed to ponder that, then shook his head. "Gosh, Lee, I can't do that."

The boy's face fell, and he said, "Well, I can do it for less."

"No, sir, Lee," Reno said with a shake of his head. "I intend to have good help, and I couldn't think of having a helper that earned less than two dollars a week. It just wouldn't do! You'd have to take on a little extra responsibility, but I think you're the one who could handle it."

"Gee! Two dollars a week!" Lee began to go into a little dance and he said, "I'll start right now!"

"Sure. Your first job is to show me all the horses we have to rent out. And after that, I feel like we better go down to that store I saw on my way here." Reno shook his head and allowed a sad expression to pass over his face. "I might as well be honest with you from the start, Lee. I have a real problem."

"Oh?" The boy's thin face changed and he seemed to shrink. Reno realized he had jumped to the conclusion that his new employer had the same problem as Ralph.

"The thing is, Lee, I'm just real bad about candy."

"Candy?"

"Yes. Isn't that a terrible thing for a grown man?" Reno

looked the boy right in the face and added, "I have to have a little candy every day, Lee, and that's all there is to it. So when I say, 'Let's go to the store and get some candy, Lee,' don't you give me any arguments, see? Just hush up and go with me, boy. I don't intend to reform. I'm just too far gone. So you'll just have to put up with it!"

"Golly, Mister Reno—"

"And you don't call me that unless other people are around. Jim was the name my mama gave me."

Lee nodded and the fine lines of worry that Reno had noted were smooth in the boy's face, so he said, "Well, let's see what you know about this stable. Maybe I can get most of it learned before I have one of my sweet-tooth fits."

"Jim, you close this place down and come home this minute!"

Reno turned, holding a bucket of grain in his hand, to find Rachel glaring at him angrily. He put the bucket down and asked, "What's wrong?"

"Do you know what time it is, Jim Reno?"

"Well, . . ."

"It's nearly eight o'clock—and you've been at this place since early this morning." She shook her head and took him by the arm, shaking him and adding, "You'll be back in that bed again if you keep this up."

"Well, I meant to come in, but people kept coming. I had to take care of the horses. I think every stall is filled."

"Then you can come with me right now."

Reno grinned and said, "I reckon I can." He turned the lanterns out and locked the door, and for the first time he was aware of the burst of noise that was emanating from Dance Street. "Pretty lively tonight."

Rachel held his arm as they walked along. "Two big trail herds camped just outside of town. Dad's already got the jail packed, and they haven't even started yet."

A series of shots rang out, and there was a wild cry that ended suddenly. "I hate all this, Jim!" Rachel said soberly. Her face was highlighted by the yellow lanterns, and he was aware again of her beauty. "Ever since I can remember, Dad has been walking down streets like this. And I never stop thinking about what could happen to him."

"A lonely job," Reno agreed, "but your brother, Jeff, thinks he can change that."

"Do you think so?"

"Not likely. I've seen it tried in towns like this before. The town fathers holler a lot about wanting peace and quiet, but when it cuts into their pocketbooks they back off. Then when somebody has to lay his life on the line walking down the street like this one, you'll find them all home behind locked doors."

They had come to the spot where the main street crossed Dance Street, which was crowded with jostling punchers, gamblers, and a few farmers. The shills outside the saloons monotonously called out the enticements of their places, and there was all the activity of a seething caldron that kept the nerves rasped raw.

A tall, skinny cowboy mounted on a wild-eyed horse rode right down the middle of the street waving a six-gun. He let out a wild screech and sent several cursing men reeling as he sent his mount right into a saloon. There was a wild explosion of sound from inside, and he came out almost at once, firing his revolver as he cleared the wooden walk and dashed down the crowded street.

Reno pulled Rachel back as the cowboy skirted the sidewalk, reeling in the saddle, and then Rachel called out, "Lee! Get back!"

Reno swept his glance around, catching sight of the small form of Lee Morgan right in the path of the drunken horseman. He had been trying to cross the street, dodging elbows and boots, but he was bumped suddenly and fell sprawling in the dust of Dance Street.

In one split second Reno took in the situation, then he moved in a burst of energy. The drunk did not see the boy who lay right in his path, and Reno knew that the only hope was to turn the horse. In one smooth motion he drove his lean body toward the street, hitting the edge of the sidewalk and launching himself toward the galloping horse just as the rider sped by. He had only one chance, and if he missed, he would fall under the hooves of the horse himself.

But he didn't miss. He hit the horse's head, wrapping his arms around, and when he locked his hands he let the force of his body twist the head so violently to one side that the horse lost his footing. Reno was thrown to the ground, and the rider shot wildly over the mount's head as he went down, rolling over in the dust.

Reno took a hard blow to the head as he hit the ground, but he got up and made his way to where Lee was picking himself up, his face pale and his eyes big as dinner plates.

"You all right, Lee?"

"Sure, Jim! Boy, I thought I was a goner!"

"Lee! Are you hurt?" Rachel arrived and grabbed at the boy.

"No, Miss Rachel—but did you see what Jim done to that horse? He just bulldogged that sucker!"

Rachel turned to give Reno an open-eyed look, the shock still in her eyes. She nodded and said, "Yes, I saw it."

She would have said more, but just then there was a wild cry from Reno's left, and he wheeled to see the drunk, his hat missing and dirt all over his face, come charging toward him, windmilling his arms and cursing. He was wild-eyed and his gun had been lost in the fall, so he charged at Reno wildly.

Reno set his feet and let one wild swing go over his head, and then twisting his body he drove a left hook into the drunk's stomach. The force of the blow doubled the man over, and his voice was cut off abruptly as he fell into a ball in the dust, hoarsely gasping for breath.

It had happened so quickly that not many saw what had happened, but there were two who did. They must have been very close, for no sooner had the man gone down than Jim was flanked at once by the two men he had seen in the saloon earlier.

Both of them were drunk, and there was a cruel light in Jack Canby's dark eyes as he said loudly, "Well, lookee here, Riley."

Riley Doucett's face was flushed, and he moved to the other side of Reno, flanking him. "Yeah, Jack, we got us a pig farmer, ain't we?"

Both of them were armed, as they had been earlier, and the crowd broke away, men backing off to watch from a safe distance. It was like wolves circling to watch a helpless victim brought down by one of the pack.

"You're pretty rough on drunks, ain't you, pig farmer?" Canby said with a wide grin.

"That joker nearly hit a boy," Reno said. He was bracketed by the two men, and he knew what they would do.

"Why, I guess Donnie was a little drunk, but he's a friend of ours, so I guess we'll have to rough you up to make it right."

"I wouldn't do that if I were you," Reno said.

"He wouldn't do that if he was us! Did you hear that, Riley?" Canby suddenly dropped his smile and his eyes were dark with cruelty. He said, "You ain't gonna walk away from this one, pig farmer!"

Reno had turned to watch Canby, judging him to be the more dangerous of the two, but he caught a glimpse of movement and heard Rachel cry out. He ducked, catching the blow of Doucett's fist on his neck, but before he could recover, Canby caught him directly on the temple with a knobby fist and the world went red as he was driven to the dust. He had only time to curl into a ball before the boots of one of them caught him in the ribs, driving the breath from his body.

Rachel screamed and threw herself at Canby, who was drawing back his boot to kick Reno again, and Lee grabbed at the leg of Doucett, who cursed and knocked him off with a hard blow to the head.

Reno caught a glimpse of Rachel being driven back into the dust by a backhanded blow, and he struggled to his feet. He had no breath and the world was filled with bright whirling lights, but he knew that he would be stomped to a pulp if he didn't act.

He was still wearing the heavy work boots and with all his might he twisted and kicked Jack Canby in the small of the back. The force of it bent the skinny gunman backward, and he screamed as he fell clutching at his back in pain.

Riley Doucett stared at Canby in the dust, and with one smooth motion drew his gun and lifted it toward Reno. "I'll kill you!" he shouted.

"Hold it right there or you're a dead man!"

Doucett swiveled his head around and looked right into the muzzle of a sawed-off shotgun. He froze as Jesse Lindsey stared at him, his eyes catching the gleam of the lanterns. "One move and I'll cut you in two, Riley. Drop that gun—*now!*"

With a gasp Doucett dropped his gun and stood stock-still, paralyzed by the bore of the shotgun.

Jesse lowered the gun and walked over to pick up Doucett's gun. He said to Zane, "Lock all three of them up."

There was a protest on Doucett's lip which he shut off as Jesse said, "I wish you'd say something. I would really like an excuse to rub you out!"

Doucett looked at the face of Jesse Lindsey, swallowed hard, and waited until Zane had pulled Canby to his feet. The gunman's face was pale as death, but there was an unholy light in his eyes as he whispered to Reno, "You're a dead man! I'll kill you!"

Zane took the three of them off, and Jesse said, "Boy, you sure are a problem to me."

"I reckon so," Reno said. "Never felt so happy to see a shotgun in my whole life! Thanks again."

Jesse shrugged. He looked across the street and said, "Jail's full already. And they'll all get off with a fine." He added, "You better believe what Canby said. He'll do it, Jim."

"I expect he'll try," Reno answered carelessly, and then he said, "Must be some place where a man doesn't have to think about somebody killing him, Jesse. Sure wish I could find it."

The marshal of Rimrock nodded and said sadly, "Me too, Jim. Me too." He turned and there was a stoop to his shoulders as he walked down the middle of Dance Street—the loneliest man in Rimrock.

FIVE
Lee Takes a Stand

"Says something about us, don't it now, Jim? We got seventeen saloons, half a dozen fancy houses—and one church that ain't even finished yet!"

Reno took in the half-finished building, noting the unpainted boards beginning to warp, the windows only holes in the walls, and said, "Too bad. When I was a kid I never did understand why people let the church building fall down when they took care of their own places."

He had eaten a late breakfast with Jesse and Rachel, then argued that he had nothing decent to wear to church.

"Wear what you got, Reno!" Jesse snapped. "If your clothes is good enough to wear in a stable, they ought to be good enough to worship God in!"

"Yes, sir, Major," Reno responded with a grin.

Jesse stared at Reno. "I'm not a major any more. How'd you know I was one?"

"Oh, I guess I must have heard someone say so," Reno said, then he grinned and added, "The way you gave me that invitation to go to church, why, it sounded like a major I had one time in the Third Arkansas. This was in the winter of '62, and we wasn't in any action. A revival got to going, and our major was about as rough as a man can get. But when he heard about it, I heard him ask a lieutenant, 'How many converts did the Texas regiment baptize?' The lieutenant said, 'Why, I think about ten more than our regiment, Major.'"

Reno leaned back and winked at Rachel who was listening. "That major cussed and said to the aide, 'You detail twenty men to be baptized after breakfast! Ain't no rag-tailed bunch of Texans going to have more converts than this outfit!'"

Rachel laughed and said, "That's about the way Dad's invitation sounded, isn't it? But come on anyway, Jim. You'll like Brother Joe's sermons. He's been in hot water with his superiors for his preaching for a long time."

"He sure has!" Jesse said with a grin. He got up from the table and said, "He only came to work with this church a few months ago, and there's already a bunch organized to get him defrocked!"

Reno got up and helped Rachel clear the table. "I like that, Major. Any preacher who doesn't have a bunch after his hair just ain't preaching!"

They sat on the front porch until the sound of a bell had summoned them to join a few families on their way to the church. As they entered the building, Reno looked around and said, "Things don't change much. Looks just like the church my folks made me go to every Sunday when I was a kid."

Long bars of sunlight shot through the windows, highlighting the swirling motes of sawdust raised by dragging feet, and there was a steady hum of flies, a drone not unlike the talk of the worshipers sitting on the crudely built pine seats. On a raised platform, Brother Joe sat on a kitchen chair, his eyes counting the house, and across from him a thin young man with a long neck decorated by a string tie was blowing into a pitch pipe.

Reno took his seat halfway to the front with Jesse and Rachel, and smiled to see that the economics of the town were strictly reflected in the seating. Up close to the front sat the well-dressed, more prosperous element, while about halfway back the clothing got plainer, less expensive. On the very back row—for the very poor—sat Lee Morgan, twisted around trying to see over the heads of the more affluent element. In a balcony several black families huddled together, peering down at the platform.

Reno whispered to Rachel, "I ought to go sit with the rest of the ragpickers. Some of the folks think I'm in the wrong pew."

He was wearing his only decent shirt and butternut trousers, both thin with wear. Over to his left he saw Jeff Lindsey and his mother, both looking somewhat surprised.

Rachel followed his glance, and nodded with a smile to them. "Don't worry, Jim. Brother Joe doesn't put much stock in what folks wear on the outside. It's when he spots something on the *inside* you'd better watch out!"

The song leader stood up and said, "Now I want you all to sing as to the Lord this morning. We'll start out with 'Old Hundred.' You all know that one, so sing loud."

He spoke the first line of the song—"Praise God from whom all blessings flow"—in a natural tone, then the congregation sang it. He gave the second line, "Praise him all creatures here below," and the congregation joined to sing that. So it went, in what was common enough practice. So many people could not read that "lining out" a hymn was almost universal in Southern and Western churches.

As the song service went on, Reno found himself joining in with songs he hadn't heard for years. Rachel noted his clear baritone voice and smiled at him. "You've been in church before."

"Long time ago," he whispered, and he added, "Guess this is one thing in the world that doesn't change much."

Finally Brother Joe got up, and there was a stern set to his lips and a peculiar light in his deep-set eyes. "Watch out, Jim, he's loaded for bear!" Jesse leaned across Rachel and whispered. "I know the signs!"

Without hesitation Sheridan said in a strident tenor voice, "I have ten churches to watch over, and I do not propose to dally around with you people. God has put me in this place as your pastor." He paused to glance around at his flock, then said in a tone that left no doubt as to his position: "Some of you think that is not the case. I will tell you right now, you will find me a difficult man to get rid of. I propose to stay in this place until some of you pious hypocrites repent! You will either cease to be the generation of vipers I have plowed up, or I will stomp you to bits!"

Reno murmured softly so that only Rachel heard him, "Why doesn't he quit being polite and come right out and say what he means?" She shushed him, but there was a smile on her lips.

Brother Joe opened his Bible and began to read with great emphasis. "Ezekiel, chapter forty-seven and verse one. 'Afterward he brought me again unto the door of the house; and behold, waters issued out from under the threshold of the house eastward, and the waters were to the ankles; and he measured a thousand, and the waters were to the knees; again he measured a thousand, and the waters were to the loins;

afterward he measured a thousand, and it was a river, waters to swim in, a river that could not be passed over.'"

A bewildered silence reigned as the congregation tried to fathom the strange Scripture. The pastor looked out at the faces turned up toward him, and said, "You can find out more about this river by reading the last ten chapters of Ezekiel, but this morning I propose to tell you about these verses.

"The things of God do not usually come all at once. Every mighty river has a beginning as a small trickle somewhere. Not one of us will ever live years enough to see an acorn become a towering oak. Did any of you ever plant cottonseed one day and pick cotton the next?" From some longsuffering farmer came a groan and a whisper, "Lord, I reckon not!" A suppressed laugh swept over the room, but Sheridan went right on.

"I tell you, God speaks to us first in whispers, but most of us don't listen. We are so all-fired busy with other things we don't even know the voice of the God who made us! But if we ever *do* stop ourselves long enough to listen to God when he whispers, why, soon he will speak loud and clear.

"Folks, if there is a want-to in a man as big as a nit, that little stream of life that most of us plug up with all kinds of god-less logs and trash will clear up and that river will rise up from our ankles to our knees—it'll come up to the loins, the source of life!" His voice rose and he pounded the flimsy desk which served as a pulpit. His eyes glowed as they swept the congregation, and Reno felt the power of his gaze.

"You can be fruitful and productive. You may have gone through your whole life not knowing there's a God in heaven. This may be the first time you've ever heard about a God who wants to give you a life with real meaning in it. Maybe right this very minute you are hearing inside a voice that is saying to you to come and live, and you may not know what it is." Brother Joe smiled then, and his whole face lit up as he added, "I think some of you are feeling the river beginning to lap around your ankles!"

For over an hour he went on, sometimes in a voice of thunder, raking them for their sins like a fierce-eyed Old Testament prophet, but often pausing to woo them to a life of honor in a gentle voice that revealed a deep love for his flock. Time and time again he brought them face-to-face with their duty—to love God and man.

Finally he shut his Bible and his voice took on a hard edge as he said, "I'm no prophet, but I have a warning for you people, which I will give in no uncertain terms. I will not have your blood on my hands!"

"I have spent many happy hours fishing on Reelfoot Lake down in Arkansas. Some of you know it. It's an oxbow lake which was at one time part of the Mississippi River. Once it was just a sharp bend in that river, and then one day there was a breakthrough. Part of the U-shaped curve got close to the other bend, right where the river turned back on itself, you see? Then the river broke through at the top of the U, and the Mississippi took a new course. The river kept on flowing down to the Gulf—but there was this U-shaped lake which was left off to one side. I call your attention to verse eleven of this chapter which says, 'The miry places thereof and the marshes thereof shall not be healed; they shall be given to salt.'"

Sheridan stared down at the congregation with a stern face. "In the river that the prophet tells of, there was a flood of good fish and life-giving waters." He paused and asked rhetorically: "Do any of you know what you catch in an oxbow lake which has got cut off from the main stream and has become a swamp?"

Reno had been so caught up with the story that he said out loud before he could catch himself: "Turtles and alligator gar!"

There was a gasp from a few members of the congregation at his response, but Brother Joe grinned and said, "You are exactly right, Brother Reno—I can see you have been there!"

Then he stopped smiling and said, "I am bound and determined that this church will not be a swamp filled with worthless turtles and gar!"

"Amen!" several staunch voices echoed, and Sheridan went on in a determined voice: "I've come to pastor this church, and my job is to keep you—and myself—in the river that always flows out of God's temple! It may be only ankle-deep now, but in this hellhole of a town we live in, that won't cut the mustard—we need rivers to swim in!"

He had to wait until the amen corner quieted down, and Reno saw that there were several angry faces in the congregation, lips white and eyes sullen.

"Some of you are living in a swamp. You are members of this church, but you are hugging up to the turtles and gar that run the saloons and fancy houses that traffic in human flesh!" He raised his voice to a shout that pierced the ears as he finished, "You will not do so for long! You will either come into the pure river of God or you will go and live with the gars and turtles!"

He looked out over the still congregation and said in a tone that was gentle and quiet, "If you are living that sort of life now, and are sick of it, I aim to help you find the river. If you have a want to serve God, I'm here to help. If your name is on the church roll and you are living in the swamp and you intend to stay there—why, I'll do all I can to accommodate you. But if I can help it, you won't live in the swamp six days a week then try to take up residence in this church on Sunday!"

"Some of you," he said, stepping down onto the floor with his Bible firmly under his arm, "will no doubt try to run me off. You just have right at it, beloved! I was looking for a church when I found this one. I close with this—we are dwelling in a grand and awful time, not one of us having any guarantee that we'll live the week out. I tell you flat out that nothing will do for this church but the plain unvarnished gospel of the Lord Jesus Christ! No standard lower than the Book will do. I invite you to join me."

Then it was over, and Reno heard one roughly dressed puncher say, "I reckon I heard me a preacher man today."

"Are you a Christian, Dooley?" one of his companions asked.

"No, I'm a Republican," the rawboned puncher said with a grin. Then he added, jerking his thumb at Joe Sheridan, "But if I listened to that feller too long, I might get tempted to become one!"

After they had left the church and were on their way back to the house, Jesse took a swift look at Reno, and said, "You're pretty quiet, Jim. The sermon hurt your feelings?"

"I guess so, Major," Reno said with a twisted smile. He thought about it for a few seconds, then shook his head, saying quietly, "That business about living with the gars and the turtles—sure does seem like Reverend Sheridan's been reading my mail."

"Why, I don't think you're that sort of man, Jim," Rachel said seriously.

Reno gave a short laugh. "Most folks in my hometown

said I was studying for the gallows from the time I was fifteen. I guess they had some right to say so."

"Man can change, Jim," Jesse said softly. "Man can always change."

A heavy expression on Reno's face shrouded the light in his dark eyes.

By Tuesday, Reno had caught up on the work at the stable so well that Faulkner gave him a raise, saying in surprise, "The place never looked so good."

Reno smiled down at Lee, who was oiling up a piece of harness, and said, "Well, a man who's got good help has just got an edge, wouldn't you say?"

"That's right. Boy, if you want to work some at the hardware store, you come by."

"Sure, Mr. Faulkner," Lee agreed quickly.

As soon as the owner left, Reno said, "You maybe work too hard. I never see you playing games with the other boys." He spoke idly and, without appearing to do so, kept his eye on the boy. He had learned that the boy was a foundling, left on the doorstep of a poor family when he was only a few months old. He'd been passed around from family to family until finally he'd run away. He lived in an attic bedroom over a saloon, making what money he could doing odd jobs.

A flush touched Lee's thin cheeks and his lips turned pale. Reno let the silence run on, then turned and put his hand on the boy's thin shoulder and asked quietly, "They give you a hard time?"

"One of them does—a fellow named Kyle Thomas. He's the leader, see, and when he gets it in for somebody, why, the rest of 'em seem to pitch in, too."

"I was on my own when I was just a little older than you, Lee," Reno said idly. "A fellow named Mac Cartwright whipped up on me ever chance he got."

"What . . . what'd you do, Jim?"

"Mostly I ran away."

Lee blinked his eyes and swallowed, "Did you for real?"

"Sure. Didn't have a brother or a dad to take up for me. Mac was older than I was, and lots bigger."

Lee thought about that, then said, "You just ran away?"

"Well, I did until I decided one day that nothing could be worse than being scared all the time—so I did something about it."

"What?" Lee demanded.

"I got me a piece of stove wood and let Mac and the rest catch me in an alley. Then when Mac was about to start in on me, I pulled the stick of wood from behind my back and laid him out."

"You really hit him with it?"

"Nearly drove him into the ground!"

"What'd he say when he got up?"

"Said, 'You could have killed me with that stick of wood.' And I looked him right in the eye and held the stick up. 'It ain't too late for that now, Mac,' I told him."

"Golly! Were you and him always enemies, Jim?"

Reno turned suddenly to stare off at the horizon, but Lee caught the sadness in his eyes. "No, Lee," he said finally. "He became my best friend. We rode together, joined the army together. It was Mac who saved my life. Crossed an open field under the worst crossfire I ever saw to pull me to safety."

"He *did!*"

"And got killed doing it," Reno said in a voice so low that

the boy nearly missed it. Then he looked up and said, "I can't tell you what to do about Kyle, Lee, but I can tell you that there's one thing that's worse than taking a beating—and that's being afraid all the time."

The boy stood there, his face working, and he finally said, "That's right. Bein' scared is pretty bad."

"Hello, Lee."

Neither of them had heard the woman approach, but when the boy saw her he said eagerly, "Why, hello, Miss Lola."

She was a woman with a rose-complexioned face, smiling and with a bold look. The fancy riding habit she wore clung to her in a way calculated to attract male attention. She was about his own age, Reno judged, and probably knew as much of the world as he did. She moved her head with a swift gesture to meet his attention. Her eyes were greenish, her hair a rich auburn that caught the light of the sun in deep gleams. She looked at him with a steady interest, and it was obvious that she was accustomed to meeting the glances of men.

"I'm Lola Fremont," she offered in a direct fashion, then waited for his name.

"Jim Reno."

"Heard about you." She cocked her head, and there was a challenge in her glance.

"Miss Lola is teaching me to read," Lee said proudly. "We have lessons almost every day."

"We sure do." Lola's face turned gentle as she put her hand on the boy's shoulder. "And you're going to be a real scholar."

"Can I saddle her horse, Jim? I can do it all by myself."

"Sure."

Lee scrambled inside, and Lola continued to regard Reno

steadily. "Lee's pretty sold on you. He thinks you're quite a fellow."

Reno shrugged, saying only, "Boy appreciates things."

"Sure." She cocked her head and said, "You're no stable hand, Mr. Reno."

"Wrong there, Miss Fremont. It's what I am for now."

She shook her head, and in her bright green eyes there was a knowledge gained by hard experience. She knew the man before her had seen bloody battle. "No, you've been to see the elephant; I know the breed." Then she said, "You know that Canby and Doucett have been making fight talk about you."

"They got their pride hurt. Guess it's all we got, men like us, so we're pretty touchy."

"You're not like those two," she said at once. "Mr. Reno, the only reason they haven't come after you yet is they know Marshal Lindsey would have their hides if they took after you."

"Can't crawl in a hole and hide, can I?"

His smile bothered her, and she stepped so close that he caught the scent of her perfume, strong and heady. "Don't let them get you in a trap, Mr. Reno. They're both killers."

Lee came out leading a dark chestnut mare, and Reno gave her a hand up. Wheeling the horse sharply around, she said, "Come by late tonight if you want to, Lee. Good to meet you, Mr. Reno."

As she set the horse down the street at a trot, Lee said, "Jim, you think she's nice?"

Reno looked down and said with a broad smile, "I sure do, Lee. Real nice."

He sighed and said, "Me too. She was my best friend until—" He broke off, embarrassed, and ended by saying, "She's been real good to me."

Reno saw that the boy yearned to hear a good word about Lola Fremont. He made a quick guess that he'd been tormented about her, what she was, and he said warmly, "Lots of nice folks in the world, Lee, but I think that Miss Lola is right up there at the top of the list."

Lee seemed to relax, and he grinned at Reno with a warm light in his blue eyes. "Sure she is," he said as he returned to polishing the harness.

Reno did not see the woman when she returned the mare. He had taken a pair of matched bays out to a farm five miles south of Rimrock. When he got back he found Lee waiting for him, a strained look in his eyes and a faint pallor on his face.

Reno dismounted, then went about the business of unsaddling his horse, knowing that Lee would have to open the conversation.

"I . . . I met up with Kyle Thomas."

"That right, Lee? Did you run again?"

"No—I hit him with this!"

Reno turned to look at Lee who was holding out a leather blackjack with a heavy disc of lead in the end. Reno took it and slapped his palm with it. "This is pretty rough medicine, Lee. You hurt him bad?"

"I . . . I guess so." Lee's lips were trembling and there was an unsteadiness in his figure. "He didn't get up. The boys got some men and they carried him off to the doctor."

Reno nodded. "All right, Lee, you did what you had to do. Don't back up, no matter what."

"I—" Lee suddenly looked up and Reno followed his frightened glance across the street. A small group of men was striding right toward them, one of them a huge man with an angry face.

"Don't you try to run, boy!" he said loudly as the group came up to surround Reno and Lee. "Think you can act like them thugs you hang out with around decent people! Well, you're going to pay for what you did to my boy!"

He was holding a braided leather quirt in his hand, and he made it whistle through the air. He had a look of vicious pleasure on his face as he said, "Come here, you whelp!"

Lee looked very small as he stood there facing the huge man, but he stood his ground, face white but with a steady voice. "Kyle has been whipping me for a year, Mr. Thomas. I couldn't stand it no more."

"Don't you sass me, boy!" Thomas made the whistle cut through the air and shouted, "I'm going to cut the flesh off your bones!"

He reached out and took Lee by the arm, but Reno reached out and struck the massive arm in what looked like a very light blow. Thomas's arm, however, dropped to his side, paralyzed. He stared at the smaller man, not able to believe what had been done. Then he raised the quirt to cut Reno across the face, but once again Reno made a swift move, striking the thick shoulder of the man. The whip fell to the ground, and Thomas stood there, both arms dangling.

Reno watched him, and there was nothing threatening in his dark face. He regarded the larger man with a mild expression, but he slapped the blackjack against his palm in a motion that caught the eyes of Thomas and his friends.

"I hope your boy is all right, Mr. Thomas," he said easily, "and if he's got the nerve to go up against Lee himself, why, that's his business. But if I hear of you bothering this boy again, I'll take it personal." His eyes moved to the other men, who had suddenly grown very quiet.

"I'll have the law on you!" Thomas recovered his voice and moved back carefully. The feeling was returning to his arms and he began rubbing them as he backed away cursing. "You ain't seen the last of this!"

Reno waited until they faded down the street, then handed the blackjack back to Lee. "You did what you had to do, Lee, but I hope you don't have to do it again."

"Me too," the boy said fervently. "I think he'll leave me alone now. You reckon Mr. Thomas will have you arrested?"

"No. He's all talk, Lee."

"Gosh, I was scared! But you wasn't, was you, Jim?"

Reno looked down at Lee and said, "Men aren't dogs to be walking around snapping at each other. Remember this, Lee, the test of a man isn't how many other men he can beat to the draw or whip in a fist fight." A look of weariness crossed Reno's dark face and he seemed to be searching for the right words to pass along to the boy who stood before him. He said finally, "The bravest man I ever knew never fired a gun, Lee, and never hit another man in anger. I wish I could be like him. I wish you could, too."

For a long time the boy stood trying to figure that out, then he said, "I don't like fighting anyway, Jim."

"Neither do I, Lee. Maybe someday we won't have to do it any more." Then he shrugged and said, "Until that day comes, you and I will just have to do the best we can to live peacefully!"

SIX
Man without a Cause

Lola Fremont lived over the Nugget in rooms she had fixed up in a style as ornate as her wardrobe. Her bedroom was covered with a cream paper ornamented with large red roses, and a thick Persian rug was spread on the floor. There was a massive brass bed covered by a brightly colored spread.

The sitting room was no less startling with garish paper, dwarfed by a cut-glass chandelier that had been made for a much larger room. Lola had liked it, though, and as she sat at a walnut table, pointing out words to Lee Morgan, she looked almost pale in contrast to the violent colors.

She was wearing a green silk dressing gown, and as she sat there with her feet tucked beneath her, she looked very young. Without the makeup that she wore during the day, her face seemed pale, and there was a vulnerable, almost innocent air about the owner of the Nugget.

She had been having Lee in for reading lessons ever since she had noticed him cleaning the windows of the saloon and asked him who he was. Something about the total isolation of the small boy had stirred a maternal instinct, and she had asked him to her room for milk and some cake. That had become a habit, one she looked forward to as an oasis in the desert which her life seemed to have become. Lee would not go to school, so she had undertaken the task of teaching him to read. He was very bright, and she saw that soon he would be past any help she could give. The thought of losing the quiet moments with the boy disturbed her.

"All right, that's good, Lee," she said closing the book. "You want to spell for awhile?"

"Sure, I like—," he began, but the door opened without a knock, and Neal Burdick entered. There was a proprietary air about the way he came in, as if it were his own room, and his massive bulk seemed to make the room smaller.

"The next time you come in here, you can knock," Lola said, a touch of anger in her eyes.

He paid her no heed, giving Lee a frown. He nodded toward the door and said curtly, "Beat it, kid."

The look Lee gave him was a mixture of fear and hatred, but he got up and started for the door.

"Come in the morning, Lee," Lola said quickly. "We'll have George fix us some pancakes."

He turned and gave her a brief smile. "All right."

As he closed the door, Burdick walked over, placed his heavy hand on Lola's neck, and squeezed slightly. His strength was so great that the gesture brought a look of pain to her eyes and she pulled away from him.

"I don't like that kid. He's a pest." When Lola remained silent, the violent spirit that lurked within him surfaced on his smooth face in a scowl. He grabbed her by the arm, saying angrily, "He gets in the way. Get rid of him."

Lola looked up at him fearlessly and said, "Neal, nobody tells me what to do!"

For one second she thought it was too much, for he raised his hand and there was a blind anger in his hooded eyes. She had seen him beat men to the ground with his terrible strength, but she did not flinch. Finally he laughed ruefully and said in a conciliatory tone, "Lola, you can sure drive a man crazy!" He put his oaklike arms around her and kissed her, savoring her full lips as if she were a delicacy. He was a man who knew women, but this one had gotten into his system in a way none of the others had.

She knew this, he realized, and although there were times when she met his passionate embraces willingly, she could put a wall around herself that both baffled and enraged him. She did so now, enduring his caress coldly and drawing away as soon as he removed his lips.

"I'm tired." She stepped to the door and added, "Next time you come here, knock. If you don't care for that, don't come back."

He stared at her, biting his full lower lip, then tried to laugh. "Sure, Lola." He moved through the door, making no attempt to touch her, but when the door closed he went down the steps with a hidden fury that he had kept bottled up but was written on his broad face and in his eyes.

Turning to his left he entered the main room of the Nugget, where he saw the boy sitting in a chair staring out into the darkness of the night. Burdick paused and glanced quickly around. Seeing nobody, he walked to the table and looked down at the boy.

Sensing his presence, Lee stood up and faced Burdick without a word. Then the man said, "Get out of here, kid, and don't let me catch you in here again!" Lee did not move nor speak. Burdick reached out to grab the boy, but a small sound behind him caught him off guard and he turned quickly to meet the eyes of Rosy Tucker, who was standing at the bar wiping a glass slowly and watching carefully out of his small, alert eyes.

"You want something, Rosy?" Burdick snapped.

"No," the bartender said with a direct look. "You want something, Mr. Burdick?"

"You're getting pretty uppity," Neal said thickly, rage burning in his eyes. "I may have to quieten you down some."

Rosy smiled briefly and said easily, "I don't guess you'd like to do that, Mr. Burdick."

For one instant Burdick nearly went for him, but he had seen the burly barkeep in action once against three tough Texas hands, and it had been pitiful the way Tucker had wiped up the floor with them. He stared at Tucker, then put his hand inside his coat, but stopped abruptly when Rosy's hand dropped beneath the bar where he kept his gun.

Their glances locked, then Burdick said, "You watch yourself, Rosy."

Rosy smiled, keeping his hand beneath the bar. "Sure. And I guess you better watch yourself, Neal."

Burdick broke away and blindly made his way back to the Palace. He found it practically empty except for a couple of swampers and Jack Canby playing solitaire moodily. The tall gunman looked up and said, "Who's been twisting your tail, Neal?"

The big man snatched a bottle from the table, poured a large drink, and tossed it off. He glared at Canby and demanded, "What's that mean?"

Canby shrugged. "You look mad."

"Mind your own business!"

"Sure." Canby grinned across the table and said, "You hear about the plan to close you down?"

Burdick stared at him. "What are you talking about?"

"Why, you must have been left off the guest list, Neal," Canby said grinning slyly. "My name wasn't there either." He took another drink and added, "It's that new shyster in town, Lindsey's boy."

"What about him?"

"Seems like he's got a yen to clean up the town, Neal, and you're the first pile of dirt he's going to start on. Least that's what I heard. Bunch of the respectable folks had a meetin' and the thing they decided on is to elect this here feller as a prosecuting attorney so him and his old man can take our guns away and make good boys out of us all. Ain't that sweet, Neal?"

Burdick took another drink and sat there glowering at Canby. Then a smile creased his broad face, and he said, "Go get Keach."

"That whiskey-soak? What you want him for?"

"Just get him here, Canby. He was here until about ten, so you may have to throw him in a horse trough to sober him up. Don't hurt him, though." Burdick smiled and poured another drink, then said softly, "I've got big plans for the judge!"

He sat there drinking steadily for nearly an hour, staring at the table and thinking. Finally Canby came in half dragging Edwin Keach, a ramrod thin, hatchet-faced man who was still half-drunk.

"Put him in that chair," Burdick said. Canby shoved the wobbly form of Keach into a chair, and his first action was to reach for the bottle.

Neal slapped his hand away and picked up the bottle. "Keach, you've got to cut back on the booze."

Keach had been a minor judge in Missouri at one time, but his drinking habits had stripped him of all ambition except to remain drunk as long as possible. He peered at Burdick out of red-rimmed eyes and asked, "Why?"

"Because you're going to run for public office," Burdick said with a grin.

"Public office?"

"You're going to be elected prosecuting attorney of Rimrock."

Canby laughed harshly and sat down across from Burdick. "Him? Why he couldn't handle the office of dogcatcher!"

"Just exactly the sort of man we need for the office, I think," Burdick winked at Canby. "And I'm appointing you head keeper of His Honor, Jack. Keep him sober enough to put on a good act."

"Who'll vote for the old soak?" Canby asked.

"You will—and so will every man in town who wants to keep an open town."

"Wait a minute," Keach mumbled, "I ain't sure I want to—"

"You're sure you want to get all the booze you want for a year, aren't you, Keach?" Neal said, and reading the answer on the ravaged face he said, "Go to bed. It's only two weeks until election. You make some speeches and kiss all the babies. I'll see you get elected. Now get out."

Canby watched the old man stumble out and shrugged. "It's a pretty good try, Burdick, but I reckon if you count noses, we're outnumbered. You ever thought about how many hoemen there are outside of town?"

"You like to make a couple of hundred real easy, Jack?" Neal asked.

"Ain't got a thing against it."

"You see that lots of those farmers don't make it into town on election day. Get some help, and see that those who do come to town get a shove and a hint of what they can expect if they vote. You know how to handle it."

"I can do that easy enough. Like pushing sheep around," Canby said. "But I reckon we might have to do something a bit stronger to make our play."

Burdick put his fingertips together, then knotted them and squeezed. "I've got that figured out already. There's a weak link in every chain, Jack. You find that one and snap it. Then you can do as you please."

"You figure Jesse is the weak link?"

"No, he's still pretty salty—besides that would be too obvious. We want to show the town what can happen to anyone who won't fall in line."

Canby frowned and said, "You want the whelp roughed up—the marshal's son?"

Again Burdick shook his heavy head. "No, that would look too raw. Maybe later, if things don't work out, we'll see what Mister Lawbook can do when he faces up to a .44."

"Well, spit it out, Neal."

"I don't guess you've forgotten Jim Reno, have you, Jack?" he asked shyly and found exactly the reaction he sought. Canby's chair legs hit the floor and his face flamed instantly.

"You know I ain't!" he spat out, then he stopped and a grin slowly spread across his face. "You mean you want me to bust Reno?"

"I think he's the one. He's the marshal's pet ever since he roughed up you and Riley." Burdick said this to spur the rage of Canby, and it was successful. "He's been pretty free with his mouth, Jack, about how he kicked you like a yellow dog. Says he'll do it again."

Canby stared at Burdick, then he said in a controlled voice, "Yeah? Well, we'll just have to see about that. Yes, sir, we'll just have to see!"

"He made some people take notice the way he stopped Thomas with a couple of licks with a blackjack. I don't care what you do to him, Jack, but you better make it good or your reputation's not worth a dime in this territory. One thing—make it *look* good. Make him start the fight, then get him in a crossfire or whatever you like."

"Crossfire?" Canby snapped. "I don't need no help with Reno."

Burdick leaned back and said, "That'll do it. We keep the settlers cowed, wipe Reno out, win the election, and send Jeff Lindsey back to Texas!"

The citizen's meeting that had included not only the council but several other responsible citizens had been set up by Odell Bracy, and he had orchestrated the affair so smoothly that only a few saw his fine hand controlling it.

Jeff had found himself acclaimed as the man of the hour, and he had rushed to tell his mother the results. She was waiting for him at the café, sipping a cup of tea at a table. He sat down and said excitedly, "I can't believe everything is happening so fast!"

"Slow down, Jeff," Ada said. "I want to hear all of it." She sat there, growing cold as he went through it all, and finally she said, "What about your father?"

Jeff's face fell, and he shrugged. "He'll come around, Mother."

"Jeff, I've known your father for forty years, and I've never once known him to 'come around.' He's the most stubborn man who ever walked the face of the earth."

"Well, he wasn't against the idea. He just thinks it won't work. But when he sees it does, why, he'll be happy."

Ada nodded and said slowly, "Yes, I'll give him that. Jesse was always a generous man, no matter what other faults he might have had. And he wants a son more than anything else. He always has." A sad look crossed her face. "I took that away from him, Jeff," she said softly, then shook her head. "Any other man would have hated me for doing that—but not Jesse."

Jeff watched her steadily, then said, "No, he loves you, Mother. A blind man could see that."

She nodded and said in a whisper, "As I have said, Jesse is not a man who changes—about anything!"

"What about you? How do you feel about him?"

She twisted the fine lace handkerchief into a knot and said nothing, but he saw the struggle written across her thin features and in her blue eyes. "Why, I thought you knew, Jeff," she said simply lifting her gaze to him with some surprise. "Jesse is the only man I ever loved—or ever will. It was for your sake I left him—to give you a chance."

Jeff stared at her and said, "That's putting a pretty heavy burden on me, Mother. I'm not sure it's fair."

She smiled sadly. "I'm not certain either. I thought once it was the only hope. Now it seems that my decision will stand or fall according to what you do here in this town."

He nodded slowly and his jaw hardened. "I'll do it, all right!"

He would have said more, but at that moment a movement caught his eyes and he looked at the door to see Rachel and Jim Reno enter.

Rachel saw him and came over with a smile, followed by Reno, who was carrying a large paper bag. "Hello, Jeff. How are you, Ada?"

"Did you hear about the meeting?" Jeff blurted out. "I'm going to be the new prosecuting attorney!" Suddenly he felt like a fool and sat there with his face burning.

But Rachel said, "Dad told me, Jeff. He's a little doubtful, but he'll be for you all the way."

"Sit down, Rachel," Ada said as she stood. "Jeff can tell you all about it. I must be on my way."

Reno spoke up, "I'll just take this grub back to the house, Rachel." He nodded to Jeff and Ada, then left the café.

"Why don't you sit down, Ada?" Rachel urged with a smile. "We haven't had time to talk. Is that tea you're having?"

Ada signaled and the waitress brought them all fresh tea while Jeff went through the story again, but this time he was more subdued. "I don't think it'll be easy, but it's the job I came to do."

Rachel smiled at him, and Ada did not miss the effect it had on Jeff. She saw he was interested in Rachel Lindsey, and that was a threat to Ada's plans. She fully believed that he would rise to prominence, and the proper wife was essential—like dressing well and a law degree. As the two talked on, she became quiet, observing that the girl had a rare beauty, and that although she was educated poorly, she had wit and charm.

Then she raised her eyes and looked out the window. "Mr. Reno seems to be having a difficult time finding his way home," she said with a smile.

Looking through the window, Rachel and Jeff saw Reno engaged in a conversation with Lola Fremont. They were both laughing, and the two made a striking picture—Lola all color and flare, Reno with his shabby clothing and dark hair and eyes.

"Who is she?" Ada asked.

"Lola Fremont," Jeff said. "She owns the Nugget Saloon."

"She's very beautiful," Ada commented.

"That's her trade, Mother," Jeff said curtly.

Rachel's eyes met his, and he thought he read a critical light in her gaze as she said evenly, "Lola's not so bad, Jeff. She's had a hard life."

It put Jeff on the defensive and he made the mistake of arguing the point. "They're all alike, Rachel. She's the enemy in this war."

"Things aren't black and white like that, Jeff," Rachel said. "Lola doesn't pretend to be something she's not, and she keeps her word. That's more than some can say who were at the council meeting."

Ada saw that Jeff was strongly stirred, but she did not interfere. He was doing a good job of driving a wedge between himself and the girl.

"She's part of Dance Street! You can afford to be generous, but when the trouble comes you know who's side she'll be on. And look at Reno!" he added angrily. "You and your father save his life and he takes up with her and her kind." Jeff had always prided himself on his self-control, and he saw with part of his mind that he was making a fool of himself, but he seemed powerless to prevent it.

"Why does the fellow keep hanging around?" he asked doggedly.

"You afraid he'll be on the wrong side, Jeff?" Rachel asked, and there was a stubborn anger in her face as she got up. She nodded to Ada, then walked out the door, and they saw her go directly to speak to Lola and Reno.

When Jeff saw her go to them, he turned pale and started to get up.

"Jeff, I think you've done a pretty fair job of making a fool of yourself already," Ada said in a level voice. "I'm embarrassed for you."

Jeff suddenly shook his head and wiped his brow with his handkerchief. He stared at it, saying in a low voice, "I don't know why I said what I did."

Ada patted his arm and said, "I do, dear. Come on. You'd better walk me home." As they left the restaurant, she led him directly to where Rachel was still standing with Lola and Reno. Ada bowed gracefully and said, "Good afternoon," with all the grace of a Southern belle. Jeff did not do quite so well, but he managed to nod and say, "Good to see you all."

When they were out of earshot, Ada said, "Much better! You must learn to keep your feelings concealed, Jeff. They will get you into deep trouble."

"I don't think there's any fish in this ol' river, Jim!"

Lee sat on the bank of the small river, staring with disgust at his cork that had not bobbed in two hours.

It was only a week before the election, and Reno had brought Lee and Rachel out to fish in the swollen stream.

"Put a new minnie on your hook," Reno suggested. "You can't catch a fish on a dead minnie."

"Ah, there ain't no fish in this ol' river!" Lee got up and picked up the lard can with the minnows Reno had seined out of the shallows. "I'm going to try down by them willows. If I don't get something soon, I'm going home."

Reno watched him make his way down the bank and then lay back, relaxing in the shade of a big cottonwood.

"It's nice out here," Rachel said. She stretched and lay back on the dry grass. "I haven't been on a picnic in a long time."

They lay there listening to the call of a hawk and the breeze stirring the branches overhead.

Reno had pulled his hat over his eyes, but she sat up and poked him in the ribs. "Jim, don't go to sleep. I don't want to waste the day."

He grunted and answered sleepily, "That's what you're supposed to do on picnics—waste time."

She sat there watching Lee for a time, then she said, "I'm worried about Dad." He sat up then and noted the air of concern in her face. "He'd never admit it, but he's not the man he used to be."

"He's still Jesse Lindsey," Reno murmured.

She nodded, but then she bit her lip and said, "What if this thing Jeff wants to do won't work? Or what if it *does* and Dad feels like he's become useless? More than anything else in the world he wants Ada and Jeff—and there's about a thousand things that can mess that up!"

Her eyes filled and suddenly she began to sob. She leaned forward blindly and Reno put his arms around her protectively, and there was a sudden release. All the fear and anguish she'd kept bottled up was loosed, and she wept like a child.

Finally she looked up, her eyes wet with tears. He became conscious of her slim young body pressed against him, and her face so close was fresh and lovely. Her eyes met his, opened wide with surprise, then they came together. Which of them made that decision was never clear, but as his arms drew her close, he felt her hands on his shoulders, and she met his kiss with eagerness. Her lips were fresh and sweet under his, and there was such a sudden surrender he was taken off guard. Then he pulled back and said in wonder, "You're quite a woman, Rachel!"

She lay quietly in his embrace for a long moment, then pulled away and sat up. She touched her cheek, then asked in a quiet voice, "Jim, what are you going to do?"

He realized at once that she was not asking an idle question, but the answer did not come easily. For years he had been without the ties that other men had, and now he found it difficult to explain his life.

"I guess I've been lost for a long time, Rachel," he answered. "Most men find something to tie to, something that they give themselves to. I had that during the war." There was a longing in his dark face. "But since the war ended I've just been riding to see what's over the next hill."

"What was over all those hills, Jim?"

"Why, as I think on it, it was never the finding something, but the looking for it that was fun."

"Jim," she said, and there was a plea in her voice as she took his hand in her own, "don't be that kind of man! You won't survive unless you find your place."

He nodded. "Yes, I've thought about that a lot lately. But—"

"Hey, look, I caught a fish!"

They looked up to see Lee running toward them holding a small fish in the air and beaming with pride.

"Find your place, Jim!" Rachel whispered as they got up to admire the fish, and he gave her a direct stare.

"Let's go cook him for supper," Lee said.

"Well, we might have to have about twenty more like him to make a mess," Reno said with a critical look at the small fish. "But I been studying the matter, and I think I can answer for it. Would you believe me, Lee, if I told you that in no time at all I can catch enough fish to feed the whole bunch of us?"

"No!" Lee snorted.

"You just hide and watch me then," Reno said grinning. He pulled off his boots, then stripped out of his shirt. He had a lean, muscular torso, with a deep chest and wide shoulders that tapered to a narrow waist. His stomach was flat as a board, packed with squares of muscle, and there was a rippling of sinew when he walked to the bank and slipped into the water.

An old tree had fallen into the water, and he knelt beside it, thrusting his hands underneath, feeling for something.

"Jim, what on earth are you doing?" Rachel asked in amazement.

"Back in Arkansas we call this 'hogging,'" he replied. He moved along the length of the tree, then when he got to the end, said, "Nobody home. But I think that cut-off bank yonder will be pretty good."

He went to a low bank about twenty yards upstream, and began probing around in the muddy water while Lee and Rachel stared at him.

"Ah! The old grandpa of them all!" Reno said, turning his face toward them. "He's a little deep, but he's here all right!"

"What is it?" Lee asked.

"Big old catfish," Jim said. "I'm tickling his tummy now, and soon as I get him calmed down, I'll slip my hand in his mouth and flip him to the bank. You get ready to catch him. Don't let him get away, now!"

Rachel stared at him, a skeptical look on her face. She had been taken snipe hunting once and she felt that this was the same sort of thing. "I don't for one minute believe that you've got a fish there, Jim Reno!" she snorted. "Why, I never heard—"

Reno suddenly wrenched his torso upright and a flopping shape came sailing through the air, striking Rachel in the stomach with such force that she said, "Wuff!" and fell over backward. The fish landed beside her, and as she was trying to get breath and strength enough to scramble to her feet, the catfish dealt her a hard swipe across the mouth with its mossy tail.

Lee shouted, "I'll get that thing off you, Miss Rachel!" and ignoring Reno's shout he ran over and made a grab at the flopping fish. At once he yelled and jumped back, sticking his thumb in his mouth.

Reno came splashing in hollering, "Watch out for those spines, boy! They're poison!"

He grabbed the fish again, dodging the spines, and he gave a heave that sent the two-foot long fish far up the bank. Then he turned to look at his fellow fishermen—and burst out laughing.

Lee was jumping up and down sucking his thumb, and Rachel had a streak of slime across her face. She was so mad she wanted to scream, but hadn't breath enough for it. Reno roared with laughter, saying, "I thought I told you not to let that fish get away, and here two of you couldn't even handle one little old bullheaded catfish!"

"I'll *kill* you, Jim Reno!" Rachel screamed, getting her breath. She threw herself at him, swinging her arms in wild flailing blows.

"You can't," Reno said, laughing. "You're too little." He held her off with one hand and finally she stopped flailing and started giggling. Then all three of them fell on the bank and laughed until they hurt.

Finally they got up and headed home. It was after dark before they got the fish cleaned, cooked, and eaten.

Jesse sat back and said, "Jim, that's the first bite of catfish I've had in a coon's age. But I tell you right now, you can have my share of hogging fish! You couldn't *hire* me to stick my hand in a hole without knowing what's there!"

Reno smiled at hearing this from a man who'd gone through the bloodiest battles of the war!

Reno walked back to the Nugget with Lee, and when they got to his door, the boy said, "Gee, that was something the way you caught that fish! I wish I was like you, Jim—not afraid of nothing!"

"Why, Lee, everybody is afraid of something."

Lee stared at him and asked, "Are you?"

"Sure."

"What are you scared of, Jim?"

Reno said slowly, "I guess I'm afraid of coming to the end of my life and dying—and finding out I never really lived." He gave a small smile as Lee looked mystified and added, "What I mean, Lee, is that I'm afraid that I won't ever find the place I'm supposed to be—that I'll be just a footloose drifter all my life."

"You won't be that!" Lee said. "I know you won't!"

"Then there's another thing that scares me," Reno said. "I've led a pretty wild life. I've seen some men get to liking that sort of thing, Lee. What if that happened to me? Using a gun gets into the blood of some men. They can't seem to stop." Then he said, "Those things scare me—never finding my way—and going the way of the wild bunch." He smiled then and said, "Get some sleep." He left then, but something in his manner troubled the boy. Lee slept poorly that night, and he thought about Reno all morning as he worked at the hardware store for Mr. Faulkner.

As soon as he finished his work at noon he ran to the stable, where he was surprised to find a crowd gathered outside. He stopped, then squeezed through the legs of the men who made a circle. He saw Reno backed up against the barn, his lips dripping blood and dirt all over his shirt. He'd been knocked down, and Jack Canby was standing in front of him.

"You've made talk about what you were going to do to me, Reno. Now back it up!"

Lee waited for Reno to plunge toward the other man, but he just stood there, saying nothing.

"Talk, you yellow dog!" Canby grated. "What does a man have to do to get a fight out of you?" He stepped forward holding his hands over his guns and shouted, "You're going to fight!"

"I'm not armed, Canby," Reno said slowly.

Canby sneered and said, "Shorty, give him your belt and gun."

A stocky puncher with a broad grin unbuckled his gunbelt and offered it to Reno. "Take it, yellow belly!"

"I won't fight you, Canby," Reno said. There was a pallor on his face and his lip was covered with perspiration, but he shook his head and added, "I'm not going to put on a gun for you."

He wheeled and started to leave, but at a nod from Canby, Shorty pulled his gun and struck Reno to the ground with the barrel of his weapon.

Canby stared at him, and when he looked at the crowd he said, "I aim to teach this sneaking coward a lesson. He's going to learn what it means to buck a real man! Doucett, go get some of that tar old man Williams is fixing his roof with—and get a pillow from somewhere."

"I gotcha, Jack. A little tar and feathers is what this joker needs."

He scurried off, and there was a nervous movement in

the crowd. Some of the men looked scared and began to fade away, but Jack whirled and said, "Nobody leaves!" His voice and the look on his face froze them in their tracks.

To Lee what happened then was a nightmare. They stripped off Reno's shirt and poured hot tar over his head and body, then slit a pillow and let the white feathers stick to the tar. They forced him to mount a rail and carried him down the length of Dance Street jeering and cursing.

The hot tar glued Reno's eyes together so he did not see Lee run blindly into an alley and throw up. He didn't see Lola turn pale beneath her paint and flee to her room, nor did he see the hawklike face of Rossiter who reached for his gun as Canby passed by, but who was stopped by Rosy who said, "You wouldn't have a chance, Al."

They took him out of town to the cemetery, and he heard Jack Canby say, "You might as well just die now, Reno. It really ain't worth the trip back—because I'll kill you the next time I see you! And I'll kill any man who helps you. You all get that?"

Then Reno received a smashing kick in the back that drove him to the ground.

He lay there in the darkness, blind and alone as he had never been in his life.

SEVEN
Man in Hiding

The fire which destroyed the jail at Hays gave Marshal Lindsey a great deal of trouble. Until a new jail could be built, all the prisoners awaiting federal trial had to be held in surrounding small towns. Usually a federal marshal would move such prisoners, but the McMillan gang had been kept together in the Rimrock jail, so Jesse and Zane had been asked to get them back to Hays for their trial.

Leaving Clarence Palmer and Bub Hartley in charge, they had left before dawn on Tuesday and by pushing hard got back the next day before noon. Palmer was a retired railroad man who had been a deputy in his younger days; Hartley was only nineteen and for a year had been begging Jesse for a chance to wear a star.

As they pushed their tired horses down Grant Street toward the jail, Jesse looked around and said, "Well, it's still here."

"Shouldn't have left town with only Bub and Clarence here," Zane grumbled.

"Probably not. Wouldn't have if a trail herd had been in

town." They passed the hardware store, and Jesse said, "Morning, Fred. Hello, Nance."

The two men glanced at the officers and nodded briefly, then both of them left the walk abruptly to enter the store.

"What's wrong with those two?" Zane asked in surprise. "They look like a pair of egg-sucking dogs caught in the act."

"Dunno, Zane." Jesse sat straighter in his saddle, his eyes moving alertly as they traversed the wide street, and as they approached the jail he said, "Something's happened. Nobody wants to look at us."

"Yeah," Zane grunted as he slid off his horse. "Let's see what's up."

Tying their horses to the rail, they went inside to find the two deputies nervously waiting. "What's going on, Clarence?" Jesse asked at once.

Palmer was a tall stooped man with thin sandy hair. He said, "You won't like it, Marshal."

"Don't tell me what I won't like—tell me what happened."

"Well, Canby braced Reno down by the livery stable—"

"A shoot-out?" Jesse asked swiftly.

"Naw, Marshal," Bub broke in, "Canby was on the prod, but Reno wasn't wearing no gun."

Jesse relaxed a little and said, "Just a fist fight, was it?"

The two deputies glanced at each other, each waiting for the other to speak. Finally Palmer cleared his throat and said, "Well, it wasn't exactly that way, Marshal. . . ."

"Come on, Clarence, what happened!" Zane snapped.

"Well—they hit him over the head, and when he was out they—they tarred and feathered him, Jesse." Palmer's lips were trembling and he spoke unsteadily, not able to meet the harsh stare of the marshal. "Then they rode him on a rail and run him out of town."

Bub's face was pinched and his voice was reedy as he said, "It wasn't our fault, Marshal."

"Where were you two when all this was happening?" Jesse asked, and there was such disgust in his voice that both deputies flinched.

"Never mind, Jesse," Zane said. "I expect Canby had a mob of his buddies with him. You couldn't expect Bub and Clarence to go up against them."

Jesse stared at the two. "My fault, Zane. I should have listened to you. Where's Reno?"

Bub said, "We've looked all over the place, Marshal, but he's gone."

"Canby said he'd shoot anybody who'd give him any help, but me and Bub went out where they dumped him, and he wasn't there."

"Well, he's got to be somewhere," Jesse said angrily. "Get out there and find him."

As the two scooted out, Zane watched as Jesse went to the gun rack and picked up his favorite sawed-off shotgun, then started for the door. He didn't ask any questions but checked the loads in his Colt and followed as the marshal walked directly to the Palace.

Pushing the doors open so hard they slammed against the wall, Lindsey saw at once Canby and Doucett standing at the bar, and there were at least ten other hard cases scattered around the room. In his favorite chair at the far end of the room, Neal Burdick was playing solitaire.

Jesse heard Zane enter and move to cover his flank. He did not glance at Burdick but locked his eyes on Canby. He walked slowly toward the bar, noting the jeering smile that Canby did not bother to conceal. He said, "Why, hello, Marshal Lindsey. See you made it back from Hays all right."

Jesse had been carrying the greener over his arm pointed at the floor. In one smooth motion he tilted it up and pulled both hammers back. The click sounded abnormally loud in the room, and Canby's face froze in shock as he stared into the deadly muzzle.

"Hey, watch out!" he said nervously, and his hands fluttered up away from his guns. Fast as he was, there was no way he could beat the pull of Jesse's finger. "That thing's got a hair trigger!" he said uneasily.

"Yeah, I knew a fellow once got cut right in two in a situation just like this. Still have nightmares about that. Give me your gun, Canby, you're under arrest."

"What for?" Canby asked. He was a tough customer, for even with the greener pointed right at him, his eyes darted to someone behind the marshal's back in a signal.

Jesse lifted the shotgun, and when he pulled the trigger, the blast shattered the mirror and a line of whiskey bottles. The bartenders were showered with glass, and Canby's mouth flew open as the shotgun lowered so that he stared right into the black muzzles.

"This gun *has* got a hair trigger!" Jesse said as if surprised. "Little accident, Neal. You want to argue about it?"

He did not turn to look at the owner of the Palace, but kept his eyes fixed on Canby.

Burdick got up and said smoothly, "Accidents can happen, Marshal—to anyone."

"Get his gun, Zane," Jesse said. "You'll get off with a fine, Canby, but maybe I'll get lucky and you'll try to escape." When Zane disarmed him, Jesse wheeled to face Neal Burdick, saying, "The judge will be through day after tomorrow. You'll have to do without your two-bit hired killer until you pay his fine."

He spat on the floor, cast a look around the room, and walked out after Zane and Canby.

Burdick stared after him, slowly took a cigar, and bit off the end. His eyes smoldered, and when Doucett began to curse the marshal, he said slowly, "Never mind, Riley. I don't think we'll have to worry about Jesse Lindsey much longer."

"Lock the scum up, Zane. I'm going home." Jesse handed the greener to the deputy, and as he headed down the street to his house, he felt more worn-out than he liked to admit. More and more he realized that he was not young, but he shoved the thought aside and plodded slowly to his yard.

The door opened and Rachel came out as he climbed the steps. She came and put her arm around him. "You heard?"

"Yeah, I heard."

"Jeff and Ada are here."

"You know where Jim is?" he asked as they went through the door.

"No. Nobody does."

Jeff was standing by a window, fidgeting with his watch chain, and his face was tight with strain. He could not meet Jesse's eyes as he said quickly, "Hello, Dad." He started to say something, then seemed to change his mind, so there was an awkward silence in the room.

"Jeff has been having a bad time, Jesse," Ada spoke up. Jesse saw she was not at ease either, but he did nothing to help them. "He thinks he's responsible for what happened."

Jesse sat down and leaned back in a rocking chair. "Could I have something to drink, Rachel?" She moved to get something and only then did he add, "Maybe you *were* responsible, Jeff. Somebody was."

"He's not the law in this town, Jesse! What could he do

against an armed mob?" Ada spoke with a steady determination.

"Why, nothing much, I guess, Ada," Jesse said slowly. He closed his eyes and put his head back. "That's what I been trying to tell all of you."

"Now wait a minute, Dad!" Jeff was defensive, his thin face flushed, and he shook his head angrily as he said, "The reason nobody did anything is *because* that mob was armed. When I get a no-gun ordinance passed, it'll be different!"

Jesse took the glass of water Rachel brought to him, drank it slowly, then said, "Canby won't be any different. Neal Burdick won't be changed. And you better be thinking about one thing, son."

"What's that?"

Jesse got to his feet and said, "I'm going to get some sleep, Rachel. Get me up at six o'clock." He moved heavily across the room, and just before he passed through the door he turned and said in a sad voice: "You better be asking yourself: 'When the no-gun ordinance is passed, who's going to make it stick?' Anybody can say, 'Let's bell the cat,' Jeff. Problem is to find a man to do the job. And I'm telling you something I never thought I'd hear myself say—I'm too old to do the job!"

He left, and Ada said, "He's never said anything like that—not ever."

"He's tired, Ada," Rachel said. Then she asked, "Who is going to do the job, Jeff? You?"

"That's not fair, Rachel," Jeff said stiffly.

"Nothing much is, I'm afraid." Rachel tried to smile, saying, "Sorry, Jeff. I'm not feeling very charitable."

He stared at her. "You think I should have stopped that mob, don't you?"

She looked at him with a level stare and nodded. "Yes, I do. I think Jim would have made a try if he'd seen you in that condition."

Jeff jammed his hat on his head. His lower lip trembled slightly, and he said in a tightly controlled voice, "Are you ready to go, Mother?"

Ada rose and followed him to the door, saying as she left, "Good night, Rachel." She paused then and did something she had never done; she put her arms around Rachel and held her tightly, then she released her and said, "Try to be patient with us, will you, Rachel?"

Rachel was caught off guard, so that they were gone before she could do more than say, "Of course, Ada. Come back soon."

She took the glass back to the kitchen then stood staring blindly out the window. Finally she leaned on her hands, shut her eyes, and cried out softly but desperately, "Jim! Where *are* you?"

He lay there in the darkness, his eyes glued together with the oily tar. His face was pressed into the dust, clogging his throat, but every time he tried to get up, the pain at the base of his skull shot through him so violently that he could not do it.

He managed to roll over and clear his throat, but the blinding stabs of pain made him so nauseous he could only lie on his back helplessly.

Time passed and his head stopped swimming. He had no idea how long he had been there, nor even if it were night or day. He had taken a musket ball at the Wilderness, but it had been nothing like this, and he realized that the shame of the thing would never leave him.

Finally he heard someone coming, and he tried to brace

himself for another attack, but the hands that touched him were gentle as they stroked his face.

"Jim! Jim, are you all right?"

He did not recognize the woman's voice, nor the other, a man who said, "Hold the lantern, Lola. I'll get him into the buggy."

He felt himself being lifted from the ground and carried lightly by a pair of mighty arms. "Be careful, Rosy!" the woman said as he felt himself being lowered gently onto a hard surface.

He knew them then and his voice was a croak as he said, "Lola?"

"Yes!" He felt her hands touching his face, and she said, "Be still, Jim. I'll take care of you. Hurry up, Rosy!"

He lay there until the buggy pulled up, and at once he felt himself being lifted again. The pain shot through his head, but he heard Lola say, "I'll go first, Rosy. There's nobody on the street. I'll see that the place is empty."

There was a short wait and then he heard her call from far off: "Now—hurry!" His head bounced painfully as Rosy carried him at a run across a level stretch, then across a wooden surface. They went up a long set of stairs, then through a door which closed instantly behind them.

"Put him in this chair. We've got to get his face cleaned off."

He slumped into a straight-backed chair and Lola said, "Go put the buggy up, Rosy, then come back here." The door closed quietly, then there was a strong smell of kerosene in his nose, and a damp cloth touched his face. He drew back gagging, but Lola said, "I'm sorry, Jim, but we have to get this out of your eyes." She worked quickly, deftly, touching him gently with the oil-soaked rags, then wiping the tar from his face with a clean cloth.

He cautiously lifted his eyelids, and there was a fierce burning that caused him to flinch. "Wait!" Lola cried, and she left his side to return with a cool dripping cloth. "This soap and water will get that kerosene out of your eyes," she said gently. As she worked on him, she drew his head to her breast, holding him with one arm while she carefully cleaned his eyes. "There—try to open your eyes."

He found that he could open his eyes with almost no discomfort. "That's better," he whispered. His throat was raw, but now that he was no longer blind, he felt immensely better.

Her face was only inches away from his, and he was still resting in her firm embrace. By the dim lamplight her eyes seemed enormous, and he saw a compassion on her lips that made him wonder. Her hand touched the back of his head, and the world spun around, making him sway and close his eyes.

"Get into bed," she said at once, and her strong hands helped him stand up, and led him the few steps to the bed. "You've got a concussion, I think. Lie down, and go to sleep if you can." He felt himself being put to bed like a small boy, and as he lay back he said, "What place is this, Lola?" The room was beginning to slowly turn, and he closed his eyes quickly, but he was asleep as she said, "This is my spare room, Jim. You'll be safe here." She turned and set the kerosene and soapy water on the table beside the bed. Tenderly she began to removed the sodden feathers and sticky tar from his body. Once she stopped and looked down into his face for a long time.

He slept fitfully, but each time he woke Lola was there, soothing him back to sleep.

A strong light awakened him, and he opened his eyes to see the sun coming through a curtained window. The noises of the street below told him the town was coming to life, and he tried to roll off the bed but stopped stock still when familiar pain hit him. He sat there, his eyes closed, then carefully got off the bed. He would have moved to the window, but stopped when he caught a glimpse of himself in a large mirror over a dressing table.

He had no shirt on, and there were streaks of tar still clinging to his sides and blotches of the sticky stuff gumming his hair in a wild pattern. His face was blotched, streaked with tar that was too deeply ingrained to remove, and his eyes were inflamed, with fiery lids that still burned and itched.

A shock ran through him, and it was not just the sight of what he was; he remembered the jeers and curses of the crowd, and he felt naked and totally humiliated as he thought that the whole town had been a witness to the sight of him bouncing on the rail. He tore his gaze from the mirror so violently that his head throbbed, and he swayed in the middle of the room, trying to drive the memory of it from his mind.

The door opened and he looked to see Lola enter followed by Doc Mitchell. She closed the door and said, "Doc needs to look at your head, Jim."

Mitchell stopped dead still, staring at Reno with surprise, then glancing at Lola.

"Nobody can know he's here," Lola said. "I know you can keep a secret."

Mitchell grunted and stepped over, saying, "Let's have a look at you." He turned Reno's head, and his stubby fingers probed at the lump, and he pulled Reno's eyelids back, looking into his eyes, first one, then another. He grunted and stepped back. "You having any trouble seeing?"

Reno frowned and said, "A little. Sometimes I see double."

"That's not good. You'll have to take it easy. Rest for a few days."

"I can't stay here," Reno said.

"I expect you can," Doc Mitchell said soberly. "If Canby or one of his pals saw you, they'd finish you off, Jim. You can't travel, and anyway, where would you go?"

"He'll be here, Doc," Lola said, and there was a high color in her cheeks as she added, "I'll see he takes care of himself."

The eyes of the old man took in her high color and the nervousness with which she plucked at a button on her dress. She was, he knew, not a nervous woman, and as his gaze rested on her, she said quickly, "Don't tell anybody he's here."

"Not even Lindsey? Him and that girl of his feel pretty bad, Lola. Got everybody running around like bird dogs looking for Reno."

"If nobody knows, nobody can tell," she answered. He need any medicine—stuff like that?"

Mitchell shook his head and turned to leave. "No. Just all the rest he'll take."

Reno suddenly grinned sourly and said, "I feel like a kid who's been spanked and put to bed."

"You mind Lola, Reno," Mitchell said as he opened the door. "Looks to me like you make a career out of gettin' sick."

"I ought to get out, Lola," Reno said after he left. "Wouldn't do you any good if somebody found me here."

Lola stared at him and a bitterness arched across her lips. "Don't worry about my reputation, Jim," she said in a strange, taut voice. "I lost that a long time ago!"

He stared at her, seeing for the first time what lay beneath the paint and the smile she gave the world. She kept a guard up, letting no man beneath the bright smile, but now she was open to his gaze, and there was a helplessness that left her vulnerable.

"Don't leave, Jim," she said, and her eyes lost the last trace of hardness, letting him see the depth of passion that she kept buried deep.

"I don't want you to get hurt, Lola."

"I've been hurt most of my life. I will be again, I expect."

He smiled and there was a touch of wry wisdom in his dark eyes. "I guess I know why, Lola."

She stared at him and whispered, "Why, Jim?"

"Because you care about people. And when you do that, you're going to get hurt by somebody sooner or later."

"How do you know I care about people?" she asked, and there was a wonder in her green eyes as she leaned toward him.

"You're a loving woman."

She stared at him, as if testing his words, then said with a sadness in her voice, "Too loving, Jim."

"Not possible, Lola."

She smiled then, and there was a lightness in her manner as she said, "Sit down, Jim. I'm going to get some of that mess out of your hair."

He was not good at waiting, and the next few days were not easy. He slowly improved, his headaches becoming less intense, and by Sunday morning he knew that he was able to travel.

He was watching the small groups of people headed for church when Lola came in with a tray. She smiled as he turned, saying, "I brought enough for both of us."

She had done this several times, and he smiled as she

spread the food on the table. "I expect you're worn out waiting on me, Lola," he said.

She gave him a quick smile and shook her head. "No. I hated cooking and things like that at home." She salted the eggs and put butter on a biscuit as she talked. "But I've found out it's sort of fun."

She sat on the bed, holding the plate in her lap while he sat on the chair. A bell sounded in the morning air, and he said, "Church time."

She nodded. "I used to go when I was a little girl. Sang in the choir." She fell silent and there was a sadness on her face. "Never can go back to that."

He said at once, "Sure you can."

She laughed and there was bitterness in the sound. "How can a saloon girl sing in a church choir, Jim? Be sensible."

"Quit being a saloon girl, then," he said calmly. There was a solid look to him, his chest and shoulders filling the shirts she'd found for him, and he faced her with a straight stare.

"How would I live?"

"You'd live, Lola," he said. "If you want to sing in a choir, do what you have to do to get there."

She shook her head, saying, "No, you can't go back to what you used to be."

Reno said, "Most people couldn't. But you could, Lola."

"No. They wouldn't have me."

Reno shrugged and said, "I'm getting out of here, Lola."

Her eyes widened and she moved her shoulders in a restless fashion. "You're not well enough."

"I can make it."

"Where will you go?" she asked.

"Don't know. Just need to get away from here."

He got up and came over to stand beside her. "Saying thanks is hard for me, Lola." She stood close to him, and he found it hard to go on. "What can I tell you?"

She put her arms around his neck and held him tightly. "Don't go, Jim!"

He stood there for one instant, then pulled back. "I have to."

She stared at him, and said, "You would never want me anyway, would you, Jim? You couldn't forget—what I've been."

He said gently, "I know what you are, Lola—a beautiful woman with a loving heart. Whatever you've done, I've done worse. But I have to go."

She saw that he was set, and she said dully, "How will you get out of town?"

"Rosy's got me a horse—or will have by tomorrow. Seems to think I'm good for an outfit."

She got up, and there was a stiffness in her back as she picked up the dishes. "Good luck, Jim."

He stood there, watching her leave, then sat down on the bed and waited for night to fall.

The streets were deserted as he made his way that night to the marshal's house. He kept to the shadows and stood uncertainly at the door, almost changing his mind. Then he knocked softly and stood there waiting.

The door opened and Rachel stood there. She could not see his face and said, "Yes?"

"Hello, Rachel."

"Jim!" She called over her shoulder, "Dad, it's Jim!" then opened the door and pulled him into the room.

Jesse came across the room, wonder on his face. He stopped in front of Reno and asked, "You all right, Jim?"

"I'm fine, Jesse."

"Where've you been?" Rachel asked.

"Upstairs at the Nugget. Got a pretty bad concussion that kept me pretty quiet."

"Wish you'd gotten word to me," Jesse said, a rebuke in his voice.

"Wasn't my say, Jesse," Reno apologized. "Lola was taking a pretty big chance as it was."

"Lola?" Rachel said in an odd tone. "She's been keeping you?"

Reno seemed to be angry with something. "I been nothing but a burden to people since I came here. I'm pulling out, but I wanted to tell you good-bye."

"You're leaving?" Jesse asked.

"Nothing else to do, Major," Reno said, a streak of rebellion in his tone.

"You could stay, Jim."

"No, I couldn't, Rachel. I can't ever forget what happened. Being shamed like that, why, it scars a man."

"I've always said we can't get enough of what we don't really want—and we run fastest and farthest when we run from ourselves," Jesse said. "There's no place to run, Jim. You know that as well as I do."

"I just can't face it. What if I stayed? I'd be forced to take up the gun again."

"Jim, what was the best time in your whole life?" Jesse asked.

The question caught Reno unprepared and he fumbled for an answer, but Jesse said, "It was the war, wasn't it? Oh, I know it was bad, but it gave you something you'd never had— and still don't have."

"What was that?"

"It gave you a vision. You were a part of something that had meaning. You were in something with other men, and you had to trust them like they had to trust you. And ever since you got out of the army, you've felt alone and lost. You've had no cause."

Reno thought of it, and his dark eyes were serious as he nodded, "Maybe you're right, Major. But there's the other side of it. I maybe liked the bad side of war, the shooting and the raw action. And lately I've been afraid that there's something in me I've got to guard against."

Jesse said, "You aren't a killer, Jim. I've been facing them all my life and I know the breed."

"Jim, don't run away," Rachel said. She touched his arm and there was a plea in her eyes that caught and held him. "Stay and fight!"

He almost agreed, but the memory of the tarring swept over him, and he said abruptly, "Thanks for all you did for me." He wheeled and left the room without another word, and fled back to the Nugget like a criminal in flight.

EIGHT
Honor in the Dust

Election day offered the farmers a break in the dull monotony of grinding labor, and the dusty streets of Rimrock began to fill up early on Monday morning. Jesse and Zane watched glumly as the pace picked up. By noon the wide street was lined with spring wagons, buggies, and horses packed along the tie rails. A milling river of settlers, cowboys, and children of all ages caught by the excitement of the day swept along Grant Street.

Two trail herds had come in over the weekend, and the hands, hungry for color and excitement, had already poured into town, getting shaved, bathed, and primed for a wild night to wash away the boredom of the long drive.

Since it was a county election, the town swelled as wagons kept threading their way through the packed streets, emptying loads of plainly dressed women and a host of barefoot youngsters. By noon simply getting from one end of Grand or Dance to the other involved squeezing through a wall of stirring people.

Jeff Lindsey made his way through the crowd, using his height and wiry strength to create a space for Rachel. He had

seen her every day, taking the time from a twenty-hour daily
work schedule. She had become more important in his life
than he cared to admit. It was painfully clear to him that her
feeling for him was not so strong. He had a tenacious spirit,
however, and he went about courting her with the same air of
determination with which he had pursued the top spot in his
class at law school. There had been several who were smarter,
but he had succeeded by a single-minded attack on the goal.
Rachel saw, of course, what he was doing, and said once with a
small smile, "You don't do things halfway, do you, Jeff?"

He pulled her closer as the crowd around Miller's Empo-
rium thickened. Miller was adding to his store, and the voting
took place in the half-finished building. He pulled her through
the door, accepting the greetings of half a dozen supporters
who thrust their hands at him or slapped him on the shoulder.
He was in his element, Rachel noted, for there was a real interest in his face as he met people—not just a political heartiness
assumed by most office seekers.

A long table along one wall was occupied by the election
board, which included Ernest Faulkner, R. G. Tyler, and Bones
Morehouse. The room was crowded and Morehouse said,
"Howdy, Jeff."

"Hello, Bones," Jeff said. He looked around the room and
added, "Looks like a good turnout."

"Best we ever had," Tyler said. "Take this ballot, Jeff, and
I'll record your name."

Jeff took the ballot, and as he wrote he suddenly noticed a
skinny farmer dressed in overalls worn white by countless
washings. He was standing before Ernest Faulkner, who was
writing his name on the list before him. As he was writing, a
voice suddenly cut through the room: "You ain't been in this
county long enough to vote, Jenkins."

Riley Doucett stepped out from where he had been leaning against the wall. He moved to stand beside the farmer, a
scowl on his face, and it seemed accidental when he brushed
against the man.

Jenkins stepped back and looked nervously at the sinister
figure, his eyes darting to the .45 worn low. He said in a stum-
bling voice, "Oh, sure—I been out on my place—"

"You callin' me a liar, Jenkins?" Doucett said. The off-set
eye lent a sinister air to his hatchet face, and he let his hand
drop to the gun in what could have been a careless gesture.

R. G. Tyler looked up, taking in the scene with one
shrewd glance. He got up and walked over and picked up a
paper lying at Faulkner's elbow. Running his eyes down it, he
found the name and said, "No, you're all right, Bob." He stared
at Doucett and said, "You want to see the list?"

"I don't care about no paper," the gunman said. He leaned
toward Bob Jenkins, making the farmer seem very small, and
he said, "You watch it, Jenkins!"

There was a silence in the room, and everyone saw what
was happening. Jenkins slowly turned, and there was a stoop
to his thin shoulders.

"Come on, Jenkins," Tyler said. "You've got a vote."

The small man did not look around, but mumbled as he
shouldered his way through the crowd, "Guess not."

Jeff was shocked at the scene. He was accustomed to elec-
tions, and he had never seen such a violation of the right to
vote. He stepped forward and said, "You can't intimidate voters
like that. Get out of here!"

Doucett pulled a plug of tobacco from his shirt pocket,
drew a knife, and carefully pared off a thick slice. He examined
it carefully with his good eye and slipped it into his mouth.

Only then did he lift his face, and a light of pleasure scrolled across his rough features.

"Who says I got to git? You?" He spat on the floor and turned to face Jeff. The room grew so still that the buzzing of flies became audible.

Jeff stood there, his face washed of color. He seemed to be frozen, and his mind raced as he sought for an answer. He was terribly aware of the gun at Doucett's side, and equally aware that everyone in the room was waiting for him to handle the situation.

"Well, you gonna put me out, sonny?"

Once Jeff had been struck in the stomach, and the blow had left him completely helpless—unable to breath or speak. He felt the need to act, but the will was drained. He stood there so long that R. G. Tyler finally said, "Jeff?"

He forced himself to meet Doucett's jeering face, and said uncertainly, "We'll see about this, Doucett."

He turned to go, ignoring the gunman's parting shot, "You gonna go and tell your daddy on me, sonny?"

As Jeff pushed his way down the street he trembled in a delayed response. He did not hear the greetings of those that called his name and was brought up short only when he saw his father standing with his back against Hall's Shooting Gallery, keeping a close watch on the street.

"Afternoon, Jeff." Jesse would have said more, but one look at the young man's face held him still.

"Riley Doucett's got to be moved out of the polling center," he said breathlessly. "He's intimidating the farmers."

Jesse stared at his son and said, "He breaking any laws?"

"Well, he's standing there with that gun of his, and people are afraid."

"Tell him to move along."

Jeff squirmed and there was a red spot on each cheek as he said, "I . . . I did."

Jesse stared at Jeff and waited, but he knew the story. "You see how it is, son? You want to bring peace to this town, but how you going to do that without force? I'll tell you something else—you're going to lose this election."

"No! There are enough votes to win!"

"Sure, but lots of them won't even come to town. Don't you know Neal has had his bunch out hittin' every settler in the county? Not breaking any laws. A farmer knows what will happen if he votes wrong."

"But we've *got* to win!"

Jesse slumped lower and there was a sad look in his face. "I said that when I was in the Confederate army, Jeff. We just *had* to win. I couldn't even imagine losing!" His faded old eyes fastened on Jeff as he said softly, "But we lost."

Jeff stared at his father and there was a childlike quality in his voice as he asked, "Dad, what will I do?"

Jesse shook his head. "Do what most of us do, Jeff. Learn to lose."

Rosy tapped on the door of the room where Reno was staying, stepping inside at once when it opened. "The horse is at the stable, Jim, and your gear is right beside his stall."

Reno stood there, his face still as he considered the big man. "What makes you think I'm good for it, Rosy?"

A small smile touched Tucker's battered lips. He shrugged his massive shoulders and answered, "I bet on worse odds. Don't be in no hurry to send the money back."

"Thanks, Rosy." Reno walked over and glanced out the

window at the busy street below. "Worst time I could have picked to try to ride out unnoticed."

"Yeah, it's a hummer all right. But by midnight the respectable folks will be off the streets, and the trail hands will be too drunk to see. Shouldn't have any trouble. Well, I got to get back."

"Rosy," Reno said putting his hand out. "Thanks."

"Sure." Rosy shook Reno's hand and said, "Stay out of jail, Reno!" and then he ducked out the door. Reno locked it, then went back to the window to watch the flow of life on the street below. A constant drama was unfolding, and the actors were all unaware that they were being observed. Many of them Reno knew, and it came as a shock to realize that the world beneath his window was one he had put some roots into—and one he would miss as he rode off toward another place.

He saw Ralph Toler standing with his back against the harness shop, glaring with jealous eyes as his archrival, Al Simmons, squired pretty little Maureen Moore along the boardwalk. Reno watched as Ralph left his spot and trailed along behind the pair. Sooner or later the two would lock horns. They would batter each other until one of them would confess himself beaten, but then, Reno thought with a wry smile, Maureen might just take the beaten one instead of the victor. *No way to figure a thing like that!* he mused.

Jeff walked past with Rachel on his arm, and Reno sat for a long time wondering if the feeling on the young man's face was returned by the girl. Ten minutes later his eyes narrowed as Jeff walked past without the girl. Reno saw him encounter Jesse, and they had a brief conversation, and finally Jeff left looking angry, heading back the way he'd come. Jesse watched him go and gave a look of such hopelessness after

Jeff that it caught at Reno, and he thought again about sticking around to give the old man some support. Then he saw the figure of Neal Burdick, and he watched the big man walk through the crowd, using his bulk to brush people aside. He was followed by three or four toughs including Jack Canby. Reno bit his lip as Burdick nodded toward the bent figure of the marshal and said something to Canby, who nodded and faded away into the crowd.

"No chance," Reno said, shaking his head. He heard a sound behind him, and turned to see Lola step in and motion to him. "Jim, I need to see you."

He stepped out into the hall, and when he was safely in her room, she turned and asked, "Are you still leaving?"

"Going tonight."

She bit her lip and nodded, then reached into the top of her dress and pulled out some notes carefully folded. "I want you to take this—as a loan."

He looked at the money, then shook his head. "Lola, how can I take that? I owe you too much already."

She slowly lowered her hand and the money dropped to the floor. "You took a beating and got your pride hurt. Now you're running away to keep people from looking at you."

"In that, I guess you're right."

She was a strong-willed woman, but there was a curious weakness in her face as she said in a whisper, "What about me, Jim? I've been taking a beating in one way or another since I was twelve years old. And you think I don't know what people think when they look at me? You think I don't care?" She turned and walked away from him, and as she put her hands to her face her body began to shake.

Reno was drawn to her, and when he put his hands on her

shoulders, she turned at once and said, "Jim, look at me!" Her large green eyes glistened with tears, and her lips were soft and vulnerable as she said intently, "No matter what anybody says, there's something in me that's not bad, Jim. All my life I've known that if I had the right one to love and to love me, I could be good! I could pour myself out for you, Jim, and never look at anyone else!" She stopped, and as he looked into her face, there was an innocence there that had nothing to do with what she was or what she had done. It was the quality of purity that she had never been permitted to keep, but which, he knew with a strange certainty, was part of her nature.

"Jim, I love you!"

He was holding her, and it was the most natural thing he had ever done to pull her close and kiss her with a great gentleness. She leaned against him, and there was a response in her full lips that stirred him, made him totally aware of the rich fullness she offered him. She was weeping, and finally she drew her head away, a smile of joy on her lips. "Jim—," she said, but before she could say anything else, the door swung open and they stepped apart turning to face Neal Burdick who stood there, a look of rage on his broad face.

He had murder in his eyes, and without a word he reached for the gun he carried inside his coat. It caught in the fabric, and that brief delay gave Lola time enough to throw herself at him. She grabbed his gun arm with both hands and as the gun came free her weight forced his arm toward the floor. "Jim! Run!" she cried throwing her weight on the arm.

Reno saw the tremendous muscles in Burdick's arm flex, and even with Lola's weight the gun began to rise. In one smooth movement, Reno picked up the brass candlestick on the table by the bed and with one sweeping overhand blow caught Burdick over the ear. There was a dull sound and the big man's eyes rolled upward as he fell to the carpet like a pole-axed steer.

Lola stepped to his side and said, "Get out of here, Jim! When he wakes up he'll kill you!"

"I can't leave you here with him, Lola."

"I'll have Rosy here by the time he wakes up. Don't worry about me, just leave!"

He looked at Burdick, then said, "Lola, I'll—"

"Don't make me any promises!" she said, and a pain flashed out of her fine eyes. "I guess I knew nothing would come of it—but I thought I'd try. Now get out! Hurry!"

He ran to the corridor and went to his room to get the clothes Rosy had brought him. He hurried to the back stairs, and when he saw they were empty, he descended to the alley. He ran to the end of it and ducked at once behind a large crate when a couple of cowboys went past. There was no way he could move without being seen, so he waited until several individuals passed. As he urgently looked for a way to get out of town, a group of trail hands ambled out of a saloon and walked his way. There were at least seven or eight of them, part of a crew just come to town. They would know no one. Reno waited until they had passed the opening of the alley, then stepped out and fell into step behind the last two, who were arguing drunkenly about a horse.

They made their way the length of the street, crossed over to Dance Street and crossed right through the middle of a crowd standing outside the Palace. One of them said, "Hey, we ain't been in this one yet."

Reno saw several men just inside the door who knew him, and he turned to take his chances alone.

Pulling his hat down over his eyes, he forced himself to

stroll along the sidewalk in a lazy fashion, even pausing to look at a display of knives in a shop window. His goal was the end of the street, which opened to a clump of cottonwoods. Once he made that, he could hole up until night, take the horse, and ride out.

The street in front of him was fairly empty, but just as he came even with the Miles Feed Store, Riley Doucett rounded the corner not twenty feet away! The sound of voices behind him told Reno that if he turned he would run face-on into them, so he turned into the feed store, running into a short figure so hard that he had to grab an arm to keep the boy from falling.

"Jim! It's you!" Lee Morgan stared up at him in blank astonishment, but before he could speak again, Reno stepped into the store just as Doucett walked by. Reno kept his back turned, and the tight expression on his face warned Lee that something was happening. Reno halfway believed that Doucett had recognized him, but the steps never faltered, and as they faded, Reno said, "Let's get out of here, Lee!"

"Where?"

"I've got to hide until dark. Burdick is after me."

Lee said at once, "Jim, you can hide in my room."

"In the Nugget?"

"Yes, up in the attic."

Swiftly he considered other possibilities, discarding them one by one. Then he thought how unlikely it was that Burdick would expect him to return to the Nugget.

"All right, Lee. I'll have to get there without being seen."

A man was unloading sacks of feed at a dock in the rear, but he paid them no attention. Lee said, "Jim, put this on your shoulder and sort of hide your face with it." He pointed to a sack of feed, and at once Jim picked it up and slung it over his shoulder. "Now pull your hat down over the other side of your face," Lee said. He looked at the results and said, "That's good! Come on, I know a short cut through the vacant lot."

Lee led him through a weed-clogged lot, through a loose board in a fence, up the same stairs he'd come down, then up a shorter flight to his tiny room. Reno stepped inside, put the sack on the floor, and glanced around.

The room wasn't over ten feet square. The ceiling slanted up following the pitch of the roof, and the furniture consisted of a homemade bed, a battered trunk, a table, and a chair with the legs wired on. Pictures cut from magazines served as wall decoration, and there was one small window looking down on the street.

Lee's eyes were big as he came to stand beside the man, and he said in a voice of wonder, "I thought you were dead! Where you been, Jim?"

Reno put his arm around Lee's shoulder and said, "Sit down, Lee, and I'll tell you all about it."

The two sat down, and for a long time Lee listened as the man spoke of where he had been. And as he talked, Reno discovered a curious thing: As he went over the story, the shame that had bound him seemed to evaporate. By the time he got to the end, he was able to look at the incident as he had at certain battles—terrible, but not a crippling thing.

"And Miss Lola grabbed his gun and you laid him out!" Lee said. He shook his head and said, "Gosh, do you think he'll hurt her when he comes to, Jim?"

It was something that Reno had not been able to be at ease with. He knew Rosy was a tough, competent man, but he was no match for the guns of Burdick and his crowd. "I don't know, Lee."

It was sweltering in the tiny room, and he asked, "Could you go get some cool water? I'm pretty thirsty."

"Sure." Lee dashed out the door and Reno walked over to peer out at the street.

Going to be pretty tough to slip out of this town. Burdick will be watching like a cat at a mouse hole, he considered.

It was a tight spot, and he thought of a time when he had been pinned down by Yankee sharpshooters at Cold Harbor. It had seemed then, as it seemed now, unlikely that he would pull free of the trouble.

Lee was gone for so long that he began to worry. He considered trying for a new hideout, but nothing offered itself.

Ten minutes later he heard shots that seemed to come from down the street. There were two of them, then another, then four or five more. After the last shot there was a silence, then a shout. He peered out the window, even risked sticking his head out to try to see down the street, but he saw the running crowds turning off on Dance Street.

He stood there, wondering what had happened, knowing the explosive nature of the town, and convinced that something serious had taken place.

A clatter of feet on the stairs alerted him, and he stepped beside the door, lifting the chair for a weapon, but Lee burst through the door, his face white.

"Jim, they got him!"

"Cool off, now," Reno said, putting his hands on the boy's shoulders. "Who?"

"Marshal Lindsey, he got shot—and Zane Williams, he's dead!"

Reno froze for one instant, then he said, "What happened, Lee? Tell me all of it."

"I didn't see all of it, but Billy Murphy did. He said that some men started a fight down on Dance Street—right in front of the Palace, and then when the marshal and his deputy came running, they got shot!"

It was an old story to Reno, and he knew with a cold certainty that it had been a trap. Burdick had lured Jesse and Zane into it, probably made some sort of attempt to make it look like just a wild brawl, then cut them down in a crossfire.

A slow rage began to build up and he turned and went through the door, racing down the stairs.

"Jim, watch out!" Lee cried out and tried to keep up with him.

Reno ignored the stairs to the alley, running through the big barroom, which was practically empty. Rosy was standing at the doors, looking out, but he whirled suddenly.

"Jim! Where you going?"

"Give me a gun, Rosy!"

"Jim, don't go out there!"

Reno turned and raced to the bar, pulling Rosy's .45 from beneath the bar. He shoved past the bartender who called after him, "Wait, Jim, I'm coming, too!"

Reno ran down the street and turned the corner to find a big crowd making a wide circle. He shoved his way through and saw Zane Williams lying in the awkward position of the dead, his gun in his hand and his face in the dust.

Rachel was kneeling beside Jesse, with Jeff on the other side. Beyond them stood Jack Canby, and across the circle Doucett was flanked by two of the men he ran with.

Reno ignored them and walked toward the spot where Jesse lay. A mutter ran around the crowd as he was identified, but he ignored it, stopping to kneel beside Rachel.

She turned blindly to him, and when she recognized him, she said, "Jim! They've killed him!"

"No, they ain't!" She whirled to see Jesse's eyes open, and although he gasped with pain, his first words were to Reno.

"You're—still here, Jim."

"Yes, Major." Reno put his hand on Jesse's shoulder and added with a steely light in his eyes, "I'll be here. You just take it easy."

Jesse closed his eyes, then he smiled and said faintly, "That's good to hear!"

Someone was approaching, and Reno looked around quickly to see Doc Mitchell running toward them. He dropped to his knees and ran his eyes over the limp form of the marshal, then pulled his clothing back, searching with sure hands. He looked up at Rachel and gave a tight smile.

"He isn't gonna die, Rachel." Then he said, "Let's get him to my office."

Volunteers gathered quickly, and under the direction of the doctor the unconscious man was carefully carried down the street. Rachel was at his head, but she looked back and said, "Jim, you come with us."

"You go on. I'll be right there," he said, and gave her a smile. "I promise."

Jeff turned and asked, "Want me to stay, Reno?"

"Better stay with the marshal." They left, and the crowd pulled away from the tense figures of Canby and Doucett. The two did not look at each other, and Reno saw over by the door of the Palace the bulky form of Neal Burdick.

There was an electric silence in the air as Reno stood there, the gun held loosely in his hand. He ignored Burdick and fastened his eyes on Canby, who stood there with his arms held close to his sides.

"Hello, Jack," Reno said softly. He began to walk in catlike stealth toward the gunman, which made Canby pull his hands in an abrupt movement over his guns.

"You want to try it?" Reno said, still moving forward, not more than twenty feet away.

Canby almost drew, but there was a deadly air about the man in front of him, and Canby was a man who had lived longer than most in his trade by taking no chances. He knew what he could do, but the gun in Reno's hand was already clear of leather, and he was shaken by the confident smile on the lips of the man who seemed to be enjoying the idea of a fight. Canby was accustomed to toying with his victims, and now he licked his lips nervously as Reno stopped not ten feet away and said, "Well, Jack, what's holding you back?"

Canby shot a quick glance at Doucett. Seeing a nod from the man, he turned to face Reno, knowing that he had a backup. Then he heard somebody say, "You ain't in this one, Riley." He glanced around again to see Rosy Tucker holding a shotgun under Doucett's ear. Doucett was completely still, his face pale beneath the tan.

"I'm giving you a break, Jack," Reno stuck the gun in his belt and added, "Anytime you want, just let 'er flicker."

In the silence that followed, Canby tried desperately to make his move. Reno stood there smiling, his arms relaxed at his side. Everything seemed frozen, not a stir from the crowd, not a word spoken.

Then Canby said in a hoarse croak, "I . . . I got no quarrel with you, Reno."

"No? Let me give you one then, Jack."

With one smooth motion he drew his gun and whipped the barrel over Canby's ear with such terrible power that it sounded like a ripe watermelon being hit with a hammer.

Canby fell to the dust in a limp heap, and Reno whirled to face Burdick, calling out, "Come and get him, Burdick! He's just the tail—you're the yellow cur that wags it!"

Burdick looked up, a red bump on his forehead, and gave Reno no answer. He said, "Get him to the doctor," in a toneless voice, then disappeared inside the Palace without another word.

Reno looked over the crowd and there was a steely quality in his gaze as he said, "I hope you all come to the hanging." He went over to the body of Zane and kneeling beside the still form he touched the dead man's face.

Looking up he said, "Help me get him out of here. I won't see honor in the dust like this!" Then he said softly to the dead man, "You did your best, Zane. I'll take care of you."

NINE

Reno Finds a Cause

A sharp wind whipped through the small group that stood around the open grave, plastering the women's dresses against their bodies and ruffling the hair of the men. When Sheridan opened his worn black Bible, a keen, fitful gust ripped at the thin pages, fanning them loudly in the morning silence.

As the preacher found his place, Reno let his gaze drift around the circle, noting with a stolid expression the lack of care in most of the faces. Faulkner, Morehouse, Tyler, and their wives along with a few other merchants were there, their faces gray in the feeble morning light. Three punchers, unshaven and wearing rough range wear, stood to themselves, and the two deputies, Palmer and Hartley, stood to their left. Jake Smiley, the burly blacksmith, had been one of those who had helped carry the pine coffin from the wagon to the grave, and there was genuine regret on his square face. Standing ten yards behind the small group were Al Rossiter and Rosy Tucker.

"Zane Williams went out of this life the way he lived it— doing what he thought was important." Sheridan's iron voice pulled their thoughts toward the rough coffin with the two ropes looped around it, and for the next five minutes they all listened as the preacher spoke of the dead man's good qualities.

The marshal was the one man who would have mourned Zane Williams deeply, but he wasn't there. Rachel was, however, and there was something in her face that caught at Reno—a gentle grief, mirrored in her gray eyes, that went deeper than tears. As Sheridan read a verse from his Bible, she reached out, laying her hand gently on the rough wood in a gesture of farewell that was mute and eloquent—a simple grace that Reno knew he would never forget.

Jeff Lindsey stood beside her, looking too well-dressed for the crowd. There was none of the concern in his lean face that Reno saw on the faces of some of the others. He moved closer to Rachel as she touched the coffin, causing her to look up at him suddenly, and there was a small smile on her trembling lips as she touched his arm.

A brief pause cut across the air, and Reno looked across to see Sheridan gazing down at the coffin with an expression of pain on his wide face. He closed his Bible and said gently, "Jesus once stood at a grave and said, 'Lazarus, come forth,' and that's what happened." Sheridan shook his head and said in a strange tone, "I don't know if he'll ever say to this man, 'Zane Williams, come forth.'" He paused, and the air was punctuated by the shrill cry of a red-tailed hawk falling onto a helpless rabbit who had time for only one frightened squeal. "We knew this man, and we loved him, some of us. And all I can say is that God loves him more than any of us did." He nodded to the men by the ropes and as the coffin descended into the raw earth, he picked up a clod of red clay and dropped it into the gaping cavity, saying, "Dust to dust."

After the final prayer, most of the townspeople got away as quickly as they could. Reno waited for a time, then went over to pick up a shovel.

"Jim, Dad wants you to come by the house." Rachel turned from saying a word to the preacher, and asked, "Will you come?"

"Sure."

He watched Jeff lead her across the broken ground of the cemetery, then began to help Jake Smiley fill in the grave.

"Good man," Smiley said. "I'll miss him."

"So will Jesse." Sheridan had come to stand beside the two men, and he peered at Reno with a sudden intensity. "Still here?"

Reno said nothing, and then he saw Rossiter and Rosy come to stand across from the preacher.

"Hello, Reverend," Al said with a wry smile.

"Hello, Al—Rosy." The minister smiled at them and said, "Glad you came."

"He was a good lawman," Rosy said. "Not too many of that breed around."

Rossiter moved his thin shoulders impatiently and said as he suddenly moved to go, "Need to talk to you, Reno. Come by when you get a minute."

"Sure, Al." The two wheeled and made their way back toward town, skirting the wooden markers that rose up out of the earth. Rossiter's slender form looked childlike next to the bulk of Rosy, and Reno remarked as he began his work, "A gambler, a saloon bouncer, and a down-at-the-heels drifter— not much of a crowd for Williams, was it, Preacher?"

"I've seen worse crowds, Jim," Sheridan remarked quietly. "I held a funeral once in a big church in Chicago for one of the nicest old men I ever met. Nobody but me came for that one. Not a soul."

Reno paused, leaned on his shovel, and said, "People don't care a lot, do they, Sheridan?"

"Most don't. Some do."

"Zane could have had lots of friends," Smiley said. The work was nothing for his huge blacksmith's muscles, and he worked steadily, handling the large shovel like it was a teaspoon. "If he could've got Rachel to marry him, why, he'd have had a good life."

"Expect you're right, Jake," Sheridan said with a nod. "He wanted that girl so bad he'd never settle for second best."

When the chore was done, Reno handed the shovel to Jake and said, "See you later."

He picked up his coat and turned to leave. Sheridan said, "I'm leaving town later today, Reno." He paused, and when Reno made no response he asked directly, "You thinking of staying?"

"No. I'll be moving on."

"Too bad, Jim." They said nothing until they came to the path that led to the church. Sheridan suddenly reached out and took Reno by the arm, his fingers biting into the flesh. "Hate to see a man waste his life, Jim. Zane didn't have much, but he at least had a job he felt was worth doing."

"And what did he have to show for it, Reverend?" Reno looked back toward the ranks of markers, and his face looked old in the morning light. He shook himself free from Sheridan's grasp and said almost angrily, "He put his life on the line for this town. Well, where was the town this morning? Too lazy to walk to his funeral! He died poor and nobody cared or ever gave him anything!"

Sheridan did not move, but there was a light of pity in his eyes as he finally said, "You might say the same thing about Jesus Christ, Jim. How did you put it? 'He put his life on the line. He died poor and nobody cared or ever gave him anything.'"

"That's different!" Reno said angrily.

"Not completely. Jim, you must have seen a few men in the army who gave up their lives to save somebody else?" Sheridan's sharp gaze did not miss the sudden effect this had on Reno, and he added, "They did it because they cared about something more than they cared about themselves." He paused and then said sharply, "You're a hard customer, Jim— but you're feeding on yourself, living for no one else."

"Good-bye, Parson!" Reno said harshly, and he shook his shoulders, breaking into a fast walk as he left Sheridan abruptly.

Anger ran through him, drawing his full lips into a thin line that scored his dark wedge-shaped face. He had the instincts of a born fighter, and to lash out at a man who challenged him was a reaction that lay close to the surface. The bridge of his nose that showed a small break and the pale track of some old cut on his right temple were memorials to the reckless side of his nature. Action was simple when it was a matter of fist or gun, but as he drove himself along the empty street he could find no outlet for the anger that the preacher's words had stirred in him.

For half an hour he walked, circling the frame buildings on the outskirts of town. Finally, he lifted his head, glanced toward the open plain and said half to himself, "Time to make tracks."

He made his way to the Lindsey house, and Rachel met him on the porch. "He's awake, Jim."

"How is he, Rachel?"

"Doctor Mitchell says he's worried." She bit her lip and said in a whisper, "He's not young anymore, Jim—and he'll eat himself up with worry about the job." She shook her head and said, "It's not good."

She opened the door and Reno stepped into the bedroom. He was a little shocked at the wan face of the marshal, who was flat on his back in the old iron bed. There was an unhealthy pallor on his face, and a trembling in his hands that lay outside the coverlet.

"Here's Jim, Dad," Rachel said.

"Hello, Jesse." Reno pulled the single chair in the room beside the bed and eased into it. "You feeling better?"

Jesse turned his head to face Reno and said, "Glad you went to Zane's funeral, Jim. Rachel told me."

"A good man," Reno said quietly.

"Yeah, he was that, all right." The effort of speaking brought a fine film of sweat on the old man's brow, and Rachel moved to the other side of the bed and wiped it with a handkerchief. "Where's Jeff?" he asked.

"He's meeting with the town council."

Lindsey gave a short laugh and then gasped at the pain it brought. He waved Rachel away and said, "That bunch of weasels?"

Rachel smoothed his hair back and said, "Since Jeff didn't win the election, they're trying to figure a way to get something done."

"That bunch can't find their noses with both hands! I know what they'll be doing, Rachel—appointing a new marshal!"

"Well—" Rachel shot a worried look at her father and bit

her lip. "There was some talk about that, Dad. You won't be able to work for a few days and somebody has to fill in for you."

"It'll be Jeff, that's what they'll do! And that'd be the end of him."

"But Dad—"

"No!" Lindsey raised his hand and waved her aside, and there was a strain of fear in his voice as he said, "They'd *use* him, Rachel! He'd be the one they'd stick out in front, don't you see that? In a little while, after he had some experience, why, he could handle it." The old man sank back in the bed and shook his head hopelessly. "He'll either have to go along with Burdick and his crowd or get shot."

For Reno it was a painful thing to see this proud man who had never been afraid of anything suddenly helpless as the things he loved most were in jeopardy. Jesse Lindsey was a legend, and one built on fact, not a dime novel creation. He had paid the price with his blood and given up the things most men have in order to be a peace officer in some of the roughest territory on the planet.

And now he was helpless. Reno felt a strange kinship with Lindsey, and as he stared down at the old man, he knew what he had to do.

"Jesse," he said quietly, "you want me to stay on until you get on your feet?"

Jesse Lindsey lay perfectly still for a moment, then he turned his head slowly to face the younger man. A light of hope was ignited in his fine old eyes, and he swallowed hard and said steadily, "Mean that, Jim?"

"Yes."

The single word brought a smile to Jesse's pale lips and he nodded. "Didn't want to ask, but I'm mighty proud you're going to be here."

"What about Jeff?"

"You'll be my chief deputy—which is to say you'll be the marshal until I can get on my feet. Jeff can get on with his rat-killing with the council. Maybe they'll do some good."

"He's going to be a good man for this town, Major," Reno said.

"Sure, but he's got to stay alive first." Lindsey mustered a small grin and added, "I reckon you've had a little experience along those lines, Jim."

"My habit."

"I'll get the word out that you're wearing the star. Rachel, get mine right now, will you?"

"Yes." Rachel moved to the chest beside the door and picked up a silver star with the simple word *Marshal* on it, and asked, "Want me to pin it on him, Dad?"

"Might as well." There was a smile on Lindsey's face as Rachel put the star on Reno's shirt and he said, "You promise to be the best deputy marshal in Kansas, so help you God?"

"So help me, God," Reno said, and the words sent a strange sense of the past through him. He smiled and looked down at the star with an odd expression in his dark eyes. "Haven't done this since I joined up with the Third Arkansas, Major."

"Does something for a man, to swear to be faithful, doesn't it, son?"

Reno sat there and looked at the thin hand that Jesse held out to him. He took it, and it felt fragile in his own grasp. He held it a moment, then smiled suddenly. "You're wondering why I'm doing this, aren't you, Major?"

"Well, I guess I am, Jim. Thought you'd light a shuck, to tell the truth." Jesse's eyes were shrewd and he said, "Know it ain't for money or glory. What you doin' it for?"

Reno released the thin hand and moved his hand across his face absently. There was a far-off light in his hooded eyes as he answered slowly, "You don't remember me, but you're one man I don't guess I'll ever forget."

"We met before?" Jesse shook his head and said positively, "Don't think so, Jim. I'd remember you."

"You maybe never even saw me, Major, but I saw you clear enough." He smiled at the marshal and said, "And you were pretty busy at the time—at Little Round Top!"

"Round Top!" Jesse tried to sit up. "You were there?"

"Right in the middle of it, with a bullet through my thigh," Jim said. He sobered and shook his head. "You know how the Third Arkansas and a lot of good Texas boys climbed that hill under the worst fire in the war. Well, we almost took it, but there just wasn't enough of us, I guess."

"It was a noble effort, my boy," Jesse said gently. "A noble effort!"

"I suppose. But I got down and our troops pulled back, and I was sure to spend the rest of the war rotting in a Yankee prison."

"What happened, Jim?" Rachel asked, leaning forward with bright eyes.

"Why, I was lying there, bleeding to death, when I looked up and there was this wild-eyed major and a bunch of crazy Texans come to save the world!"

"Didn't quite do that, Jim," Jesse said with a fond smile.

"No, but you got me out of there—and a bunch more of us who had all given ourselves up." Reno stood up and said, "So I look on this deputy business as a way of paying off a debt, Major. I'll do my best for you—just like you did for us that day on Round Top."

A sudden firmness touched the lips of the old soldier, and he looked at Reno with a freshness in his cobalt blue eyes. "Jim, I can tell you been totin' a load lately, but let me tell you this: Any man that went up that hill has got what it takes. Some mighty good boys didn't make it that day, and I've always sort of figured that those of us who did owe them a debt."

"What kind of a debt, Major?" Jim mused softly.

"Why, just to take whatever we get handed and do the best we can with it."

"Not a bad way, Major." Reno smiled, and said as he followed Rachel out of the room, "I'll report to you tomorrow—if I don't get shot first!"

Rachel's face beamed as she led Reno to the door. Then she suddenly said, "I've just *got* to hug you, Jim Reno!" and threw her arms around him with such a robust strength that he grabbed at her to keep his balance.

"That's the trouble with all you Southern belles," he said with a quick smile. "You're too reserved."

"Jim, it's just what Dad needed, to have someone like you on the job."

She was still clinging to him, looking up into his face with a bright smile, when the door opened. Jeff stood there, stock-still at the sight of Rachel and Reno. He saw the star on Reno's shirt and his lips grew thin. "See you got a new job, Reno."

"Oh, Jeff, isn't it wonderful?" Rachel said, and in her happiness she failed to see the cloud on Jeff's face. "Jim's going to be a deputy until Dad's able to get up and around."

"The town council asked me to take over," Jeff said stiffly.

"But you can't use a gun, Jeff."

A flush touched his cheeks then, and the full lower lip revealed a touch of childishness. "There's a little more to the law than playing with pistols, as I've tried to tell you, Rachel."

"But, Jeff—"

"Reno, I think you'd better meet with the council right away. As I said, they want me to step into Dad's place."

"You better talk to Dad, Jeff," Rachel said at once. She had sensed the anger in Jeff, but there was no way he could handle the job, and she dreaded the scene between the two. "Don't go now, though. Come tomorrow when he's stronger."

"All right." Jeff's voice was strained, and he wheeled and left the room abruptly.

"He doesn't understand, Jim," Rachel said slowly. The light of joy that had filled her eyes faded and she shook her head. "He's going to be stubborn about it, and Dad's not able to handle it right now."

"We'll make it work, Rachel," Reno said. He touched her shoulder gently, and she swung to meet him, hope springing into her face at once. "Jeff's just young, that's all. Time takes care of that."

"Jim, I'm . . . I'm so glad you're here!"

"Well, don't break out the brass band yet, Rachel. We have a long way to go."

"I know. But I was so frightened, Jim, and now, well, I'm not!"

He said gently, a light in his rugged face, "I'll be around, Rachel."

He left the house and went directly to the Nugget. Al Rossiter was sitting at a table playing solitaire with his back to the wall, and Rosy was standing at the window close to his table. Both of them looked up and saw the star on his chest.

Al threw his cards down and took a drink of whiskey from the bottle in front of him. "Don't look now, Rosy," he said, "but a dumb rider with all his brains kicked out just walked into the room."

Reno grinned and sat down at the table. He surveyed Rossiter's face and said easily, "Aw, come on, Al, you're just mad at me because I thought of it first." He looked up at Rosy, who was glowering with disapproval, and said solemnly, "I really came to hire you two on as my deputies. Won't we make this old town hum, though?"

"Joke all you please, Jim," Rossiter said with a glum shake of his head. "Neal is going to get you. Ask Rosy."

"That's right, Jim," Rosy agreed nodding. "I been hearing things. You won't have a chance."

Reno sat there grinning at them, and there was an ease in his manner that neither of them had seen before. Always there had been a tension, a wire-fine quality just beneath the surface. He had been in trouble since he'd hit town, but now that he was headed for the most dangerous situation of all, there was a lightness in his manner that overflowed. His dark eyes seemed lighter, and there was an ease in the way he lounged at the table that they did not understand. He saw their uncertainty and grinned broadly, looking young and reckless.

"Neither of you was in the war, were you? Well, it was a wild thing, but for me the hard time was waiting. I got jumpy and nervous before a battle, but once we were on our way it, why, it all left me. Guess that's crazy, but I feel better now that I know what the job is."

"I guess you still believe all the storybooks, Jim," Rossiter said quietly. He stared moodily across the dim light at Reno and a streak of dark cynicism that ran deep in him was traced in the hollow contours of his thin face. He slumped deeper into his chair and said, "What is it with you, some kind of holy cause?"

Reno smiled faintly and murmured, "That's close enough, Al."

Rossiter snorted and said bitterly, "You should have had all that shot out of you when the South went down!"

"I thought it had, Al," Reno said gently. A strange light touched his face, softening the sharp planes and washing the hardness from his features.

Rosy watched him closely, not understanding the change in Reno. He saw the worst of men from his position behind the bar, and he asked suddenly, "You look pretty happy for a man who's going to be the target for the wild bunch, Jim."

Reno thought about that, then said with a smile, "Well, Rosy, they may kill me—but they won't be able to kill me but once. That's what we used to tell each other just before we went into a big fight."

"Once is plenty!" Al Rossiter said bitterly. "You're a sucker, Jim."

"Guess that's what I was in the army for, Al," Reno said lazily, and as he got up, he laughed suddenly, his teeth very white against the bronze of his cheeks. "Yep, guess in America we got a right to be wrong!"

He left the saloon and Rosy asked in a puzzled voice, "What's that all about, Al? He got religion or something?"

Rossiter stared at the cards scattered on the table and picked up one, staring at it. He threw it down and took a drink before hc said bleakly, "I think so, Rosy. And it's going to get him killed."

Patterns come easily for a man with a job, and wearing the star brought order into Reno's life very quickly. Exactly at seven he came to Rudy's for breakfast, occupying a table that gave a full view of the room. After a full meal, he strolled down to the stable and mounted a bay gelding, then rode out of Rimrock. He rode west into the timber, letting the solitude of the wild country wash the tensions out of his system, and stopped at the small stream to water his horse and look for signs of beaver.

This time of day was a brief interval when he was free from the petty treacheries of the town, from the pressures of the townsmen and the saloon crowd. Here he could escape the thoughts of dark alleys and lightless windows and breathe the air sharp as wine coming through the pines.

Then he would ride slowly back, enter Dance Street, and wait for the night to come on. A shave at Larry Sneed's Barbershop, a time to sit around and watch the town carry on its business, and then by one o'clock he would go to the jail and see what sort of fish the night had brought in.

Clarence Palmer was on nights, and he had watched Reno carefully, waiting for him to show some weakness, but had found none. Palmer was devoted to Jesse Lindsey and jealous of any attempt to usurp the marshal's authority, but he had grown to admire Reno during the five weeks of Lindsey's time off.

"Anything new, Clarence?"

"Naw, just three drunks. Was some kind of argument over at Flora's place about three this mornin'—but nobody got shot."

Reno nodded. "Nice day."

Palmer took a critical glance at Reno, noting the broad shoulders, the steady gaze, and the light in the dark eyes. Reno wore a low-crowned black hat, a gray shirt, and dark gray trousers. He had full long lips and raven black hair matched by heavy eyebrows. He had a catlike quickness about him and the strong juices of a young man's vitality bubbling in him. He could play it soft or hard. Palmer had seen him face down the roughest challenge with a steady force, and he had seen him flare out with a wild explosive anger that shocked even the toughs who'd seen practically everything.

"Get some sleep, Clarence."

"Yeah. See you later."

For an hour he sat at the desk going through wanted posters, writing letters, taking care of the book work. Finally he got up, stretched, and left the office to make his first round of the town.

He was set apart by his office, but he answered everyone who spoke to him, having learned the names of practically everyone in town. There was a pleasure in this part of the job, but he knew that as the darkness fell and Dance Street opened up, he would close up his natural openness and shield himself behind a wall for his own protection.

He stopped by the Nugget and his eyes went to the table where Lola usually sat. He saw that she was there and joined her with a smile. "Hello, Lola."

"Jim, you look tired."

"No, just getting old."

She smiled at him, and it struck him not for the first time how he had come to count on the time he spent with her. She never mentioned helping him, nor the closeness his trouble had brought them, but he knew that there was something the two of them shared that would have to come out one day.

She never spoke of Neal Burdick, but his presence was a very strong thing. He knew she was still seeing Burdick, but he never inquired into that side of her life.

They sat there and talked idly, mostly about Lee. "He's getting too smart for me, Jim." Lola bit her lower lip and shook her head, "He needs to go to school."

"He'll have to want it, Lola."

"I know. Can't you talk to him? He'll listen to you."

"I'll have a try."

The door burst open and Ernest Faulkner burst into the room. He was pale, and his eyes lit up when he saw Reno. "Marshal, come quick!"

Reno was out of his chair and beside Faulkner at once. "What's up, Faulkner?"

"It's Jeff Lindsey, Reno! There was some trouble at my store, and Jeff tried to stop a couple of Texas drovers—"

Reno didn't wait for Faulkner to finish. He left the room at a run, pushing several riders out of his way. The hardware store was around the corner, and he saw that a small crowd had gathered outside. He used his strength to plow through the press, using his elbows roughly. A cowhand was blocking the door, and Reno caught the man by the coat collar and slammed him back, then entered the store.

Jeff Lindsey was facing two punchers, both of them armed. There was a thin trickle of blood on Jeff's cheek and his face was pale.

There were two other punchers in the store, grinning at the two in front of Jeff, and Reno guessed they were all from the same outfit. It was dangerous, for these trail hands stuck to their outfit.

Jeff saw him then, and something in his face caused the two men to whirl and face Reno, their faces alert. They were both young, just off the trail, and probably could have been easily handled if Reno had had a free hand.

But Jeff said, "Arrest these two, Marshal!"

It forced them to prove their toughness, and one of them said, "He ain't arrestin' nobody—and I'm gonna stomp you, sonny."

"Settle down, cowboy," Reno said easily. "What's the trouble, Jeff?"

"These two came in here and started forcing themselves on the clerk!"

Reno would have laughed it if hadn't been so serious. The clerk was Annie Farmer, a homely spinster who would have enjoyed nothing better than being accosted by two full-blooded young cowboys.

"You fellows just move along," Reno said, and it would have gone all right, but Jeff said angrily, "You may let them go, but I'm not going to!" He grabbed at one of the punchers and was knocked down instantly by a roundhouse right.

The puncher who had knocked him down shouted, "I'll stomp you good!" and raised his boot over Jeff's unprotected face.

Reno leaped at him and threw him against the harness hanging on the wall. Instantly Reno was struck in the back of the neck by one of the other punchers and driven to his knees. He took a kick in the side from a third puncher and then he lost control, a curtain of red rage falling across his eyes. He swung his fist, catching someone in the mouth. A pair of arms locked around his head and he reached back, grabbing two handfuls of hair. He nearly scalped the first puncher as he dragged him over his shoulder. The man hit the floor and as he struggled to rise, Reno struck him in the face with a knee that put him out of action instantly.

Out of the corner of his eye he saw one of the other punchers pull a gun. He instantly pulled his own weapon and whipped the man across the wrist, sending the gun flying.

"That's it!" he yelled at the fourth man who reached for his gun too late. "All of you are going to the pokey. Pick him up, you two." He motioned toward the man he had put down with his knee, and he got them moving, herding them like sheep down the street.

When they were locked up, he found Jeff and Faulkner entering, both of them angry.

"You shouldn't have done that, Marshal," Faulkner said, wringing his hands. "They're with the Bar T outfit, old John Taylor's brand. They bring lots of business to town."

"I could have handled it if you'd stayed out, Reno," Jeff said angrily.

Reno said, "They stay in jail until somebody pays their fine. And Jeff, you better watch yourself. Some of these trail hands are pretty rough. One of them will ventilate you for a dime."

"I'm telling you, Marshal, Taylor will be in to get his crew, and he'll pull your jail down if he takes a notion," Faulkner insisted, his face pale. "He's done it before in other places."

Reno stared at the two men and said, "You let that crowd call the shots and you might as well hand them the keys to the town. You think Jesse would let this pass, Jeff?"

The mention of his father seemed to anger the young man, and he said bitterly, "I won't argue with you, Reno—but the town council will! There's a meeting at eight tonight, and you're to be there!"

He walked out, followed by Faulkner, and Reno watched them go, his face grim. He stood there, and he touched the star on his chest, wanting nothing more than to toss it on the desk and ride away from Rimrock. But he shook his head and forced himself to leave the office and walk the streets, where he was rewarded with glares from the businessmen and sly grins from others who saw his authority sliding away from him.

TEN
Fight at the Palace

"Blast it all, Ada, I wish you'd stop treatin' me like a month-old baby!"

Jesse Lindsey glared at Ada, who was holding his bathrobe; she smiled sweetly and said, "You're more trouble than ten babies, Jesse. Now put on your robe and slippers. Jim's here."

"Where's my pants?" he demanded crustily, searching the room with bright eyes. "Man without pants is a plumb worthless critter!" He took the robe from her and threw it across the room, the sudden action bringing such a sharp stab of pain to his healing tissue that he gasped and turned pale.

Ada stared at him, and there was a gentleness in her face that soothed away the lines he had noted when she first came to Rimrock. Her voice had softened, too, and when she said, "That make you happy? Now behave and put your robe on," it brought back memories from a past that he treasured.

He stared at her and gave her a sudden smile as she picked up the robe and held it up to him with a determined look on her face.

"You always had to have your own way, Ada."

She faltered then, dropping her gentle expression in the confusion that had come to her recently. Her single intention had been to accompany Jeff so that she could help him climb to some great career, but it had not been that simple. If it had not been for Jesse's injury, she might have kept her distance; but she had begun sitting with Jesse so that Rachel could have some relief, and his presence had shaken her. Old emotions that she had buried years before surfaced, and she was dismayed to find that the powerful attraction of their youth, which she thought was gone, had only been dormant.

She forced herself to look up into his eyes, and there was a sudden tremor in her firm voice that he did not miss, "Jesse, I . . . I don't think I can come to sit with you any more."

He stared at her, and her face burned. Others she could deceive, but he had always been able to read her heart. She tried to turn, but he caught her by the arms and forced her to look at him. "Ada," he said in his direct manner, "I lost you once. I don't want to lose you again."

She trembled suddenly in his hands, and the customary serenity of her ivory face broke. Her eyes swam with tears and she let him pull her forward, but she whispered in a voice tight with pain, "Oh, Jesse, it's too late! Too late!"

He said nothing for a time, but held her firmly against his chest. "No, it's not too late, Ada."

"We're old!"

"You're a child!" He smiled and kissed her with a tenderness that carried the flavor of the fierce passion of a youthful love, then he said, "Now, get my pants."

She broke into a startled laugh, and reached up to pull his hair in a gesture he remembered. "Jesse Lindsey, you're awful!

I believe you're just sweet-talking me to get your own way like you always did!"

He laughed then, and as he put on his pants and shirt there was a new expression on his seamed face, which was mirrored in Ada's eyes.

"Jesse, don't say anything to Jeff about . . . about us."

With a laugh he reached out and pulled her around so that she could see her reflection in the mirror. "Don't have to say a word, Ada. Look at you! You look like a bride."

She blushed like a girl, touched her cheek and said, "I'm afraid for Jeff."

He sobered, nodded and said, "I know. But he's going to be all right, Ada. You did a good job with him."

"No, I should have let him have a father. I see that now."

"Well, he's got one, and he's young enough and smart enough to learn."

"You know he's in love with Rachel?"

"Sure. Dumb as I am, I saw that right off. And you don't think it's a good thing?"

She took a few short paces across the room, then threw her arms out in a defenseless gesture. "I was so ready to match him up with a woman who could help him do great things, help him have a career. But I've changed, Jesse. We have such a short time here, and—I don't want him to miss out on the real thing."

He put his arm around her. "Well, she may not love him. I've thought she looked at Jim Reno like a woman looks at a man."

"Yes, and that's what's driving Jeff to play the fool. He's jealous of Reno."

They stood there, caught up with the problem, then Jesse

said, "Well, we'll have to let them work it out, Ada. Advice to the lovelorn was never too well received."

They went out of the bedroom and made their way to the kitchen, where Rachel was serving pie and coffee to Reno and Jeff. When she looked up, Ada saw that she recognized at once the change in their attitude. The girl smiled at once and said, "Hello. I see you made her let you put your pants on, Dad."

The two men laughed, but there was a quickness in the girl that Ada had not expected. Rachel came to her and put her arm around her in a warm familiar way saying with a pixieish glint in her eyes, "Don't tell me you've fallen under his spell?"

Ada looked directly at Rachel, and there was a sudden intuitive flash between the two women. Ada smiled and kissed Rachel on the cheek with an impulsive gesture that froze Jeff in the act of lifting a piece of pie to his mouth. He had never seen his mother so free and open with anyone on such short notice. He glanced at the wide grin on his father's face, and the expression came so close to being exultant he suddenly swallowed too big a bite and began to choke.

Rachel laughed and slapped him on the back, saying, "That's what you get for being a pig, Jeff."

Reno smiled and pushed his empty plate back on the table. "Guess I'm worse than Jeff." He got up and said with an air of regret, "Sure would like to say you're a good cook, Rachel. But the truth is the worst pie I ever ate was good! I'm no judge at all!"

"Things going all right, Jim?" Jesse asked. He looked at the figure of Reno and thought again how the man was built to be a lawman. He had the bulk of shoulder, muscled arms, and heavy legs to bull his way through a crowd, but still there were the catlike quickness and hair-trigger reactions that kept him constantly vigilant. His deep-set eyes were protected by a shelf of heavy bone above and high cheek bones below, and there was enough bulk in his chin to take a punch without going down. There was in the man an inner toughness that would never let him quit, and Lindsey knew he'd need it soon enough.

"Two new trail herds came in yesterday. Guess Dance Street will be a little lively tonight."

"Heard about your run-in with old man Taylor."

"He hollered a lot, but he paid the fines."

Jeff said suddenly, "He said he'd be back and take the town apart, too."

"Big Texas talk."

"No," Jeff argued. He shook his head stubbornly, and added, "We need that gun law, Jim. If they don't have guns, they won't cause any trouble."

"Can't see Taylor doin' anything like that, Jeff," Jesse said. "If we passed a no-gun ordinance in this town, he'd ship his cattle from another spot—which is just what the merchants don't want—nor Neal Burdick for that matter."

"I don't care what Burdick wants!" Jeff argued heatedly.

"He's got lots of muscle in this town. Look how he kept you from getting elected."

It was a sore spot to Jeff, and he flushed to the roots of his hair. "That old fool Keach is nothing but a joke, Dad! Anytime any of Burdick's crowd gets arrested, he just fines them five dollars no matter what they've done."

"Well, he's the people's choice, Jeff," Jesse said with a glint in his blue eyes and a suppressed grin on his lips. "It just shows how much power Burdick has."

"Well, I'm not going to put up with it!"

"You going to shoot the old buzzard, Jeff?" Reno asked lazily.

"No!" Jeff shot back angrily, stung by Reno's manner. "I'm going to get the attorney general to impeach him. I've been collecting evidence, and I've got enough to get him dismissed."

"Steve Hanna, the Attorney General?" Jesse asked.

"Yes!"

"Him and Burdick go elk hunting together in Colorado most every year." They all saw how that hit the young man, stripping him of his assurance, and Jesse said in a kindly manner, "We'll just have to wait for a break, Jeff. Burdick will make a mistake. His kind always does."

"We'll nail him, Jeff," Reno said. He turned to leave, adding, "Jesse's right. I'll keep an eye on him."

Ada saw an expression on Jeff's face that she had seen before when he was put in a bad light, and usually he lost control. To her dismay he blurted out, his face suddenly pale, "You hanging around that tramp in the Nugget just so you can keep your eye on Burdick? Everybody knows she's his woman!"

"Jeff!" Ada said instantly, for she saw Reno's eyes flash and the muscles swell beneath his tight shirt.

"Well, it's true, isn't it?" Jeff's brow was suddenly damp, and there was an unsteady quality in his tone. "Why are you upset when I tell the truth?"

"It's not the truth, Jeff!" Rachel said evenly. She too had seen Reno's reaction, and unconsciously she put her hand on his arm to restrain him. "Lola keeps a saloon, and she's had a hard life." She paused then and said gently to Jeff, "You've never been hurt, Jeff. I don't think you ought to judge people until you've stood in their shoes."

The rebuke seared the young man, and he could not stand the pressure. He headed for the door saying in a muffled voice, "I didn't know we had so many bleeding hearts around this house!" He deliberately shoved against Reno as he left the room, but Reno merely stepped back and watched him go.

"He should know better," Ada said quietly, pain in her eyes. "I'm ashamed for him. Jim, I'm sorry."

Reno was a dark shape outlined against the wall, and there was something wolfish about him at that moment. He could be a dangerous man, and all of them knew that he was putting himself under an iron control, an opaque light hooding his eyes, and his mouth a cruel slash across his dark face.

Finally he found a smile and said, "Not altogether his fault, Ada." He did not look at Rachel, but they realized he was aware of Jeff's feeling for Rachel and of the jealousy the young man felt.

"When I was his age," Reno said, and he allowed a wry smile to touch his broad lips as he mused in a gentle voice, "I felt like it was a wasted week if I didn't make a fool of myself at least twice a day."

"Yeah," Jesse said slowly, but there was a dark apprehension in his face, "but we're playing for keeps this time, Jim. If Jeff made a bad play with Burdick or one of his crowd, like he just did here, it could get him killed."

Reno nodded and said slowly, "Jeff will come out all right—if he doesn't get sucked into something too big for him. Mad as he is now, he may do something foolish to prove himself."

"Could we get away, Jesse?" Ada whispered.

"Too late now, Ada," Jesse said at once. "This thing is going to break soon. I've got to get better!" He slapped the able with his hand and there was a frustration in his eyes. "Jeff needs me!"

Ada slipped her hand into his and said, "I need you, too, Jesse. We all do."

The last of Reno's anger drained away as he watched this, and he said, "I'll keep an eye on the boy. He's good stuff." Then he wheeled and left the room, and there was a sudden urgency in him to break the stronghold that Burdick had on Rimrock. Reno was basically given to action rather than thought, and he knew that he had to do something to break the stalemate.

A taste of snow was in the air, and before he made his way down Monroe Street to turn onto Grant, steely fragments began to sting his face. By morning the cattle milling around in the stock pens would be coated with snow, their horns glittering with a coating of ice. He shivered and hurried down the street, stepping into the warmth of his office in time to catch Bub Hartley slipping into his coat.

"Hi, Marshal. I'm goin' to get some grub for the prisoners. You want something?"

Reno looked at the skinny deputy, and asked, "You sick Bub? Looks like you got something."

Hartley's face was pale except for two spots on his cheekbones that blazed like fire. His eyes were dull and he croaked like a bullfrog as he said, "Aw, just a cold. Get one every first snow."

Reno took the coat from Bub's hand and hung it back on the rack. Picking up his own sheepskin jacket, he gave the young man a slap on the shoulder, saying, "Get in bed, cover up, and I'll have Rosy make you a hot toddy according to my old granddad's secret remedy—half a lemon in a quart of whiskey!"

Bub grinned weakly, protesting as he allowed himself to be shoved toward the small back room they used for naps. "Aw, Jim, just bring me some of *that* and I'll be OK." He paused at the door. There was something in his eyes, dull as they were with sickness, that revealed his admiration for Reno. Unconsciously he had taken on several of Reno's mannerisms, as he had done previously with Marshal Lindsey. At nineteen Bub longed desperately to have the tough assurance and easy manner of Reno, but he had never proved himself under fire. The fear that he might fail haunted him.

"Get some rest, Bub." Reno smiled and added, "Too cold tonight for much trouble." Both of them knew better, for the falling temperatures would send the trail hands seeking the warmth and excitement of the saloons all the more eagerly.

A layer of snow lay on the ground, smoothing the corrugated mud of the streets to a broad white ribbon, and already the graceful crests and crowns of snow were forming atop the rough frame buildings of Dance Street.

The beauty of it caught at Reno, and he stopped to admire the symmetry imposed by the falling flakes. The sky was a gray background which served as a foil, transforming the stark, raw fronts of saloons and sporting houses into castles glittering with a diamondlike brilliance. All was smooth, clean, pure, and it suddenly depressed Reno to consider the grimy activities beneath that beauty. *Sure is pretty. Too bad things can't always stay clean,* he thought. But he was too much of a realist to allow more than a passing regret to interrupt his immediate task, so he ducked his head in the sweep of easy wind and downy flake and did not pause until he entered Rudy's Café.

Al Rossiter sat alone drinking a cup of coffee, gave Reno a moody look, and pushed a chair back with a kick of his foot. "Howdy, Jim. Have a seat."

Taking off his sheepskin coat, Reno called to Rudy who had come out of the kitchen, "Need grub for three prisoners, Rudy. And bring me a steak."

"Comin' up."

"What's going on, Al?" he asked, taking his seat and soaking up the warmth radiating from a potbellied stove close by. "You fleecin' enough dumb trail hands to keep yourself in socks and cigars?"

Rossiter responded with a grunt and took a sip of coffee. Reno noted that there was a restless air of discontent in him. Rossiter pulled a thin cigar from his vest and studied it morosely. He bit off the end, lit it, and finally said, "Where you been, Jim? You been out of pocket lately."

"Had to make a trip to Hays." He studied Al, leaned back, and asked, "Anything wrong?"

Rossiter's thin face was usually expressionless, a mask that concealed whatever was inside him, but something about the set slash of his thin slips and a smoldering glint in his slate-colored eyes declared a streak of anger.

"Nobody told you?" he asked suddenly.

Reno stared at him, mystified. "Told me about what?"

"About Lola and the kid."

A premonition struck Reno, stiffening his body, and he stared at Al with a sudden predatory cast to his gaze. "What about them, Al?"

"Guess people don't know exactly how you and Lola stand, Jim. You two have been pretty close lately."

Reno had spent several evenings in Lola's room, always with Lee there doing his studies. He had gone at first to encourage the boy, but it had come to something more than that. He'd been drawn to Lola in a way that surprised him. She

had allowed a warmth and gentle wit long concealed beneath a
shell of cynicism to flow during those times. Reno, who had
been totally conscious of her luscious body and the startling
beauty of her face, had come to those evenings with a deep
pleasure in the long talks, sometimes going on after Lee had
dropped off into sleep.

He had known, of course, that he was observed by curious eyes. He was only acting marshal, but the invisible but adamant line that separated the sheep from the goats had been
violated. And although nobody had ventured to question him
directly, he had noted the response in many people.

Bones Morehouse, the most outspoken of the council,
had said only, "Marshal has to walk a pretty fine line where his
connections are concerned, Reno." But a direct stare from
Reno's dark eyes had cut off his next statement abruptly.

Jesse had never mentioned Lola, nor had any of his
friends—except Jeff.

In the course of his duties, Reno encountered Neal Burdick often. Half expecting a challenge to his authority, Reno
soon realized that the burly saloon keeper would use one of
his underlings when the time came for a challenge. There was
an incongruity to the man that Reno did not miss. Outwardly
Burdick had the earmarks of one who would batter down anything that stood before him. His broad face was undergirded
by a massive bone structure built to take punishment, and the
muscles of his upper arms and shoulders swelled and strained
against the shirts and coats he had to have specially made to
accommodate his bulk. He had thick legs, and there was a pon-
derous air to all his movements. Despite this physical power,
there was a slyness in the man which was revealed in the
greenish glint of his small eyes and the full, mobile lips that

kept the large white teeth covered. He was capable of terrible violence, and that part of his character had been displayed enough for the town to beware of his rare rash moods.

As Reno stared across the table at Al, he knew what was coming, and realized suddenly with a sick feeling that he had been in part responsible for it.

"Tell it, Al."

Al said evenly, "I wasn't there, but Rosy gave it to me straight."

"Let me guess," Reno said. He looked down at his fists which were clenched tightly and went on, "Burdick pushed them around, didn't he?"

"Yeah, that's it."

"How bad?"

"Way Rosy told me, the kid wasn't really hurt—more scared than anything."

"And Lola?"

Al shifted and the angry light in his eyes grew fierce. "Nobody knows—except Doc Mitchell, and he won't say anything."

"What did Rosy say?"

"Said that Lola and Neal had been clawing at each other for a week. You know, both of them mad enough so you could tell a break was coming. Then night before last they got into a brawl in the Nugget. Neal got so loud that everybody in the place heard him—which is unusual for him."

"What were they fighting about?"

Al gave Reno a straight look. "You," he said bluntly. "Burdick told her to stay away from you, and Lola told him to mind his own business. Then she got up and went to her room. Later that night Lee went to her room, and about ten Burdick came in, pretty drunk, Rosy said. He went right on up, and it wasn't but a few minutes when Lee came running into the bar crying. A big red mark was on his face. Rosy had a feeling, so he grabbed a bung-starter and ran to Lola's room."

Rossiter took a few nervous pulls at his cheroot, then threw it violently on the floor and cursed bitterly.

"Finish it, Al!"

"You can guess, Jim. The big ape was pounding her, and I guess if Rosy hadn't knocked him away with that bung-starter he'd have killed her. He took Neal's gun away, and threw him out on the street—which is going to get Rosy killed sooner or later—then he sent for Doc Mitchell. That's it."

Reno's jaw was set. He looked past Al, staring at nothing. "No, that's not the end, Al."

Rossiter smiled grimly. "Didn't think you'd let it drop, Jim. Wish it had been me that caught up with that skunk instead of Rosy. I'd have stopped his clock!"

"Well, something may happen to him someday, Al," Reno said softly, and the fierce glint in his dark eyes belied the mildness of his words.

Al grinned wolfishly, and there was an understanding between the two. "You understand Burdick won't go against you himself. He'd use one of the gorillas he's got cluttering up the Palace. Any one of 'em would shoot their own mother for a free drink."

"That's what he'd like. I remember Stonewall said just before the Valley campaign: 'Never give the enemy what he wants.' Guess that's what I'll have to think on."

"Don't get yourself in a pocket, Jim," Rossiter said swiftly. "You got no friends here. The town fathers would crucify you if you cut into their profit. The trail drivers hate your guts, and you know how you stand with Burdick and his crowd. If you had any sense, you'd walk away from it now."

"Never thought to win any popularity contests, Al." Reno looked up as Rudy brought his steak. "Looks good, Rudy—but I've got a little chore that won't wait. Have someone take the grub to the jail, will you?"

As Reno went outside pulling on his coat, Rudy called out, "Hey, Jim, you want me to keep this warm for you?"

Rossiter got up, threw a bill on the table and said, "You better eat it yourself, Rudy. I think the marshal may take longer than he thinks with his errand."

Stepping outside, Al pulled his gun from the folds of his coat, checked the loads, and hurried through the swirling snow toward the Palace saloon.

A sullen rage had burned in Burdick since he had been thrown out of the Nugget by Rosy, and the red mark on the side of his temple seemed to glow as the anger inside increased. His first impulse was to send Canby to gun Rosy Tucker down, but he forced himself to wait. When Canby himself suggested such a move, he had said through clenched teeth, "We'll wait."

"He made a sucker out of you, Neal. You can't let it slide."

"He'll go down, Jack,—and he won't go alone!"

Canby exchanged glances with Doucett, but neither of them cared to mention Reno. It was common knowledge that Lola had dumped Burdick, and everyone jumped to the conclusion that she had opened the door to the new marshal. Burdick caught the look on their faces and the red spot on his temple seemed to glow afresh. "I know what the town's saying. I'll wait, though. My turn will come."

There was an Indian-like patience in the big man, and he moved through the town facing up to the stares with a killing glint in his eyes that made others avoid him. He had been unchallenged for so long that there was a wildness in him that he kept suppressed with an iron will, but he knew that sooner or later there would come a time to settle matters.

When Reno stepped out of the driving snow into the Palace, Burdick knew at once that he was in a killing mood. "Riley," he said quietly around his cigar, "move over against the wall—and move some of the boys around toward the door."

Doucett took the situation in with one quick glance, and with a grin he melted into the crowd that packed the saloon, dropping a word to a couple of the housemen.

Reno didn't miss any of this and an alarm triggered inside his head, but he was through with the waiting game. Making his way down the room he put himself at the bar, the crowd making way for him. Turning to put his back to the massive mahogany bar, he stood there quietly, but there was a tension flowing in him. Burdick was to his right, seated at a table. Reno caught sight of Riley Doucett lounging in the rear, and he knew he could expect trouble from the man. He saw a houseman slip to the swinging doors, and one of the bartenders moved to his left, letting his hand fall below the level of the bar.

Reno deliberately put his back to all of them and advanced along the bar until he stood five feet away from Burdick. He realized that he could take a bullet in the back, but he stood loosely in front of the saloon owner and said, "Hear you had a little trouble with your love life, Neal."

The audacity of the remark drained the color from Burdick's face, and the red mark on his temple jumped into prominence against the sudden pallor of his broad cheeks.

A mocking smile touched Reno's wide lips, and he said louder, "Hear you couldn't hold onto your woman—so you beat her up."

With a violent curse Burdick came to his feet, sending the table skittering across the floor. He pushed it out of the way, and there was a murmur from the men who watched. As Burdick took a step toward him, Reno said sharply, "Hold it right there, Neal. You may slap women and kids around, but I'll drill you if you pull that gun you're reaching for."

Burdick stopped dead still, his hand half-hidden beneath his coat. There was a rigidity in Reno's frame and a sudden wildness in his eye that caused Burdick to move cautiously. He pulled his hand from beneath his coat and his eyes moved over the room. The sight of Doucett and the others at Reno's back reassured him, and he pulled his coat together saying, "You made a mistake coming here, Reno! But you won't have to worry about leaving, because they'll carry you out feet first!"

A confident smile creased Burdick's meaty lips as he said, "You're pretty proud of your draw, Reno." Hate flickered in his hooded eyes. Confident that one of the men flanking the lawman would never let him clear leather, he said, "Well, let's just see how fast you are. I'll let you go for it first."

This, Reno knew, was to give the trap a thin guise of legality. The story would be that Reno had forced his way into the place and began shooting wildly. And there would be no lack of witnesses ready to back up any statement Burdick cared to make.

A familiar feeling came to him, one he had often had during the war, always just before the command came to charge into action. He decided to drop Burdick with one shot, throw himself to one side, and hope to stay alive long enough to make a fight of it against Riley and the others who would be laying a hard line of fire on him. He had little hope of coming out of it alive, but there was no fear—only a regret at the loss of a few things. Even in those last seconds he thought of the things he had loved—a new world at sunrise in the mountains, the first warm breath of spring after a bitter winter, a few friends—not much, actually. Then he thought of Lola, and a deep sense of loss struck him as he thought of never seeing her again.

Just as his nerves flickered and his hand was posed over the .44 at his side, a change crossed Burdick's face. An uncertain cast on his broad cheeks caused Reno to risk one quick look over his shoulder.

Al Rossiter had stepped inside, and although his hands were hidden, Reno knew by the face of the houseman Doucett had set to cut off his retreat that the gambler had put a gun in his back.

He hadn't come alone, for the burly figure of Rosy Tucker shoved through the crowd. He came to stand by Riley Doucett and said audibly in the gunman's ear, "You scratch for it this time, Riley."

Doucett whirled around, but the pistol in his ribs brought a look of caution to his face. He saw also the shotgun in the oversized hand of Jake Smiley, who raised the muzzle to cover the men standing at the bar behind Reno.

The scales had tipped so abruptly that a look of shock formed on Burdick's face, and he stood there so long that Reno laughed and said, "What's the matter, Neal? You afraid to fight without your army?"

The desire to kill came over the big man, but he pulled his hand away from his coat. "I'm not going to draw on you, Reno. Fellow has to be a fool to play another man's game."

He started to turn, but Reno stepped forward and cracked him across the face with a swinging blow. The noise sounded like pistol fire in the silence of the Palace, and a gasp went up from the crowd as Reno said in a voice edged with raw contempt, "You're a dog, Burdick—a yellow dog with no guts!"

Knowing now that Reno would not draw on him, Burdick reached slowly into his coat, removed the small hideout gun he always carried, and laid it on the table gently. Then he slapped his meaty hands together and said, "I'm unarmed, Reno. If you want to try me with fists, I'm ready."

He had no thought that a man of Reno's size would take up such a challenge, but he wanted to get his gun out of the holster to be certain that a gun fight would not occur. To his surprise, Reno unbuckled his gunbelt and laid it on the bar.

Rossiter wanted to shout, "No! Don't do it!" for the sight of Burdick's massive form loomed ominously against the slim figure of Reno.

Burdick shouted, "All right, you sucker! I'm going to bust you up!"

He moved with a speed that was incredible for a man his size. The distance was only a few feet, and he covered most of it in two lunging steps, his massive arms half-circled to grab Reno and trap him in a killing grasp.

If he had done so, it would have been over, but as he closed the gap, Reno picked up a half-full bottle of whiskey and brought it down full on Burdick's skull. The bottle broke, cutting a jagged trail down the side of the ear, and it drove the larger man to his knees. It would have knocked a small man unconscious, but Burdick merely shook his head and got to his feet.

Reno took a step backward, fists clenched and held waist

high. Burdick was a fearsome sight. He weighed at least fifty pounds more than Reno, and topped him by a good six inches. Reno knew that if he went down, Burdick would kill him with his bare hands.

He backed away as Burdick made a swift feint with his left fist and sent a hard right from the opposite direction. It was an easy blow for Reno to duck with his swift reflexes, but when he countered with one of the hardest blows he'd ever struck right in Burdick's stomach with no effect at all, he knew he was in a fight.

The only sound in the room was the scraping noise of the feet of the fighters and the rasp of Burdick's breathing. Their shadows moved along the wall in a ghostly dance, and their reflections in the long mirror behind the bar were made brilliant by the huge chandelier.

Time and time again Burdick would advance, arms outstretched like oak limbs, then he would send a tremendous blow through the air which would have finished Reno had it landed.

Reno had landed several punches, one a crashing blow right in Burdick's mouth that had not dimmed the fire in his eyes at all. Reno began to fall back as Burdick advanced, and he raised both hands to ward off the left jab that came at him. It caught him on the temple and he fell backward, his shoulders striking a table. He rolled sideways at once to avoid the kick he knew would follow. It caught him on the thigh, sending waves of pain to his brain, but he ignored it and kicked a chair in Burdick's way. The big man stumbled over it and fell with his feet tangled up in the rungs.

Reno rolled free, and as he got to his feet he smashed a chair down on Burdick's head. The seat shattered, and the bloodied head of the big man was driven through the shattered fragments. His hoarse breathing increased, and he got up slowly, moving like a man under water. There was something almost comical about the way he stood there trying to get free of the chair he wore around his neck. But there was no laughing, and as he finally freed himself, he peered through the hair matted with blood and sweat at the man across from him.

"I guess we're about even now, Neal," Reno said, and he advanced to meet the battered form of Burdick, still dangerous as a wounded grizzly. This time Reno struck first, throwing a long looping left that caught Burdick in the throat. He followed this with two lightning-fast rights to the belly that drove the breath from the larger man.

He misjudged the man's stamina, however, and a powerful fist came from nowhere, raking the flesh from his eyebrow and driving him into a scrambling fall. The world roared as Burdick pounded him with a couple of thunderous blows. Reno grabbed one of the huge arms and swung Burdick against the wall. The big man fell, but he got up slowly, with no sign of quitting.

Reno was desperate now, for he knew that his own strength was almost gone, and the bull-like endurance of Burdick would wear him down if the fight didn't stop. He ran straight at the man and caught him with a roundhouse right before Burdick was off the floor. It drove him down, but he caught Reno's shirt with his free hand. Knowing he was a dead man if he fell in the iron arms of Burdick, Reno wrenched back, leaving a handful of his shirt, and drove a mighty blow straight into Burdick's face. Twice more he struck, throwing his waning strength into the effort. At the last blow, Burdick's eyes went dull and he slumped to the floor.

Reno's rasping breath was painful, and he could not stand. As he slipped to the floor, he felt hands pulling him up, and someone said, "You fellows be real careful about coming through that door. You might get real dead."

As he was half-carried out of the Palace he heard Al say in a fierce tone, "You should have killed him, Jim! You'll have to do it anyway!"

Burdick said nothing for several hours, and when he came to he whispered through broken teeth, "Doucett—get the Blantons."

Doucett bit his lip and hesitated. "You sure, Neal?"

"Get them!" Burdick whispered. "Tell them it's five thousand for Reno's head!"

ELEVEN
Before the Storm

The winter which had lurked up in the north for so long finally clawed southward, closing in on Rimrock with an iron embrace. Biting winds and subzero temperatures shut down the trail herds from Texas and reduced the town to a deserted crystal shell. Snow piled up four feet deep against houses, and except for expeditions to bring in wood, everyone kept inside next to stoves and fireplaces.

Reno had little to do during the freeze. He remarked wryly to Rossiter, "Guess this is the answer to sin, Al—get it cold enough and it shuts down just like everything else."

Rossiter had given him a cynical grin, saying only, "According to that little theory, the Eskimos must be downright holy!"

They were sitting downstairs in the Nugget, eating bacon and eggs that Rosy had cooked in his small kitchen in the rear of the bar. Despite the cold brilliance of the morning sunshine that lay in long bars of light across the room, there was a ghostly air about the place, produced in part by the humpbacked shapes of chairs and tables covered by white sheets.

Reno finished the last of his meal and poured fresh coffee into his cup, then walked over to peer out the window. "Wonder how long this will last?"

Rossiter didn't answer. His long face was paler than usual, and he pushed his plate away, the food hardly touched. "I hate cold weather. Ran away from home to get thawed out."

Lighting up a cigar, he glanced toward the stairs leading up to the second floor and asked suddenly, "You been to see Lola?"

"No. How is she?"

"Well, I ain't seen her myself, Jim. I tried a couple times, but that girl Doc Mitchell's got sitting with her said she didn't want to see anybody for a spell." He stared at the glowing tip of his cigar and a frown creased his high forehead. "From what Rosy said, I'd guess her face is marked up. You know how it would be with a fine-looking woman like that. Hope it ain't permanent."

"Here comes Doc now. Sheridan, too. Maybe we can find out something."

The burly form of the doctor filled the door, his black overcoat and matching derby whitened by thick flakes of snow. Sheridan entered behind him. Doc shucked loose from the heavy coat, threw it on a chair and said, "You wait here, Preacher." He glanced at the two men in the room, nodded, and moved up the stairs with a surprising quickness for a man of his weight.

"Have some coffee, Bishop?" Rossiter said.

"Believe I will." Sheridan removed his buffalo coat, took the steaming cup of coffee from Reno, and sat down with a sigh.

"Hope you don't get contaminated, Bishop," Rossiter said,

dropping a wink in Reno's direction. "Eating and drinking with sinners like Jim and me in a gambling den."

A quick grin touched Sheridan's wide lips. He looked around the room and said, "Spent more time in places like this than in the pulpit, Al. If I had all the money I've dropped in poker games, guess I could buy a new horse."

Rossiter stared at him, a question forming on his lips. He hesitated and said, "Lola ask to see you?"

"No. I want to see her." He sipped his coffee, then added with a rueful laugh, "If I waited until people asked to see me, I wouldn't be much of a preacher."

Al Rossiter stared at the tall form of the preacher, and his habitual sardonic expression was replaced by a sudden smile which made him look young. "Well, not to be disrespectful, but I've heard one or two remark that they didn't think you were much of a preacher anyway."

Sheridan threw his head back and laughed loudly. "Not hard to hear that. One of my superiors asked me last time I was in a meeting in St. Louis how many folks in my congregation were workers. I said, 'One hundred percent! Fifty percent for me and fifty percent against me!'"

Rossiter grinned, and as they sat around drinking coffee and talking, Reno saw that, despite the thin gambler's frequent caustic remarks about religion, he saw some genuine quality in Sheridan and was drawn to the man. He sent a few barbed remarks on the subject of religion designed to irritate the bishop, but the easy manner of the preacher did not change; he often adopted a bantering tone, making fun of himself. His quick wit and rock-bed humility drew a warmth from Rossiter.

Doc Mitchell came down and poured himself a cup of coffee. "Who made this mess? I could stand in a barrel of it and not see my toes!"

"You're getting so fat you can't see your toes for that belly of yours, Mitchell," Sheridan returned. "How's the patient?"

The burly doctor shrugged, and there was a frown on his face. "Can't say, Preacher. She's not in bad shape physically, but seems like she's down in the mouth. No spirit at all, and that's not like Lola. Go on up. I told her you wanted to see her."

"What'd she say?"

"Nothing much, but she agreed. Go on and save her soul, Parson. Then you can start on me."

"Don't think I won't try, Doc."

After the bishop disappeared up the steps, the doctor shouted, "Rosy! Rosy!" When the bartender appeared he said, "Give me some of that awful rotgut you serve."

Rosy brought a bottle, and Mitchell pulled the cork and filled his almost empty cup up to the rim. "Maybe *that* will make this stuff taste better!"

"What you up to, Doc?" Rosy asked.

"Everybody in town's trying to get sick," Mitchell grumbled. "I don't think I'm going to have enough medicine."

"Have some sent on the train from Hays," Al suggested.

"Already wired Hays for that, but the big trouble is, some folks is snowed in. They'll just have to get well or die without me."

"Always thought those were about the odds when it came to you doctors," Rossiter said, and the doctor gave him a sharp look, taking in the thin face and frail form of the gambler. He seemed to find something to interest him, but said only, "I guess I cure about as many as I kill, Al."

When the bishop came down ten minutes later, he got more coffee and seemed more thoughtful than usual. He listened as Doc Mitchell spoke.

"Only patient I'm really worried about is little Janet Peeples. When I saw her a week ago, I left all the medicine I had. It has to be gone now, and there's no way to get any more over there until the thaw."

"Horse can't make it?" Reno asked.

"No way. It's way back in the hills, and the snow must be at least five feet deep on that slope. Man couldn't make it either." The pudgy hand of the doctor slapped the table with a loud noise and he swore, then gave a look at the bishop. "Bad as I hate it, guess Janet will have to get along with just your prayers, Preacher!"

Reno asked, "You reckon we could scare up a pair of snow-shoes in this town?"

"Snowshoes?" Doc's eyes lit up. "Why, I think that would be the answer, Jim. But I doubt we could find a pair in the country."

"I know where some are," Sheridan said quickly. "I saw two pairs in Pete Hayes's barn, up in the loft. Said an old trapper came through two years ago, and he traded the old man a worn-out saddle for the things. Can you use those things, Reno?"

"Spent a winter in Idaho once—spent lots of time on snow. I think I can make it. How far is it to the Peeples'?"

"Why, not more than fifteen miles."

Reno got up and said, "You go get your pills, Doc, and I'll go get my kit. It'll be a two-day trip."

"Go see Lola first, Jim," the bishop said quickly. "She told me to ask you."

"Sure." Reno climbed the stairs and knocked on Lola's door.

"Come in." He entered and saw that she was standing

beside the window, dressed in a quilted robe. She kept the right side of her face away from him for a moment, then with a shrug faced him fully. "You might as well see the worst."

"You feeling better, Lola?" Jim asked. He advanced, and when she dropped her face, he put one hand on her shoulder and used his other to lift her chin. "Let me see."

The right side of her face was still swollen, and although the worst of the discoloration had passed, orange and purple splotches covered her face from her brow to chin, and when she spoke it was obvious that her jaw pained her.

"I look awful, don't I?" she said, watching his face for a reaction.

He grinned and touched her battered cheek softly. "You look good to me, Lola. I've been worried about you. Why didn't you let me come?"

"I don't know, Jim," she said, and with a small smile she added, "Vanity, I suppose. Didn't want you to see me like this."

Reno shook his head, and all the toughness that was a part of his character was transformed. His black eyes were gentle as he said, "Did you think less of me when I got beat up bad, Lola?"

A startled look touched her eyes, and she said, "Why, of course not, but—"

"I'm put out that you think I'm less of a man than you are a woman, Lola," Reno said quietly. "I never told you how beautiful you are. Guess you've been told that often enough. But I been wantin' to tell you for some time—you got something more than that."

"What's that, Jim?" Lola whispered.

"Why, it's hard for a man like me to say it right out. I'm no poet, but I've wanted to tell you that you got a beauty inside that I admire."

"Me?"

Reno was embarrassed and gave a short laugh. "Sound like a lovesick kid, don't I?"

She looked up at him, and there was a light of happiness in her wide eyes as she said, "It sounds fine to me, Jim."

There was a moment of tension between them, and he sensed her desperate need of reassurance. In her flat slippers she seemed small, and there was a defenselessness about her that made him suddenly put his arms around her. For one instant she held herself stiff and unyielding, then she leaned against him. He closed his eyes and knew that this woman had for him a glory that he had never known from anyone else.

Finally she pulled herself back and said, "It was never like this for me, Jim. Not with anyone!" Then she bit her lip and said, "I asked for you so I could tell you to leave Rimrock. Neal will kill you, Jim."

"I expect he'll try."

"You're not afraid, but I know him—too well. He can't stand to lose, and one way or another he'll have to kill you."

Reno said, "I've got to leave town for a couple of days. I'll see you when I get back. You think Burdick will bother you?"

"He'll never leave me alone, Jim, that's what I'm trying to tell you." She caught at his arm, and fear was in her eyes as she said, "Jim, go away! I couldn't stand it if something happened to you!"

He left her then, but he paused at the door, turning to face her. On his dark face there was a tough certainty. He grinned and said, "If he kills me, Lola, he'll be the first to get the chore done. Don't worry. Just get well, and I'll see you in two days."

He left the Nugget after bidding a quick farewell to Rosy

and Al. He stopped at the jail, put on the warmest clothes he had, and told Clarence to keep an eye on the town.

Doc Mitchell was waiting for him at his office, and the fat doctor cautioned him, "Now don't kill yourself, Reno. If it gets too bad, come on back."

"Sure. Want me to tell the Peeples anything?"

"I've put a note in with the medicine. Tell 'em I'll be out soon as a horse can make that road. And Sheridan asked me to tell you that Miz Franklin ought to be checked on. You know her?"

"No."

"Widow, lives in a cabin right by the road. Preacher thought she might need some wood chopped or something like that."

"I'll stop by. See you when I get back, Doc."

He stopped by the Lindsey house, and Jesse opened the door. He looked much stronger, Reno thought. "Have to take some medicine to the Peeples girl for Doc Mitchell, Jesse. Clarence can look after things."

"You can't get a horse way up there, Jim."

"No, but I can make it on snowshoes."

He left and picked up his horse from the stable. The road was open as far as the Hayes place, and he found Pete feeding his stock in the barn.

"Snowshoes?" Hayes said, scratching his head. "Yeah, I got a couple pair of them things. You know how to walk in 'em?"

"Some." He waited until Hayes found two pairs of elk-hide snowshoes and said, "OK if I leave my horse here until I get back, Pete?"

"No trouble."

Reno put on the best of the snowshoes, waved at Hayes, and plodded out of the yard, headed toward the west. It had been a long time since he had used snowshoes, and he almost tripped several times until the old rhythm returned. He found that the old skill was still there, but he knew that the unusual strain of lifting his feet high enough to clear the unwieldy and heavy webbing would give him sore muscles. But the joy of cutting across the smooth expanse of unbroken snow, and the clear, sharp air delighted him as he made his way toward the gently sloping land to the west of town.

Several times he had to stop and rest his aching legs, but by two in the afternoon he arrived at the small cabin occupied by Mrs. Franklin. She was delighted to see him cut some fresh wood and stack it under a shed roof attached to the cabin. When he finished she fed him a heaping plate of steak and beans. She sat there watching him eat, enjoying the company. She was a tall, thin woman, and when he asked if she had been afraid when she got snowed in, she had laughed and said, "Afraid? No, young man. I stopped being afraid years ago. Since I lost Benton, my husband, I been alone here, but the Lord is my keeper."

He grinned and said, "I had a stepdad who lived by that verse, Mrs. Franklin. No matter how bad things got, he'd just say that verse and keep on going."

"Sounds like he had sense. I hope you do the same."

Reno paused, put his fork down, and there was a thoughtful look in his dark eyes as he shook his head, "Tell the truth, ma'am, I've got pretty far from some of the things he tried to tell me. But lately, I been thinking a lot about him."

She patted his arm, and said, "You'll find the way, young man. Now you eat up—and stop on your way back. I been concerned about Janet lately. Been prayin' sort of extra hard. The answer came last night—and it came right sharp." Her old eyes flashed with a light that belied her years. "Yes, the Lord told me that the angels would be around that little girl. Guess you're one of 'em, Mr. Reno."

He laughed and got up to put his coat on. "Well, maybe all the angels were busy, so I got the job."

She didn't smile, but said, "You're a good man—and you'll be better when you get on the right track like your daddy told you."

He left the main road half an hour later, and the land began to lift more sharply. He followed the winding trail through several miles of heavily timbered country, but this soon gave way to stunted oak and twisted pygmy pine. His legs were aching, and he was glad to make the Peeples place just before dark.

"Hello, the house!" he called out. A door on the small log cabin opened and a man's voice said cautiously, "Who's comin'?"

"Medicine from Rimrock."

The door swung open, and a tall, gangling man with a shaggy mane of black hair stepped outside, his rifle in his hand. "What's that you say?"

A woman came out of the door and asked in a concerned voice, "You've brought the medicine for our girl?"

"Here it is, Mrs. Peeples," Reno said, taking the small package from his pocket. "Doc Mitchell put a letter in here for you. Said to tell you he'll be up as soon as the road clears."

The man's face had been hooded with suspicion. Now he nodded and said, "You walked on them things all the way from town?"

"It wasn't too bad," Reno said, but the muscles on the back of his legs were drawing sharply.

"Come on in the house, man," Peeples said. He was a Southerner, one of the mountain men from Kentucky, not likely to trust anyone quickly, but Reno's mission had broken down his reserve. "Woman, get this medicine into Janet, then set this feller a table!"

Reno was half-dragged into the small cabin by the man, whose name was Caleb. The girl, a tiny birdlike creature with huge eyes, seemed to be doing all right; but she was shy as a wild animal, hiding her face against her mother's breast.

Reno soon found himself being stuffed like a Thanksgiving turkey: deer steak, potatoes, beans, fresh-baked bread, sweet potato pie, and sweet milk.

Finally he shoved back and said, "Can't eat another bite!"

"Mister," the mother said, "we thank you for what you done—bringin' the medicine. It was good of you."

Caleb seemed to have more trouble putting his gratitude into words. He said finally, "You ever need help, Mr. Reno, I'm goin' to take it bad iffen you don't let me do the helpin'!"

Reno slept in front of the fire, refusing to take the single bed in the snug cabin. Wrapped in a thick buffalo robe, he lay watching the glowing coals for a long time, and he thought of the Peeples family. No money, isolated from town, and practically no luxuries. But he had seen the love that passed between the man and the woman. *They've got everything,* he thought just before he dropped off to sleep.

He pulled out after breakfast, and the look in the couple's eyes told him that they would never forget his simple act of kindness.

He made the trip back at a much slower clip, his legs sore

nd the urgency gone. Stopping at Mrs. Franklin's, he spent an hour idly talking over soup and coffee. He marveled again at the serenity of her face and knew that her faith was of the same quality as his stepfather's. He thought again of his own lapse from the faith.

Sunset was beginning to glow in the sky behind him as he picked up his horse from Hayes's barn and turned into Rimrock, where he rode straight to the jail. Weariness was on him, and he wanted nothing more than to have something to eat and drop into his bed.

First, he had something to do, however. He made his way to the Nugget. Going around to the back, he made his way to Lee's room and knocked on the door. It opened at once and Lee stood there, a quick smile on his face. "Jim! You're back."

The boy had been shoved around too much in a tough world to express his emotion, but Reno put his arm around the boy and gave him a hug saying, "You been staying out of trouble, son?"

He felt the boy grow rigid, then a thin arm went around him and the boy's voice was thin and breathless as he said, "Sure I have, Jim." Then he threw the other arm around the man and said, "Gee, I'm glad you're back, Jim!"

Reno slapped the thin shoulder, smiled down into the boy's thin face, and said, "Get a good night's sleep, Lee. We go to work tomorrow."

"Work? What kind of work?"

"You meet me at the café at eight for breakfast." Reno smiled and turned to leave. "Get lots of rest, Lee. I'm going to work your tail off for the next few days!"

Lee was waiting impatiently outside the restaurant for Reno the next morning. He plied Reno with questions about the job they were going to do, but Reno kept him in suspense.

"Come on," Reno said after breakfast, and led the wa
Faulkner's Store. The place was empty and Ernest looked u
in surprise as they entered. "What can I do for you, Marshal?

"Lee and I are going into business, Faulkner. Going to
run a trap line."

"A trap line?" Lee said in surprise.

"That's it," Reno said. The idea had come to him on the
way back as he noticed the heavy patterns of animals tracks in
the timbered country. He thought at once of how he could
spend time with the boy, and it had been a pleasure for him to
make elaborate plans for the venture. "Fit him out with some
warm clothes—socks, pants, shirts, and the best high-topped
boots you have. While you're doing that, I'll go through your
traps."

"Right over there, Marshal," the storekeeper said, and for
the next hour Reno got a thrill out of watching Lee get new
clothes from the skin out. The boy was thin as a bird, but if all
worked well, he'd begin to put on some muscle.

By eleven o'clock they were getting off Reno's horse in
Hayes's barn, and Reno got out the two pairs of snowshoes.
Lee spent an hour leaning how to maneuver in them, and as he
fell, rolling in the snow, the heavy look in his young face was
changed to a childlike expression of fun. Reno noted it and
said, "All right, let's get back. You practice tomorrow, and the
next day we set the trap line."

"You think I can do it, Jim?" Lee asked anxiously. His eyes
were doubtful, and apprehensive.

"You can if you want to, Lee," Reno said. There was so
much he had learned that he wanted to pour into the boy, but
he knew that it would not be easy. Time and patience were necessary, and above all, the boy had to want to grow up. Care-

looking down at the harness on one of the snowshoes, no said in a different tone, "Man can fall down, like you just nd. But if he wants something bad enough, he can get up and go after it again."

Lee thought about that, and a line of determination appeared on his young lips. He nodded and said, "I'll be ready, Jim. Day after tomorrow."

"Right." Reno had the wisdom to add nothing else, and as they rode back to town with Lee hanging onto him with one hand and clutching the snowshoes with the other, he began the boy's education by telling him in an offhanded way how to set traps.

For the next two weeks Reno spent most of his time running a short trap line in the timbered country. The town was still locked in with snow, so he had no duties that demanded his attention. It was, for him, almost like becoming a boy again, for as he watched Lee master the snowshoes and pick up the tricks of the trapper, he thought of his own lost youth. He had been once such a boy, and he wondered often how his life might have been better if he had stayed with the simple pleasures that were touching Lee.

Lee went at it with a determination that amazed Reno. He went until his legs gave out, then got up and went again. He had a quick mind, and when he was told something once, he held onto it tenaciously, hoarding up knowledge greedily. He learned how to cover his trail, where to find signs, and how to soak traps in oil to cover man-scent. He had trouble killing the first animal they took—a large marten—and Reno offered to do it.

"No! I'll do it, Jim," he said, and it hurt the man to watch his face as he put the animal away.

"Hard for me, too, Lee," he said simply, and it was all right.

He showed the boy how to take the hides and make boards for stretching them. Reno went with him for the first two weeks, then Lee said, "I'll run the line by myself, Jim."

"Sure." Reno appeared unconcerned, but he was nervous until the boy got back carrying a bundle of hides. He could see that Lee was bursting with pride, but didn't want to brag.

"Any trouble?" Reno asked making his voice careless.

"Naw. I made it fine."

Reno let his broad hand rest on Lee's shoulder, saying only, "You learn quick as anybody I ever saw, Lee."

The boy's face glowed, and he tried to make his voice deep as he shrugged and said, "Wasn't too hard."

"Let's go tell Lola," Reno said, and they made their way to the Nugget, going up the back stairs to knock at her door.

"Well!" she said when she had opened the door. "Looks like you made a haul!"

Her face was no longer swollen, but she was pale and thinner than she had been. It bothered Reno and he said, "You're coming with us tomorrow."

Her eyes grew larger and she gave a nervous laugh. "Me? Out in the woods?"

"Snow's mostly melted," Reno said with his slow smile. "We'll go to the cabin by the stream. You can cook for us while we run the line."

"I don't think—," she began, but Reno interrupted her.

"Be ready at eight. Lee and I'll be here to get you. We'll have a good breakfast and a day out will do you good."

She saw he was trying to get her out of her shell, and she said, "All right, Jim, if you say so."

"It'll be *fun!*" Lee said eagerly. "I'll teach you how to skin a coon."

"I can't wait!" Lola smiled and ruffled his hair. She watched them leave and leaned against the door, a smile on her lips as she thought about the pair.

"I can't believe it, Jim! Look at how green the grass is!"

Reno smiled at the sight of Lola pulling a sprig of emerald grass from the tender earth and held it toward him.

"Spring always catches me off guard," he said. "Last week the whole earth seemed dead. Now things are coming out fresh and green."

They had left town early, getting to the cabin before ten. Lee had been wild to see about a small line he had set himself, claiming that he was going to get a mink, so he had left Reno and Lola to seek his fortune.

They had walked along the bank of the small stream that glistened with a diamondlike brilliance in the morning sun. They shed their heavy coats soon, and Lola seemed to blossom in the fresh air. She was delighted at the sight of a family of white-tailed deer they surprised, and their magnificent leaps as they cleared the fallen timber brought a cry of pleasure to her lips.

She ran to pluck a tiny wild violet from a bed of moss under a snowbank and held it against her cheek with a gesture that was more graceful than anything Reno had ever seen.

For an hour they walked, and finally he found an old cedar lying beside the stream. It was almost dry, and he made a seat for her with his coat. "Better rest. Don't want you to do too much."

"Oh, Jim, I'm glad I came!" The light in her eyes and the fresh color in her cheeks rewarded him. He had hoped that getting her outside her room would have just such an effect.

"Doc Reno," he said with a grin. "Results guarantee your money back."

She looked up at him with a smile and said, "I wish we never had to go back. It's so nice out here."

"Maybe we could just stay here, you and me and Lee. Just be plain old squatters."

She said evenly, "We couldn't do that, Jim."

She was, he saw, totally serious, and he sat down beside her. "Don't be afraid, Lola. You've got too much going for you."

She laughed, and there was a sudden bitterness in her green eyes. "Oh, sure, I got a lot going for me. I own a saloon, and I've spent most of my life working in one. Wonderful, isn't it?"

"I've told you before, Lola, you can change."

She said quietly, "That's what the bishop keeps saying to me. Are you two coaching each other?"

"No, but he's a pretty good man, I think. I'd listen to him if I were you."

She sat there silently, and finally she said, "My father was a little man, Jim. My mother died when I was only six, and he raised me. He was just a common laborer, working at whatever he could get. But he loved me. I remember he always made me take some fruit in my lunch when I went to school. 'You have to eat lots of fruit, daughter,' he'd say to me." She picked at the front of her sweater and there was a profound sadness in her face as she looked up at Reno and said, "When I went to work in a saloon, it nearly killed him. I tried to give him money, but he never would take a penny. I mailed him money after I left town, but he always mailed it back. And you know what he'd say in the notes he'd put with the money? He always said, 'I love you, Lola. You're a good girl.'" A cry of bitterness

...ain broke from her lips and she repeated, "A good girl!" ...n she bowed her head and her shoulders shook.

"Don't do that, Lola!" Reno said. He forced her to look up, and there was an intense look on his face as he said, "I see that goodness in you!"

"Do you, Jim?" she pled desperately. "Do you see it?"

"For me, you've got everything." Then he kissed her and said, "We can make it together, Lola, you and me."

She clung to him, and they were very still. He heard the rippling water of the creek and the far-off cry of a bird, and then she pulled back and said, "Jim, if you mean that, let's leave, get away from here. I'll sell the Nugget. We can make a new start!"

He shook his head, saying what she knew he must say, "Not until Jesse is able to handle the town. Then we'll go."

She took a deep breath, nodded, and said, "I guess I knew that. It's what you are, Jim."

He pulled her to her feet, saying, "It won't be long, Lola. Then we can go."

They turned to go back toward the cabin, and she said quietly, "No matter what happens, Jim, I've had this much. It's so quiet here, but this isn't real. Neal is real—and this is the quiet before the storm."

"We'll be all right, Lola," Reno said, but she shook her head and there were tears in her eyes.

TWELVE
Hard Case

"You look like you struck gold, Jeff," Jesse observed as young Lindsey came into the dining room with a broad smile on his face. "You must have done what lawyers always do."

"What's that, Dad?" Jeff asked, bending over to kiss Ada, then slipping into his chair next to Rachel.

"Talk fellers into fightin' each other, then steal their coats while the brawl is on."

"Jesse! That's awful!" Ada shook her head and began to pile food on Jeff's plate. She had been worried about the way he'd sulked during the long weeks, pining away in his small office with absolutely nothing to do. The light in his eyes and the ready smile on his lips told her that he was himself again.

"I don't mind anything tonight, even lawyer jokes." He looked at Jesse, and there was a challenge in his voice as he said, "I finally got something done, Dad. You'll never know how close I came to packing up and leaving town this winter."

"What is it, Jeff?" Rachel asked. She leaned forward, and she had no way of knowing how attractive a picture she made in the yellow lamplight.

"I've done what should have been done a long time ago," Jeff said earnestly, his jaw suddenly set in a way that reminded both women of Jesse. "I got the town council to meet, and they finally *did* something instead of just talk!"

"I take it you talked them into passing that gun ordinance," Jesse said quietly, his head cocked to one side.

"That's right, Dad!" the young man said defiantly, casting a quick look at Rachel. "I know you think it's a mistake, but you're a fair man. You'll see what a difference it will make in Rimrock."

Jesse traced a pattern in the tablecloth, and looked up only when Ada put her hand on his arm. He gave her a smile, and then said, "Son, nobody wants it to work more than me."

Jeff began to talk excitedly, his eyes glowing, and all through the meal there was a closeness between them that all of them welcomed. Jeff had been aloof, and although Rachel had longed to see him open up, there had been no break until now. She took in the pride in Jesse's eyes, and Ada nodded at her with a plea in her eyes to give it a chance.

After the meal, Jesse said, "Let's go see what the weather's up to, Ada. Feels like spring is sneaking up on us." They stood on the porch, Jeff insisting on helping Rachel with the dishes.

The sky was a pool of black velvet, pierced with brilliant points of glittering light. A smell of new earth lay on the night, and Jesse said, "Reminds me of those spring nights in Colorado. You remember, Ada?"

"Yes, of course." She took his arm and pulled his attention from the sky. Her face was ivory in the moonlight, and the fine lines were erased by the warm darkness, so that she looked like a young girl. "Jesse, what are you going to do?"

He knew what she meant, and he said at once, "I'r
ting, Ada. It's time for that. I want us to get a little place a.
just sit and rock for awhile."

"You mean it, Jesse? You're going to resign?"

"Sure." He hesitated and added cautiously, "Course I have
to wait until Jeff's plan is working."

Ada knew him well, and she said sadly, "You think it will
fail, don't you, Jesse?"

He paused and finally said slowly, "Why, no, Ada. It'll
work all right—but it's not going to be an easy thing. All these
trail towns change. The rough bunch will move on to a raw
new town where they can do as they please." He inhaled
deeply, then let out his breath, touching his side tenderly.
"Thing is, that won't happen without somebody makin' it happen. We could have calmed this town down two or three years
ago, but we weren't ready to pay the price. I guess Jeff's forced
us to do what we should have done before."

"Can't you let Reno do it?"

"No." He did not elaborate, and she knew too well what
that one word meant. It was his pledge to stand beside a man
who wore the star no matter what, and as long as he could
walk and lift a gun he would not forsake that code he had lived
by.

She stood there, feeling isolated, cut off from the world
that he inhabited. Once before she had felt so outraged by
what she felt that she had taken Jeff and fled to the shelter of
the city. Something in her urged her to do the same now, to
flee from the future that she could see so clearly.

He knew her as she knew him, and he said quietly, "You
going to leave, Ada?" His voice was even, and in the quietness
of that moment, he felt that his future hung in the balance.

...e turned her face up to him, and he saw the diamonds ... eyes and a silver tear tracing its way down her smooth ...ek. "No! I'll never leave you again, Jesse!" And she clung to ...m as he put his arms around her.

In the kitchen Rachel listened as Jeff talked about his plans, and finally he stopped abruptly and said, "I'm talking too much."

"No. Don't stop."

He looked at her and said with a red tinge in his cheeks, "I . . . I talked too much once, Rachel." He forced himself to look into her clear eyes and added with an effort, "I made a fool of myself talking about Jim and Lola. I was wrong."

He was so much like his father at that moment that Rachel's heart went out to him. She put her hand out, and when he grasped it and pulled her toward him, she did not resist. His kiss did not take her by surprise, for she had known it was in him. What did take her off guard was the sudden gust of passion that rocked her as he drew her close.

When they parted he looked at her in wonder. "I thought it was Jim."

"I thought about him," she answered. "He's a good man— but not for me."

"Well, I guess you know how I feel about you, Rachel. Have I got a chance?"

"Yes, Jeff." She smiled, then she laughed and added, "Know what I'm wondering? How would we ever explain the family tree to our children?"

"I'm not a lawyer for nothing," he said with a grin. "You just leave the explaining up to me!"

The warm breezes that unlocked the icy streams and dissolved the crests of snow brought the trail herds into Rimrock. First

came a single herd all the way from the Texas border, then t
cash-hungry ranchers began to fill the stock pens in Abilene,
Hays, Dodge City, and smaller towns such as Rimrock with the
bawling longhorns.

Dance Street shook free from the lethargy of winter, opening its arms to receive the trail-weary punchers. Several new
saloons opened, mostly just rooms with a plank across two bar-
rels and a table for poker.

Spring winds melted the frozen surface of the wide street,
and the two riders who came in from the south had to force
their horses through a river of mud to get to the Palace saloon.

The way they dismounted revealed something of their
character. One of them simply plopped down in the thick mud
and waded to the plank walk. He was a heavy man, thick in the
shoulders, and his large muscular legs swelled his faded, dirty
trousers. He looked back at his companion and said shortly in
a rough bass, "Hurry up, Con. I got me a big thirst."

The man called Con had the same narrow space between
his eyes and the same spit-colored eyes as the larger man, but
in every other respect they were in violent contrast. There was
a feline quality in the slim figure of the mounted man, not only
in the small bones and catlike grace of his movements, but in
the face, which was sharp, pointed, and alive with an intense
readiness. This contrasted sharply to the blunt and brutal features of his stolid companion. As he swung his horse parallel
to the sidewalk with a cruel jab of his silver spurs, he slid off in
one fluid motion. He tossed the reins of his horse to the other
man saying, "Take the horses to the stable, Sonny."

"Aw, let them wait, Con, I'm—"

"Shut your mouth and do what I tell you." Con did not
raise his voice, but the huge man flinched under the sudden

pact of his gaze, and without another word he took the reins
from Con and sloshed down the muddy street toward the livery stable.

Con Blanton stepped inside the Palace, which was half-filled despite the early hour, and a tall, hard-faced rider at the bar stared at him. His eyes opened wide, and he spoke quietly to a short man on his left who turned, stared, and shook his head, saying, "That's him? He sure don't look like much."

The hard-faced man allowed himself a brief smile. "Lots of folks pushin' up daisies in Boot Hill thought the same," he said. "Last count I heard was thirty-two dead men on his record—and Con Blanton don't count Mexicans."

Blanton leaned on the bar, and when the bartender came to stand before him he said, "I'm looking for Burdick."

"He's in his office upstairs—first door to the left."

Blanton wheeled and climbed the stairs, his eyes moving constantly from side to side. When he got to the door he opened it without knocking and stepped inside.

Burdick looked up from his desk, anger in his eyes. "This is a private office—get out!"

Doucett was lounging on a couch to Burdick's left. He swung his feet to the floor, saying, "Hey, Neal, this here is Con Blanton."

Burdick stared across his desk at Blanton in surprise. He had heard of the man, as most had, but never seen him. The gunman was small, not over five-foot-ten in his high-heeled lizard skin boots, and he was somewhat of a dandy. Fawn-colored trousers, an embroidered silk shirt with ruffles, a form-fitting coat, charcoal with grey piping on the sleeves, and low-crowned beaver hat made up his costume. But if there was something of a foppishness in his attire, the gold-handled Colt

in the holster of polished calfskin was not merely orname
According to all witnesses, the blinding speed with which i.
could palm that weapon had to be seen to be believed.

"Glad to see you, Blanton," Burdick said. He put out his
hand, and Blanton hesitated for a second, then put his own
hand out. It was, Burdick thought with a shock, a hand that
was almost childlike—thin, small, but with a surprising grip.
"Took you a long time to get here."

Blanton's tenor voice was not unpleasant, but it was life-
less, totally without warmth. "Had to get Sonny out of jail.
Guess your man told you about that."

"Yes, but he was pretty sure that your brother was going
to have a tough time getting off. Way he heard it, the evidence
was pretty strong against him."

Doucett had returned from his trip to Texas with the
news that Sonny Blanton was on trial for murder in San Anto-
nio. "Con never works without Sonny," Doucett said as he
made his report. "Said to tell you he'd come, but he had to get
his brother off. Don't think he'll do it, though. Five witnesses
saw Sonny do the killin', and the guy he killed wasn't even
wearin' a gun."

Con Blanton's eyes lit for just a moment, the old icy color
touched by a sudden flash of humor. "I had to work on it a
little. Takes some doing to get five witnesses to change their
story."

Burdick stared at him. "They all did, I take it?"

"Oh, sure. One of them was a little stubborn."

After a short silence, Doucett asked, "What happened to
him, Con?" Again a flash of humor touched Blanton's eyes.
"Oh, he had an accident. Got trapped in a stall with a real bad
horse. Never saw nothing like the way his head was all
crushed. Should have been more careful."

Burdick gave Doucett a quick glance, and then looked back to the smooth face of Blanton. There was something unnatural about the lack of care, the utter smoothness of the gunman's face. The dead voice and the empty eyes completed the impression that something had been left out at his making. Burdick, despite being tough enough for anything, felt a chill as he forced himself to grin and said, "Yeah, I guess so."

"Still need the job done? I need some cash."

"Yes," Burdick answered. "Same job, same price."

"I want something now—a thousand. The rest later."

"All right—but you'll have to do it my way."

"Anyway you say, long as I get the money."

Burdick got up, walked across the room, and pulled a steel box out of the safe. Taking some cash out, he handed it to the gunman. "There's a thousand."

"Who is he?"

"Name is Jim Reno. He's acting marshal now."

"You want it done now?" Blanton put the money in his inside coat pocket and showed little interest in the matter. It was just another job to him. He had long ago lost interest in anything concerning his victims. They were only items in his business transactions.

Burdick said slowly, "I won't presume to tell you your business, but I'd be careful with Reno. He's smelled powder somewhere."

A feline smile touched Con Blanton's face, and he said with a trace of a smile, "Can he do this?"

There was a flicker, just a flash of white as Blanton's right hand moved. Doucett and Burdick heard the faint sound of flesh slapping metal, and incredibly the .45 was in Blanton's small hand, steady as stone and pointing right at Neal Burdick's stomach.

Burdick swallowed and stared at the bore of the weapon, trying to believe what he had seen. Finally he smiled thinly and shook his head. "No, Con, he can't do that—nobody can."

Another flash and the gun was back in the leather. The man was not human, Burdick decided. He had the reflexes of a cat, or a striking snake, and according to all reports he was not only fast, he was an expert shot. In one exploit he had faced three men in Arizona, flanked by two of them. But according to witnesses, Con Blanton did not even reach for his gun until one of his enemies had cleared leather. Then he had drawn and put all three of them down with three shots.

"I want you to make him crawl, Blanton—in public," Burdick said and there was a savagery in his blunt face as he spat out the words. "I don't care what you have to do, but first he crawls, then you kill him."

"Must have got to you pretty bad, Burdick," the small gunman said, and there was a jeer in his dead voice. "I can't guarantee that part about crawling. All I can promise is he'll be dead."

"All right, see to it!"

"He may not have the chance, Neal," Doucett spoke up. "I never saw such a bunch of wild drovers as we got comin' in. And I hear that old man Taylor's first herd of the season is due in any time. He's been cussin' Reno all winter, I hear, and it wouldn't surprise me none if him or one of that froggy crew of his didn't beat Con to the job."

"That so?" Con said quickly. "Then I better get to work. Hate to lose a fee to a bunch of amateurs."

"You won't be able to do much right off," Doucett said. "This is Saturday, and you'll probably have to wait until Monday to get it done."

"Yeah. Can't shoot a man on the Sabbath, can I now?" Blanton said with his smooth face totally unemotional. He left the room without another word, closing the door soundlessly behind him.

"Pure poison, Neal," Doucett said softly. "If Taylor's crowd don't down Reno, Blanton shore will!"

Neal nodded slowly and sat down, but for a long time he stared blindly at the ledger in front of him. The fight with Reno had done something to him, more than just the scars on his face, which had almost healed. He had slept badly, and he could not free himself from the suspicion that men were laughing at him behind his back. And the loss of Lola—that was the cancer eating away at him, and he knew that he could regain his former assurance only when Reno lay squirming in the dust and Lola was in his big hands again.

Downstairs Con found Sonny bellied up to the bar, a bottle in front of him. "Want a drink?" he asked.

"No. I'm going to get us a room at the hotel and get some sleep. You stay here and find out all you can about a lawman named Reno."

"He the one?"

"Yes. Drink some, but don't get drunk. Don't ask questions, you hear me? Just buy a few drinks and listen to the talk. Lawmen always get talked about."

"Got any money?"

"Here," Con said, handing a few bills to the big man. "Here's the deal: The man paying the money wants this Reno dead, but he wants him to look bad first—wants him to crawl before he gets it. So you listen, and when you get a line on him, come and tell me."

Con left, knowing that Sonny could consume unbelievable

amounts of alcohol without losing his animal cunning. A.
headed for the hotel he nodded politely, stepping aside to
two women pass. One of them whispered when he was out
range: "Who is that, Clara?"

"I don't have any idea, but he surely is a gentleman, isn't
he? Not like most of these awful cowboys!"

When Reno and Lola entered the church he heard her take a
quick breath and felt her suddenly hold back. "Don't balk on
me, now," he whispered quietly, and his smile gave her enough
courage to walk down the aisle. Every eye in the house was on
them, and the pressure was like a weight on Reno as he looked
for some seats in the crowded room. He had been to church
often, but he knew what an ordeal it was for Lola to submit herself to the curious eyes of the congregation.

Jeff Lindsey was standing up, beckoning to him, and
when Reno had maneuvered Lola past the people already in
the bench, Rachel reached out and took Lola by the arm. "You
sit here by me, Lola." The warm smile on her face was like a
flag to Lola, and she sat down quickly beside Rachel, a look of
gratitude on her face.

"You're late, Jim," Jeff whispered.

"Had to do a little arm-twisting," Reno answered.

Lola had been adamant at first, refusing point-blank to go
to the service. "Jim, they'd strip me to the bone with their
pious looks! I'd be the scarlet woman to them."

"Some might be like that," Reno had agreed. "But I want
to know one thing—is all this talk I been hearing from you
about startin' a new life just a bunch of talk? If it is, why, you're
the hypocrite, Lola!"

She had thrown her head back, angry to the bone. "That's

, Jim! I do want a new life—but not *here!* I . . . I can start
newhere else!"

"I don't think it works that way." Reno had brought his
dark eyes to bear on her and went on in a voice that sounded
hard: "I'm not the one to do any preaching, but from what I've
heard, God expects you to be the same any place you happen
to be. I knew a man once that called some people *Sunday
men*—I think because they only acted like Christians on Sunday. I reckon you won't be any better in Dallas or Denver than
you will be right here in Rimrock, Lola. If you won't stand
here, you won't stand anywhere."

She had glared at him, then with a sudden surrender, she
had said quietly, "You're right, Jim. I'm just so scared of facing
people who know what I've been!"

"Show them what you've become, Lola." Reno had smiled,
and not until they entered the church had her courage weak-
ened.

There was a trembling in her hands that she tried to conceal by clasping the small purse she held until her fingers
grew white with the strain.

By the time the thin song leader stood up and said, "Let's
have 'Old Hundred'!" she was ready to bolt. But as they sang
song after song, she felt herself relaxing. Partly it was the light
touch of Reno's hand on her arm, some of it the smiles she got
from a few when she had the courage to lift her eyes. Mostly it
was the result of the warm light in the steady gaze of the
preacher who raised his face from his Bible to seek her out.
She had talked with him often, at first with a wall of resent-
ment. She had expected him to attempt to drive her into some
sort of conversion, but he had done little but listen and encourage her. Slowly she had learned to trust Sheridan, and now,
looking up at him, she saw in his face the trust she needed.

He preached a sermon on the love of God, and when the service was over, Lola had her hand shaken by many. Even though there were sneers on the faces of some, and a few of the men she had served often at the Nugget avoided her studiously, she felt as if she had been released from prison.

At the insistence of Jesse and Ada, she and Reno accompanied them to the white frame house, and the warmth and love in the faces of the two old people brought a fullness to her breast. She knew that a remarriage was in the offing, and the thought pleased her.

The group sat in the small parlor and Ada showed them photographs of Jeff and Jesse taken twenty years earlier. They laughed at Jesse's youthful appearance and had cookies and coffee.

Finally they got up, Reno saying, "Got to make the rounds, folks."

Jesse asked, "You hear about the Blantons, Jim?"

"Heard they were in town."

"Be careful with them. They're scum and dangerous."

"Guess they'll have to check their guns like everybody else." The new ordinance was scheduled to go into effect in two days, and although Jesse and Reno had said little about it, both of them knew it was going to cause trouble.

"Sure, but don't make the rounds alone, Jim. I'll go with you."

"I'll take Bub."

"Well, all right, but we can get another man or two when the deadline comes on that ordinance." Jesse was adamant, and he added, "Don't walk by any vacant alleys, Jim. Keep your back covered. This thing is going to be plumb tense!"

"It'll be OK, Major," Reno said.

"Thanks for the meal, and for—everything," Lola said with a smile. "It was wonderful."

"We'll have to do it often, Lola," Ada said warmly, and she stood with Jesse as the two walked down the steps and turned toward the Nugget. "Do you think they'll make it, Jesse?"

"Sure hope so. They're pretty tough—and they'll have to be with what's in front of them."

When they got to the Nugget, Reno walked up the steps and pulled his hat off as they reached Lola's door. She turned and said, "It's been so good, Jim! I . . . I guess I've been thinking all kinds of things lately. I just can't believe we're going to get away from here and have a life together."

He put his arms around her and said, "I'm having trouble with that myself."

She pulled his head down and kissed him, then drew back. "You . . . you be careful, Jim Reno, you hear me! I don't want you to be some kind of hero! This man Blanton, don't you give him a break. If I thought he'd hurt you, I'd hide in the alley and shoot him in the back myself!"

Reno laughed in delight, and his eyes gleamed as he cried out, "Whoa, now! The man hasn't done anything yet!" He pushed her hair back from her forehead and said gently, "Don't worry. Things are going to be good for us, Lola. I promise."

"Do you promise, Jim?" she whispered. "Tell me over and over it's going to be good. Nothing has ever been good for me, and I want to believe it's different."

He held her gently, and said, "I promise, Lola. Trust me."

He left her then, and she went to stand by the window. For a long time she stared blindly, then she turned and fell on her knees beside her bed as she wept like a child.

THIRTEEN
Under the Gun

By Monday night the town overflowed. Every pen in the loading yard was packed with wild-eyed cattle, every hotel room was stuffed with punchers just as wild-eyed as the steers, and the saloons bulged outward with the swarms of yelling, pushing men bright-eyed with drink and excitement.

By ten o'clock the jail was crowded, and Reno had to ask Jake Smiley to guard the place while he made another round with Bub and Clarence. "Some of their buddies may get the idea of bustin' them out, Jake," Reno said on leaving. "Just fill them full of buckshot from the greener if they try it."

"Yeah." Jake nodded, the large shotgun looking like a toy in his massive hands. "You watch it, fellers. I never seen it this bad. You know old man Taylor hit town with his boys about an hour ago?"

"Hadn't heard, Jake. I'll keep an eye on the man."

The three of them left the jail, walked along Grant, and turned down Dance Street. "We'll take this end first," Reno murmured. "Fan out and keep your eyes open. Don't let fly

se things unless you have to." He nodded at the sawed-
tguns they carried in addition to their handguns.

"Jim, it's gonna be hard to see much in this mob. You
ck close to the wall," Clarence said nervously. He wiped the
sweat from his brow with a red bandana. "We need five more
men to do this."

"Most of these boys are OK," Reno said. "Just lettin' off
steam."

"Old man Taylor won't let it go, Jim," Bub said. He fingered the gun at his side nervously, and Reno saw that he had
no confidence. He had not been bloodied in battle, and until he
was, he would not be steady. Reno realized there was nothing
to do but to trust that if action came, Bub would grow up in a
hurry.

"Let's go, Bub." He faded into the crowd, edging toward
the wall, and the two deputies let him get twenty yards down
the street before they spread out and covered his progress.

Reno went into some of the saloons, letting himself be
seen. Although he felt the pressure of hard glances from
many, he let nothing show on his dark face. He nodded to
those who called his name, keeping his glance in constant
motion as he progressed toward the Nugget, which lay at the
east end of Dance. There was nothing to read in his counte-
nance. It was an old game to him, and he had learned to keep a
tight rein on his emotions.

Turning into the Nugget, he was greeted at once by Rosy
who said, "Come in the back room, Jim." He left the bar, and
when Reno followed him inside the small kitchen, Rosy said,
"They've got you set up tonight, Jim. Friend of mine who
works on the other end of town, he dropped a word to me that
your ticket's gonna be punched."

"He say how?" Reno asked.

"Didn't know much, and it was risky for him to say as much as he did. But you can bet Burdick will be at the bottom of it. Stay out of the Palace tonight, Jim. They'll wipe you out."

"Thanks, Rosy. I'll keep my eyes open."

He left the Nugget, speaking to Al as he left. Rossiter was in a big game, the table piled high with chips and cash. Nevertheless, Al asked at once, "Want some company?"

"Maybe later, Al."

Outside on the walk Reno caught a glimpse of Jack Canby on the far side of the street, half-hidden by a group of punchers making their way west. Canby ducked his head, reversed his steps, and made his way toward the other end of Dance. A sense of danger shot through Reno, an old feeling that had saved his life more than once, and he moved slowly west, his eyes searching dark alleys and upper windows vigilantly. He caught at sudden movements, and his senses filtered out the noise and the blaring music, leaving him with wire-tight nerves that he did not reveal to those who watched his progress toward the end of Dance Street.

He saw a group of riders messing around the entrance to the Wagonwheel, a large saloon owned by a man named Ray Tomlin. Tomlin had no love for Reno, who had set down on him hard more than once, and Reno swerved suddenly and made straight for the door.

One of the men, he knew, was a hand for Big John Taylor. He was a hard-eyed cowboy with a huge moustache and a white scar that started on his forehead, ran down his cheek in a ragged track, and disappeared under his collar. His name was Rambo, Reno remembered, and he recalled that he had roughed the man up the last time his crew had hit Rimrock.

They did not intend to break their ranks for him, he saw, ιd he used a trick he had used often. He put his full gaze ιard on Rambo and ignored the others. Walking right at the man, he saw a break in the scarred face, and Rambo fell back, making a break in the ranks. Reno pushed through it and stepped inside. Big John Taylor was standing at the bar, his huge frame ad florid face dominating the room. He glared at Reno, who walked up to him and said, "Hello, Taylor."

Taylor grew redder than ever, and he looked down at Reno from his great height. "Marshal, my boys are here to have a little fun. You try to interfere with them like you done last time and I swear on my mother's grave we'll pull this two-bit town apart!"

"Tomorrow at noon there'll be a new law, Taylor," Reno said evenly. He fixed the tall Texan with his dark eyes, and although he made no threatening gesture, there was a tension in Taylor. "After twelve o'clock, there'll be no guns worn. Check them in at my office."

Taylor stared at him, cursed and yelled, "You try to pull that and you'll wind up dead, Reno! You been warned!"

"Noon—that's the deadline." Taylor stood there cursing, and Rambo had his hand on the butt of his side arm, but when Reno pinned him with a glance and said, "You want to try it now, Rambo?" Rambo jerked his hand away and plunged inside the Wagonwheel.

Reno found Bub waiting for him as he cleared the door, and there was a tension in his thin face as he muttered, "Jim, don't move so fast! When you ducked into the Wagonwheel, I couldn't get to you through all this mob. We better stick close together."

"All right, Bub, I want you to listen to me. We're going to

the Palace, and I want you and Clarence to stay at m͏
There's going to be some kind of trouble."

"You think Burdick will start the ball?"

"Can't say, but I'm counting on you, Bub. If you want t͏
pull out, now's the time to do it. Once we go in, I have to knov͏
you're watching my back."

Bub's young face was pale, but there was outrage in his
voice as he said, "What you talkin' like that to me for, Jim? You
think I'm gonna show yeller?"

Reno let his gaze fall on Bub and he said, "You've never
had to stand fire, Bub, and no man knows what he'll do until
that time comes. I need to know if I can count on you—even if
you go down!"

Bub gulped and turned red, and there was a moment
when Reno thought that the boy would quit. Then his lips got
firm, and he said with an intensity he'd never used with Reno,
"I . . . I ain't gonna quit on you, Jim! I may get shot, but I'll go
down doing the best I know how!"

Reno smiled. He realized the matter of growing up was
not a matter entirely of years, and he knew that Bub was no
longer the boy he had been moments earlier.

"All right, let's go. Clarence, we're going into the Palace.
Watch close." The older man had approached from across the
street. He nodded solemnly and Reno moved ahead, walking
rapidly in the light of the yellow lantern light, and he did not
pause until he reached the swinging doors of the Palace. Without hesitation he plunged through, and as he crossed the wide
room Clarence and Bub took position near the door.

The place was full, as were all the other saloons. The gambling tables were packed two-deep with men waiting a chance,
and the bar was lined solid with drinkers.

ay Reno wheeled and caught the eyes of Neal Bur-
no sat at a table with a man Reno knew at once to be
Blanton, the hard case Jesse had warned him of. He made
. way toward the pair, noting that neither Canby nor Doucett
was in evidence. This fact triggered an alarm in his mind, for
he knew that Burdick kept one or the other of the pair close at
all times. He noted the stairs leading up to the second floor,
the small balcony at the top, the door at the end of the bar leading to the supply room. Any of these could be filled by one of
Burdick's men, but Reno knew the real danger he had to think
of was the slim figure sitting to Burdick's right.

"Hello, Reno," Burdick said tightly, and a red spot in each
cheek signaled the anger bottled up inside the man.

"Hello, Burdick," Reno said evenly. He stopped ten feet
from the table and waited. There was a sudden silence in the
room, and it sent a chill along his nerves as he realized that at
least a dozen men at the bar were not above throwing a shot at
him. But he kept his voice even as he said, "Came to give you a
personal notice about the new law, Neal."

Burdick slowly stood up and said in a tone edged with the
hate he felt for the man in front of him, "You think you can ride
me, Reno?"

"Just passing the word, Burdick—no guns to be worn
after noon tomorrow."

"You telling all the owners about it in person?"

"You're special, Neal," Reno said, and there was a mocking tone in his voice as he stood there.

"Have your fun, Reno. My turn will come. You're riding
pretty high, but I've seen better men than you who wore a
star—and they ended up dead!"

Reno was paying little heed to Burdick. He was setting

the scene in his mind, the men behind him. He knew that t
two deputies flanked the door with their shotguns cocked an
ready. No man would go up against a greener at close range,
but he knew he wouldn't be allowed to leave the room without
a fight.

"You haven't introduced me to your friend yet," he said to
Burdick.

The man in the fancy clothes was looking down at the
glass in front of him, and had not, in fact, looked up at Reno at
all. Now he slowly lifted his head, staring full into Reno's face
with a pair of cold eyes and a thin smile on his lips. He got to
his feet in one smooth motion, like a cat, stretched and said
softly, "I'm Con Blanton."

Reno took in the easy grace of the small figure, the long
tapering fingers. "Heard of you."

"Yeah?" Blanton said in mock surprise. "What did you
hear, lawman?"

Reno said evenly, "I heard you were a low-down yellow
dog who had no guts, Blanton. Anything to it?"

A murmur arose from the men around him, and there
was a scuffle of feet as a path cleared behind him. Reno knew
at once that Blanton was Burdick's weapon for revenge. He
was not a man for waiting, so he deliberately cut at the hard
case, trying to force the play. There was a wildness in Reno
that seldom revealed itself, but as he stood there in the center
of the room in the light of the chandeliers there was a reckless-
ness in his stance and in his eyes.

It made no impression on Con Blanton. The smile on his
lips did not touch his eyes, and he slowly pulled his fancy coat
back, so that the gun at his side was free.

"I take that personal, lawman," he said, a sibilant quality

ₐs voice as he stared at Reno. "I'd have to say you owe me apology."

It was an old game, one that Reno had played before. He saw the smile on Blanton's lips broaden, and a sudden noise behind him struck him like a blow. He almost turned, but forced himself to keep his eyes locked on Blanton. Then he heard Bub cry in a strangled voice, "Jim!" and he knew that the trap was sprung.

"Better take a look at your men, Reno," Burdick said with a sneer.

Reno stared at him, then half-turned to see that both his deputies had been taken out of action. Canby and Doucett had waited outside until the deputies got set, then they had stepped inside and put a gun at the back of their heads. As Reno watched, Burdick's men lifted the shotguns and pulled the side arms out of the holsters of Bub and Clarence.

Turning to face Burdick and Blanton, Reno said, "Looks like I'm the sucker this time."

"About that apology, lawman," Blanton said smoothly, "I think I might like it better if you got down on your knees and said it. Don't you think that would be better, Neal?"

"On his face!" Burdick said, his face filled with cruelty and anticipation.

"Guess I'll have it now," Con Blanton said with an edge to his voice.

Reno let his hand brush the handle of his Colt, and he answered in an even voice, "I still say you're a yellow dog, Blanton. Anytime you feel like it, let 'er flicker."

Blanton smiled and said, "I guess you all heard that, didn't you, boys? The lawman says for me to start the ball. But I'm going to show him I'm a gentleman. Reno, you go for your iron. I don't take no favors from anybody."

Blanton placed himself squarely in front of Reı. again there was motion behind him as men scurried t of the line of fire.

Several times in his life, Reno had been in such tight spots that he had simply given up hope. Now he put away anʲ hope of surviving the fight, and put his mind on one thing— getting Blanton. He knew the man was probably the fastest shooter in the West, and although he was a fast man himself with a gun, he knew he had no chance of getting off the first shot. But he had survived Little Round Top and other fights when the odds were overwhelming, so now for the first time in his life he didn't wait for the other man to go for his gun. With practiced speed he dropped his hand to the handle of his Colt.

Then he froze, for Con Blanton had pulled his gun and had it trained right on Reno's chest. A striking snake was slow in comparison to the draw of the gunman. The gun in the small hand of Blanton was steady as a rock, and Reno was caught.

A gasp went up at the draw of Blanton, and every man in the room tensed, waiting for the explosion as the gun fixed itself on Reno's broad chest.

Reno's eyes narrowed as he saw Blanton's trigger finger turning white as it curled around the trigger. There was a ringing in his ears and a tingling in his chest as he waited for death, but his face did not change.

That split second between the draw and the expected explosion expanded, and Neal Burdick shouted, "Shoot! Shoot him down!"

Reno tilted his glance up to look into the face of Blanton, and saw a strange light in the dead eyes of the gunman. He tilted the gun upward so that the muzzle was trained squarely on Reno's face and said in a queer whisper, "Beg!"

stared at him, shook his head and said, "No."

word seemed to fall into the room like a stone into a
nd, sending vibrations through the air. Con's eyes
ed wide, then, and he cocked the gun and said, "All right,
e then!"

He cocked the gun and the click sounded like a rifle shot
in the silence. Then he leveled the gun at arm's length and his
finger tightened on the trigger.

Again there was a frozen moment of time, and again Burdick said in a strangling voice, "Shoot!"

But the gunman slowly lowered the gun. He stared at
Reno, and finally said in a whisper, "He didn't blink! That's
pretty good—he didn't blink!"

Then he laughed softly, and suddenly the gun in his hand
was in the holster at his side.

"Lawman, get out of here!" he said, and when Burdick
sputtered something, he said, "Shut up, Burdick!"

Reno stared at the wild eyes of Blanton and said, "Never
heard of you as a man of charity, Blanton."

The gunman said, "You didn't blink, Reno. That's pretty
good." Then he said, "That law tomorrow?"

"Yes?"

"Don't come down here and try to take my gun, you hear?
If you do, you won't have *time* to blink!"

Reno stared at him, nodded, and said, "I'll be here at
noon, Con."

"No, you won't come, Reno. You know you ain't got a
chance. You're tough, but you got enough sense not to commit
suicide!"

Reno said again, "Noon tomorrow," and turned. He
stopped at the door and said, "Give those guns back." He

waited until Bub and Clarence got their weapons, then all three of them walked outside into the night.

None of them spoke until they got back to the jail, then Bub said, "I let you down, Marshal. Guess you'll want this."

Reno looked down at the badge Bub held toward him. He shook his head and said, "Not your fault, Bub. Put it back on."

Clarence looked at Bub's trembling hands and said, "What about tomorrow, Reno?"

Reno stared at him. "Didn't you hear what I told him?"

"But that was . . . I mean. . . ."

"Jim, we'll get a lot of help," Bub said quickly. "We'll string a line of riflemen across the tops of the buildings. We'll—"

Reno cut him off with a single hard look.

"Sooner or later it always comes to this, kid. We jockey around and try to arrange things, but when that's all done, a man will always find himself under the gun. He's got to stand or run. If he runs, he's worse off than if he dies. That's why tomorrow I'll stand in that street if I die for it. Anything's better than being afraid!"

Clarence said quietly, "Dead is a long time, Jim."

"Running away—why, that's being dead, too, Clarence." Reno stared down at the star on his chest, touched it gently and said, "Funny the things a man will do for a few ounces of tin, isn't it, boys?"

FOURTEEN
Trial by Combat

"We can't just stand by and do nothing! It'll be murder if Reno tries to take that killer's gun!"

Jesse looked up from where he sat in a cane-bottomed rocker on his front porch. Jeff's face was flushed, and there was a wild look in his eyes as he stood on the steps. His habitual air of easy assurance was gone, and he kept turning to watch the crowded street. "Look at that mob! Come out to see the show!"

Although it was only ten in the morning, Rimrock was already crowded; the hitching racks were packed and the saloons were doing a record business for a weekday morning. There was a carnival air about the crowd which sickened Jeff, and he struck the side of the house with his fist and said angrily, "You'd expect this behavior from savages, but I thought we'd gotten a little more civilized than this!"

Jesse looked down and peeled a long, thin shaving from a piece of cedar with a worn pocket knife. He watched it catch in the wind and tumble across the porch and across the yard. "You ain't learned, Jeff, that folks are about the same every-

he peeled another shaving and added, "You're learnin'
ing now that they don't teach in law school."

Jeff stiffened, and there was a defensive tone in his voice
he said, "He doesn't *have* to face up to Con Blanton, Dad."

"Yes, he does." A thin edge of anger touched the older
man's voice. He snapped the knife shut, slipped it in his vest
pocket, then stood up. He was thinner than he had ever been,
and the lines etched in his face were grooved deeper, but no
weakness touched his cobalt blue eyes as he said, "This is
what I been trying to tell you, son, but I know now it ain't something you can tell a man. Sooner or later, after all the law books
are written, and all the legislatures have met, and all the rules
are made up . . ." A thin smile touched Jesse Lindsey's lips,
and there was an ancient wisdom in his face as he concluded
softly, " . . . after all that, a man has got to go out and lay his life
on the line. Otherwise, all the rest of it don't mean a thing."

Jeff stared at his father, understanding that the words
framed the foundation of his life, the bedrock of his faith. It
was this that had kept him wearing a star for miserable pay all
of his life.

Slowly Jeff nodded, his fine eyes filled with a respect and
love for his father. "I . . . I see what you mean, Dad. Guess I'm
a little slow. But it's finally gotten through my thick skull that
somebody's got to pay the price to bring law to people."

Quite a few commendations and even a medal or two had
come to Lindsey, but nothing had ever moved him as much as
the knowledge that his son understood and commended his
life. He dropped his head, seeming to struggle for words, then
said with a slight break in his voice, "I'm right glad you can
say that, son."

The stillness of the moment was broken by the sound of

the screen door banging, but not before Jeff had r~~
and squeezed Jesse's shoulder and seen the happine~
seamed face.

Ada and Rachel came out, neither of them missing t~
transformation in Jesse's face. Stepping beside him, Ada too~
his arm, saying, "What are you going to do?"

"About Reno?"

"Yes."

"Nothing. You know Jim—he wouldn't back down from
the devil himself."

"Sounds like Jesse Lindsey," she said with a faint smile.
Then she bit her lip and nodded toward Dance Street. "You
won't let him go alone. I know that."

"No." Jesse shrugged and said, "It's more than one gunman. The town's on trial today. No matter what happens
between Jim and Blanton, the law says no guns will be worn
inside town."

"There's enough men like Taylor who'll fight," Jeff said
quietly. "I see that now."

"What will you do, Jeff?" Rachel asked, and there was a
sudden intensity in her gaze that struck Jeff like a blow. He
met her eyes, knowing that their future together was in a pre-
carious balance, in some way depending on the answer he
gave. "Why, I guess I'll put most of what I learned behind me,
Rachel. I'm going to go get as many of the town councilmen as
I can to get their guns and back up the law."

"Think any will do it?" Jesse asked.

"Don't know," Jeff said, and the softness of his mouth was
replaced by a tight-lipped smile. "But I'll be there!"

The two men smiled at each other, and Jesse said, "Come
on, son. I'll go with you. We'll give the town fathers a chance to
win some medals."

ʃ walked down the street, Rachel said, "I'm afraid,

ʃe older woman put her arm around the girl, and there
ʃ strength in her that belied her slender frame. "I let fear
ʃeat me out of so many years!" she said softly. Then she faced
ʃachel, and faith like an iron bar rested in her voice as she
added, "It will be all right, Rachel!"

The two men said nothing as they made their way along
the narrow walk, but when they turned down Dance Street and
headed for the bank, Jeff said in a puzzled tone, "Wasn't that
Ed Hoskins? He tried to act like he didn't see us."

"Like I said, Jeff, the town's on trial—only this trial won't
be settled in a courtroom." As he tried to explain it to the younger man his eyes were sweeping the street, cataloging minor
details that could be the difference between life and death.
"Look around you, son, and you'll see some men wearing overalls and some wearing chaps. Before this day's done, one of
those groups will own this town. But the fellows wearing overalls, why, they've been eatin' humble pie so long they're afraid
to be seen even talkin' to us. They want the town safe, but until
the verdict is in, why, they're playin' it safe. Can't blame 'em, I
guess. Look at that."

Jeff looked up to see Neal Burdick standing outside the
Palace, and he was flanked by half a dozen hard-eyed men
lounging around the entrance.

Lindsey stopped and turned to face the saloon man.
"Morning, Neal."

"Marshal." Burdick's face was smooth, but no threat was
necessary, for both men were wise in the ways of the world.

"Quite a crowd," Jesse said softly, running his eyes over
the street. Then he said evenly, "See you at noon," and moved
steadily down the crowded walk.

Burdick watched him go, and there was a frown on h. face. He wheeled and stepped inside the Palace, which was humming with activity. Con Blanton was sitting at a table, rea ing a newspaper, and he looked up as Burdick came to stand over him.

"I see here that Kate McGarrigle's going to be in Abilene next week. You ever hear her sing, Neal?"

Ignoring the question, Burdick said shortly, "I don't like this. You missed your chance yesterday. If you'd done your job, the thing would be all over."

Blanton's pale face did not change. He took a drink from the glass of beer in front of him, then said, "What's the difference, Neal? I been thinking about it, and this way is better. The thing that worried me was the thought that maybe Reno would run. That wouldn't answer, would it?"

"I didn't hire you to run him off, Blanton."

"No, but we don't have to worry, because I know now he won't run," Blanton said gently. "No, sir, he won't run. You get to know men pretty well in my line of work, and I can promise you at twelve noon, Reno will come after me—like a lamb to the slaughter!"

"You should have let him have it when you had the chance!"

"No, this is better," Blanton insisted. "Look around you, Neal. Town is packed with drovers, and they all know about that new law against packing iron. But I'm warning you that you might have some trouble if the town decides to help make that law stick."

"No chance!" Burdick said, shaking his head. "They're afraid they'll lose money if the herds move on to another railhead."

"But there's always a few deputies and some do-gooders
dy to fight for the right, you know? But when I drop Reno,
ow many you think will have the spine to make a fight of it?"

Burdick thought about it, then slowly nodded. "You may
be right, Blanton. I expect old Lindsey will try to back Reno
up. The old fool's lived too long anyway. But if you missed, if
you went down in front of Reno's gun, . . ." Burdick's eyes narrowed and his voice hardened as he said, " . . . *that* could
throw things the other way, put some backbone in the town."

"Come on, Neal!" Blanton had an angry light in his eyes.
"You saw how I put a gun on Reno before he could even clear
leather! He's tough enough—didn't even blink! But he'll be a
dead man in a couple of hours!"

Burdick stood there studying the gunman carefully.
Finally he said, "All right, you get Reno. And if there's other
trouble with the marshal and his deputies, you jump in on that,
too."

"Sure," Blanton agreed carelessly, and went back to his
paper.

Burdick spent the next half-hour with Doucett and Riley,
then went to the bar where the florid Texan John Taylor was
standing. "Hello, John," he said. "You have any trouble on the
drive?"

"Hello, Burdick," Taylor answered. "No trouble this trip.
Just a little brush with some Injuns after we crossed the Red."
He took a pull at his beer and glared at Burdick. "About this
new law—you gonna stand for it?"

"Why, I don't think they'll be dumb enough to try and
make it stick, John," Burdick said easily. He waved his hand
around at the crowded bar. "This is money in their pocket, and
except for a few crusaders, why, nobody wants to change
things."

Taylor's face was red with drink and anger. He w
who could not abide opposition, and he was tough enou
rich enough to have his own way as a rule. "I ain't gonna s
it, Burdick! That lawman pushes too hard. And a Texas mar
don't take pushin'!"

"What'll you do, John?" Burdick asked.

"I done told my boys to give 'im lead if he asks for it! And
Abe Reynolds just come in. You know how he is—just like me!
So I'm kinda hopin' Reno does try to make that law stick! I figure I'll sleep better if we teach that two-bit lawman a few manners!"

Burdick studied the man, then said, "You probably won't
get the chance with Reno."

"Yeah, I heard about him and Blanton—but the same
goes for any other yokel with a tin badge! I don't give up my
gun while I draw breath, and neither does my boys!"

"Way it should be, John," Burdick said with a smile. "Roy,
give John and his men a drink on the house." He walked
slowly to his favorite table, seated himself, and drank steadily
while watching the hands on the big clock over the bar slowly
advance.

Down the street Odell Bracy faced Jesse Lindsey and his
son with a strong streak of antagonism marking his face. He
sat behind his desk, shaking his head stubbornly. "You can't
march in here and tell us it's our responsibility to clean up
Dance Street, Lindsey. That's the job of the man who wears the
star."

"No, it's not," Jeff said at once, his cheeks red with anger.
"We're not talking about *enforcing* the law, Bracy. This thing is
a war, and if we have to deputize every honest man in Rimrock
to win the war, that's what we'll do!"

w, Jeff, let's think about this." R. G. Tyler spoke, and
vas a worldly air in his shrewd eyes. "This is a trail
, Jeff. If the town has the lid clamped on it and if barbed
e ever gets strung, we'll lose the biggest single source of
icome."

"That's right," Ernest Faulkner said. "If we got three
miles of wire today, there'd be thirty by next week, and that's
the end of free graze. I say we do what we've always done."

"Place is dead without Texas money," Bracy said.

Bones Morehouse had said little, but now he asked, "How
many months we got Texas money coming to town? June to
October. Five months. Rest of the time we sit around and
starve for seven months."

"Five good months make up for seven bad ones!" Bracy
said.

"Mebby so, Odell," Bones said slowly. "But I been thinkin'
on it heavy. Your homesteader is here all year. Comes to town
once a week and he buys. Brings his woman and kids."

"Not enough of them," Bracy argued.

"Wasn't once. But you seen that crowd that got off the
train yesterday? There'll be more of 'em today, and more
tomorrow." He stopped and looked around at the group, a
shrewd look on his homely face. "I done something this
mornin'. Made a count of the homesteaders. Checked the
records down in the recording office. You don't see these
people. They pass through then drop out of sight—but there's
five hundred families within twenty miles of Rimrock now."

"That many?" R. G. Tyler asked, openly surprised.

Bracy, never a man to stand opposition, turned red and
began to argue loudly, and Jesse said, "Come on, Jeff. No
sense hanging around here."

As they stepped outside, Jeff shook his head. "I thou_
they'd come around. Guess I've been wrong about just abou_
everything."

Jesse said, "Let's go find Jim. I'm going to try one more
time to get him to back off." He shook his head and laughed.
"Fat chance of that! Well, we'll try to get all the help we can to
back him up. You got any idea where he is?"

"Rachel said he took Lola out for a ride early this morning."

"Yeah—well, he'll be back in time. You can bet on that."

Just at that moment Reno was helping Lola across a
decayed tree that had fallen across the trail. They had tied the
horses and wandered under a canopy of pines down to where
the river dropped twenty feet in five hundred yards. The swift
water had cut through the topsoil into the bones of the earth,
and they stopped beside a massive pine to watch the race of
white water.

Neither of them had said much on the ride. Lola's face
was pale, and when she did speak there was a strained quality
in her speech, as if she were keeping a tight control on herself.

Finally she turned and said, "Jim, you can't go through
with it." When he started to speak, she quickly put her hand
over his lips. "No, listen to me. I know what you're going to
say—you can't let the marshal down, a man has to keep his
word. That's what you'll tell me, but it's not enough!"

Pulling her hand away from his lips, Reno said, "I guess
that's right, Lola. I know it sounds pretty dumb, but it's all I've
got. Lots of things on my record I wish weren't there. But I've
never let a friend down. You wouldn't love me if I did."

"I would! I would!" she cried out and clung to him
fiercely, as if to wrest his decision to her way. "I want you alive,
Jim! What good will it do for you to throw your life away?"

'Have to believe I'll make it," Reno said.

Lola drew back, and the tears ran freely down her cheeks. ...aking her head she said, "You think I don't know how Blanton beat your draw? Everybody knows you don't have a chance, Jim. Nobody will blame you for not facing up to him!"

"Lola, you've been talking a lot to Bishop Sheridan, haven't you?"

Taken off guard, she stood mute, then nodded. "Yes, I have." A look of wonder crossed her face as she said softly, "I never thought I'd be able to change—but with God's help I think I can."

"Sure, you've already changed, Lola. And knowing Sheridan, I'd make a guess that he told you that it wouldn't be an easy life."

"He said that."

"Well, I guess this is your first lesson. My stepdad always said no matter what's over your head, it's all under God's feet!" A sudden smile lighted Reno's face and he took her in his arms. "I think the preachers call it *faith,* don't they? And I guess that's what you and me have got to have."

"But you don't have a chance, Jim!"

"Always a chance in this kind of thing," he said quietly. He leaned forward and kissed her, and again there was the wild response that always ran through both of them when they touched.

She sighed, lay her head against his chest, and said, "I knew it would be this way, but I had to try."

"We better get back." He turned and they started toward the horses, but she paused and drew his head down again.

"Promise me again that it'll be all right, Jim!"

He gave a crooked grin, and with a strange mixture of

happiness and regret said, "I've been talking to the b[...]
some myself. Matter of fact, he stopped by early this m[...]
ing." His grin broadened at a thought, and he said, "He w[...]
me like I was on fire and he had the only bucket of water in[...]
world!"

"What did he say, Jim?"

"Why, he said, 'Reno, you may be dead as Pharaoh in a
few hours. Are you ready to meet God?'"

"And are you, Jim?"

He sobered and said, "I used to be able to say 'Yes' to
that, Lola. But I've gotten off the track somewhere. Not so
sure as I used to be of a lot of things. That's what I told the
bishop. Well, we talked about that a long time, and then I said,
'What if I don't die—and Blanton does?' So we talked about
that. It was the kind of thing we talked about during the war—
you know, is it right to kill the enemy or not."

"And where are you now, Jim?"

"Guess I'm a little confused. But the bishop said I was a
seeker. Said I was on the right trail for finding God."

"I'd be afraid of dying, Jim. Are you?"

"I guess it's like heading down a dark path in the middle
of the night. You can't see what's ahead, so it's naturally
spooky."

"Tell me again that it'll be all right!" she begged.

He stood there quietly for a moment, then he said gently,
"I believe God will take care of us, Lola."

"All right, I'll believe it, too!"

As they rode back toward town, a heaviness settled on
Reno, which he concealed from Lola. He had been by choice a
loner for a long time, and now the promise he had made
seemed to bring a tension which put a strain on his emotions.

...der no illusions about his chances in the fight. He
...d long odds many times, but never had the happiness
...ther rested on him. He had never come close to any-
...g like a normal life, and now the idea that he might never
...are a home with Lola shook him.

As they entered town, the glances of the spectators
brought him back to the harsh realities of sudden death, and
he said to Lola, "Wait for me. I'll come to you as soon as I can."

She dismounted and stood there, and there was gentleness, hope, and faith in her eyes as she said, "I'll be waiting for
you, Jim."

She turned and disappeared into the Nugget, and Reno
wheeled and made his way down the street, his face a mask.

Reno pulled a bundle from beneath his bunk and began to
untie the leather thongs. Throwing the canvas back, he pulled
out a revolver in a worn brown holster. Removing the weapon,
he checked the loads, then fitted the gunbelt to his slim waist.

"Jim! You ain't gonna face Blanton with *that* thing!" Jesse
stood at the door, consternation written on his face. "What in
the world is it?"

Reno flipped the gun out with a flick of his wrist, then
held it up for the marshal to see. "It's a Navy Colt .36, Major."

"A .36! Why, that ain't a heavy enough gun, Jim! You
ought to use that .45 you usually carry."

"Look at the barrel." Reno held it up and said, "Nine
inches long. Friend of mine had it special made. Most accurate
gun I ever saw."

"But this ain't gonna be no shootin' match, Jim," Jesse
said. "That extra long barrel is just gonna slow you down when
you're trying to match Blanton's draw."

Reno pulled a plain brown leather vest out of the bag. H slipped into the vest and fastened its single button. Jesse stared at him and shook his head. "I wouldn't think you'd be worried about high fashion at a time like this, Jim. Or is that your lucky vest?"

Before Reno could answer, the door opened.

"Jim!" Lee stopped just inside the door and tried to say something, but nothing came out. His face was pale and there was a working in his lean throat.

"Go on, Major," Reno said quickly. "I'll be right there."

"All right." Marshal Lindsey gave Reno a piercing look and said, "Son, I have to say how much I admire you, but I think you ought to back off this time. No sense in gettin'—" He looked down suddenly at Lee, stopped, then said as he left the room, "I'll cover your back, Reno."

Reno went to Lee, put his hand on his shoulder and said, "Worried about me, Lee?"

"Jim, please don't go!" Lee said instantly. He reached out and pulled at Reno's arm, his thin face taut with fear. "Even Marshal Lindsey don't think you got a chance!" He choked suddenly and turned his face away from Reno.

Reno looked at the boy and knew there was no way to explain what he felt. "Lee," he said finally, "nothing I'd like better than easing out of this. But if a man backs off from the tough things, what's left?"

"But you ain't got a chance!"

"That's what I thought when we were pinned down at Little Round Top, Lee, but the marshal came and pulled me out of there. Now I owe him one for that, don't I?"

The clock on the wall suddenly struck, and the sound struck Lee like a blow. He cried out and reached blindly for

no, who put his arms out and held him tightly. They stood
here listening to the slow beat of the clock as it counted out
the hours, and when it finally stopped, Reno drew back and
said quietly, "It's OK to cry, Lee. I do it myself sometimes."

Then he pulled himself free and went to the door. "Wait
right here, Lee. I'll be back soon." Then he was gone. Lee
rubbed his eyes with knobby fists, gritted his teeth, and
slipped outside the jail.

The streets, which had been humming all morning, were
now quiet. Only the stamping of the horses at the rails and a
low muttering of voices filled the air. Every window on Dance
Street was crowded with faces, every door outlined with
groups staring out, and a line of men stood with their backs
against the walls of businesses.

Jeff and Marshal Lindsey stood at the side of Jake
Smiley's blacksmith shop along with the two deputies. After
glancing at his watch, the marshal said, "Let's see about it,
boys." He led them down the short section of Grant, turned
left on Race, and headed toward the Palace.

When they got halfway there, Jesse said quietly, "Hold it.
There's Blanton."

The gunman strolled out of the Palace, and it was obvious
that he enjoyed being the center of attention. He walked easily,
and there was a smile on his pale face as he took in the crowd.
Walking with a slight roll to his gait, he moved along toward
where the marshal stood. Glancing up and down the street, he
raised his voice and said, "Twelve o'clock." Then he looked
down at the gun at his side and said with a short laugh, "Guess
I'm a criminal, boys, wearing a gun and all."

A laugh went up from some of the drovers who had come
out of the Palace, and one of them shouted, "Where's that lawman who thinks he's so tough?"

Blanton straightened up, looked up at the window
second floor, and said, "Guess he's busy somewhere else
today." There was a trace of disappointment in his voice, an
he shrugged regretfully, then turned toward the small group
of lawmen who stood waiting. "Up to you, Lindsey. You want to
take my gun?"

"Blanton!"

The sound came from behind him, and the gunman
whirled, his hand hovering over his Colt. He had expected
Reno to enter from the east end of Dance Street, and it shook
him to be taken off guard.

Reno had made his way through the alley that ran parallel
to Dance, until he came to the end. He had stood in the
shadow of an ancient barn until he had seen Blanton step outside the Palace, then he had stepped around the corner plant-
ing himself in the middle of the street. All eyes were fixed on
Blanton, so Reno had not been observed.

"I'll have that gun you're so proud of, Blanton!"

Reno stood at least two hundred feet from Blanton, and
his voice floated on the air with a hollow, ghostly ring. He
stood there as if carved in stone, the long-barreled Navy Colt
still in his holster and his face drawn into angular planes that
threw his dark eyes into relief.

"Reno, you'll never take my gun!" Blanton turned to face
Reno, and the smile he had lost when taken off guard
returned. "I knew you'd try to be a hero. Well, you just came to
your own funeral!"

He started to walk toward the still figure in front of him,
but Reno cried out sharply, "Hold it right there, Blanton! Drop
your gun in the street right now—or else go for it!"

A wave of surprise drove the sneer from Blanton's face.

never draw first—you know that! Now we'll just close

we ain't in the next county from each other."

Blanton took one more step. When he was in mid-stride, no suddenly went into action. He whipped his body around, exposing his right side to Blanton and his right hand dipped for the Navy Colt at his side. As Reno made his move, Con Blanton did what he did best in all the world. Jesse saw the flicker of movement in his right hand, and as Reno's gun was still clearing leather, the gun at Blanton's side leaped out and spoke.

The movement was too fast for the eye, but Jesse saw Reno stagger back and knew he was hit. Blanton's gun roared again, this time driving up a puff of dust three feet in front of Reno. Another shot passed over his head.

A cry went up as Reno was driven back, but he cleared the long-barreled Colt and assumed the classic position of the duel: turned to present the side of his body to his opponent, gun brought up to eye level, and extended at arm's length.

Jesse's agonized thought was: *Jim! This ain't no fancy duel with rules!* But the action was too swift for speech. Even as Reno's arm swept up, Blanton, with only three shots left, suddenly realized that the range was too great. He lunged forward, running toward Reno full speed, and as he ran a shot from the Colt in Reno's hand ploughed up a dust cloud at his feet.

There was a terrible resolve about the way Reno stood there that drove the cool deliberation from Blanton. He loosed another shot that touched Reno's right calf like the sting of a bee. Blanton's eyes were glazed now, and he ran raggedly, cursing and yelling, but he turned suddenly as a bullet raked his side. The slashing pain and the sight of Reno standing there in front of him, his dark face like a destroying demon, brought what he had never known—paralyzing fear that stopped him dead in his tracks.

He stopped, smelling the burning smoke from his own gun, and seeing the arm of Reno falling into place. He stared into the bore of the Colt in Reno's hand, and a mindless scream began in his head that escaped from his lips in a babbling cry. He pulled the trigger on his gun once more, then the white blossom that began at the muzzle of Reno's gun grew larger. It seemed to swell as he screamed, and there was a roaring sound in his head like a terrible blast of thunder which drowned his cries. Then the white blossom enveloped him, and as Reno's bullet struck him squarely in the heart, he threw his arms open in a strange gesture that sent his gun rolling into the dust.

The echo of the guns reverberated faintly down the street. There was a heavy silence as Blanton's body gave one last convulsive twitch that drew his hands halfway up in a grasping motion, and then he assumed that awkward look the dead have.

Reno slowly allowed his arm to drop, then he began to walk down the dusty street. When he came to the body of Blanton he paused, looking long into the staring eyes that were still clear, and then he holstered his gun and made his way toward the knot of men who stood rigidly in place, not able to accept what had happened.

Big John Taylor stood in the center of his crew, and there was a pale cast to his florid cheeks as Reno walked straight up to him.

"Your gun, Taylor!" Reno said, with a wildness in his dark eyes that held the big man motionless.

It might have worked, but one of the hands cursed and

pulled a gun before anyone could move. Reno felt the slug stir the air beside his head. He went for his gun, but a shot suddenly rang out, and the puncher grunted and fell to the walk, squirming and making a low mewling cry.

"Everybody drop their guns!" Jesse Lindsey stepped beside Reno, his gun smoking. For one brief instant it looked as though the drovers were whipped.

Then a voice cried out, "There ain't but two of them!" and a wild cry went up from Big John Taylor. His face went scarlet and he bellowed, "You killed one of my boys! It's the end of the line for both of you! You get your ticket punched right now!"

"Touch that gun and you're a dead man!" Jesse said, and trained his gun on Taylor instantly.

"Texas men know how to die!" the big man said, and he looked at the ranks of men ready to fight if he gave the word. "You boys tell them back home that John Taylor went down fightin'!" Then he turned and said, "Look at the odds, lawmen. You may get me, but my boys here will get you both."

The two men stood there alone, neither of them allowing anything to show in their faces, but it was clear to both of them that Taylor meant just what he said; he would die if that was what it took to get them.

Then, just as Taylor opened his mouth to give the signal, a voice said, "You boys better take a look at your hand before you cut your wolf loose!"

Al Rossiter came to stand beside Reno and Lindsey, and there was a cold smile on his thin lips. He was holding a gun in his thin hand and he swept it around toward his left, then his right. "Read 'em and weep, boys!"

Taylor paused and his eyes swept the street from left to right, and something in his face made Reno risk a glimpse.

A group of men had pulled around in a semicircle, all of them armed with rifles and shotguns. To the left the two deputies Bub and Clarence flanked a line composed of Ernest Faulkner, R. G. Tyler, and Rosy Tucker. On the other side, Jake Smiley, Odell Bracy, Jeff, and Bones Morehouse ranged themselves, and behind them a line of men began to form, all of them with some sort of weapon drawn and cocked. In the center Reno saw the face of Caleb Peeples. He had a heavy Spencer laid right on the group of cowboys, and when he caught Reno's eye, he grinned and said, "Told you if you wanted somethin' did, to let me know, didn't I, now?"

Slowly the small army swelled, fed by men who would never have made the first move, but made bold by the sight of the many guns which flashed in the noonday sun. The people had decided that the no-gun ordinance would stick, and they showed their support by bringing their guns to the aid of the law. All knew that after this showdown there would be no more guns worn in Rimrock.

Taylor looked down the ranks of shotguns and rifles fixed on his men, and something went out of him. He wavered, then swallowed and muttered lamely, "Who needs this two-bit town?" Then he pulled his hat down over his face and shouted, "Let's get out of here, boys!" His crew filed down the walk, keeping their hands carefully away from their guns as they mounted, and Taylor shouted, "You'll never have a Texas herd in this town after I spread the word! Come on!"

He led the way out of town, and then a wild cheer went up from the townsmen as the dust the drovers raised boiled in the street after them.

Lee came from nowhere, and Reno caught him as the boy fell against him.

Jesse turned to him and said, "You got hit, Jim. I saw you take one of Blanton's slugs. We better get Doc Mitchell to take a look at you."

"No need for that, Major," Reno said with a smile. He touched the brown vest, calling attention to a ragged scar, still fresh on the surface. "Won this vest from a bank robber who wore it for his work. Look, it's got this slab of leather an inch thick on each side, tough as iron. It'll turn a bullet, or slow it down so it won't do too much damage."

Jesse grinned, and said, "And you made Blanton fight at long range, 'cause you knew he wasn't used to it."

"Most gunfighters never have a target more than twenty feet away." Reno fingered the scar on his vest and smiled grimly. "Blanton was better than most. If he hadn't panicked, he might have got me."

While the two men were talking, the crowd was milling around, loudly talking after the action. In the confusion, Reno had not seen Lola trying to make her way through the crowd. He turned and began to walk with Jesse down the walk, and the crowd thinned out as they made their way west on Dance Street.

Lola was weeping, joy on her face, but as she broke free and ran toward the two men, a flash of light caught her eye. She glanced up to see a rifle barrel suddenly jut out of a window upstairs over the Palace.

She was almost even with the two men, and she cried out, "Jim!" and threw herself at him just as a shot rang out.

Reno whirled just in time to catch her as she was driven against him by the force of the bullet that struck her high in the back. He caught her with his left arm as he whipped out the Colt and fired the last bullet in the chamber at the window.

There was a piercing cry, and then the window shattered into a thousand fragments as a bulky form shot through it, cartwheeling madly as it fell.

Burdick struck the wooden walk with a terrible crash, but there was an animal vitality in the man. He rolled over, blood streaming from his chest, and with a terrible effort pulled the handgun from his belt. He struggled to raise it, but it was too heavy. He lifted his face toward Reno and tried to speak. Then his eyes rolled upward, and he fell face down and lay utterly still.

Reno heard shouting and there were more shots, but it was as if they were far off, in some distant place. He knelt in the dust of Dance Street and cradled Lola in his arms. A terrible fear shook him as his hand encountered the spreading dampness on her back.

She lay there as he called her name, "Lola! Lola!" and then very slowly her eyes opened. She smiled and raised her hand to touch his cheek. Her lips formed a word, and as he leaned forward to hear, he caught it only faintly.

"Jim—I love you!"

She closed her eyes. Her breast rose once—then she was gone.

People were pulling at him, and someone was telling him that the doctor was on the way, but he shook his head and held on to the dead girl.

Finally, a firm hand gripped his shoulder, and he looked up to see the face of Bishop Sheridan.

"Come along, Jim."

"I can't leave her here, you know that!"

"Bring her, then," the bishop said.

"Bring her home, Jim." Rachel was there, her hand on his arm, and behind her Ada and Jeff.

Jesse Lindsey knelt beside Reno. His face was fixed and there was compassion in his voice as he said, "Let's go, Jim."

Slowly Reno got to his feet, holding Lola in his arms. As he walked toward the house, he was not conscious of the warm sun on his face and of the mockingbird that trilled as they entered the yard.

Rachel opened the door and led the way to a bedroom, and Reno placed the still form on the bed, looking down into her face.

He said, "I promised her it would be all right."

Sheridan said gently, "Jim, I know you can't believe this now, but you will someday. Lola *is* all right. Deep down, you know she had a changed heart."

Reno made no answer, but turned and left the room.

Reno disappeared, and there was some confusion about Lola's funeral.

"We have to wait until he comes back," Rachel said. "He'd want to be there."

Sheridan had answered, "He'll be there."

And when, at ten o'clock the next morning, the cemetery was packed with most of the population of Rimrock, Reno appeared at almost the last minute. He rode up on a gray gelding, his saddlebag and bedroll behind him. He was obviously ready to travel.

He came to stand at the head of the coffin. While the bishop said a few simple words, Reno's face was drawn, his emotions veiled to keep from informing those who watched him about what was going on inside.

Finally the service was over. Reno was pale, and there was a nervous manner in the way he moved that revealed the strain.

"Thanks for all you did for Lola, Bishop," he said in a controlled voice. "I don't think I could stand it if I didn't know you had gotten Lola on the right road."

Then he said good-bye in a tight voice. Avoiding the protests that rose to their lips, he made his way to his horse.

As he started to mount, he was struck in the back by a small body. "Jim! I'm coming with you!"

Reno turned and looked down at Lee. The boy had a bundle in his hand and a battered hat on his head. There was a defiant light in his eyes, and he looked Reno straight in the eye and said, "If you don't carry me, I'll walk! You ain't leavin' me!"

Reno's face had been fixed, and his eyes had been vacant. Nothing of the man they knew had been visible to those who knew him best. Sheridan caught Jesse Lindsey's eye; they both knew Reno was dead inside, buried with that girl.

Now as he looked down at the slight figure, standing so adamantly before him, Reno's lips began to curve. The dull light in his eyes changed to a mild glow, and the rigid stance of his body relaxed.

"What makes you think I'd take you with me, boy?"

"You *got* to do it, that's why!" Lee said stubbornly. "Now, do I walk, or can I ride behind you?"

Reno tipped his hat back and assumed a stern look. "Take you with me? Why, I'd be arrested for kidnapping!"

"No, you wouldn't," Lee shot back, and he grinned as he added, "This in one kid that can't be napped, 'cause there's nobody he belongs to—except you, if you want him."

Reno slowly looked him up and down, then he looked over at Jesse Lindsey, and there was a ghost of the old humor in his dark eyes as he said, "Major, you ever hear what they used to say about the Third Arkansas?"

"Don't think I ever did."

"Used to say . . . ," Reno drawled and reached out to grab Lee and toss him up behind the saddle, " . . . used to say, 'Them boys will do to tie to!'"

Reno swung aboard the horse, looked back at Lee and said, "I guess we'll just have to tie to each other, Lee. Both of us are so ornery we need a keeper!"

He dug his spurs into the horse's flanks and gave a yell as he drove the animal across the cemetery in a wild charge, Lee clinging to his back like a burr.

"The old rebel yell!" Bishop Sheridan said with a smile. "I can remember when that sent me into a bad case of runnin' away!"

"What will happen to them, Sheridan?" Lindsey asked.

"I think they'll make it, Jesse," the bishop said quietly. "Yep, I think that pair will do to tie to!"

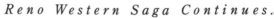

RIDE THE WILD RIVER

One
Runaway

Julie Wade stared at herself in the mirror, scowling at her reflection. Most young women close to seventeen would not have glared so sourly at such an image. Glossy brown hair with reddish highlights fell in an abundant shower down her back, and the face gave promise of more beauty to come. Olive skin, smooth and clear, was set off by a wide mouth with a full lower lip and a dimple in her right cheek. She had a straight nose, even teeth, and good bone structure, but most striking of all were her eyes, which were almond-shaped, gray-green in color, and shaded by long lashes.

As she bit her lip and whirled from the mirror, there was a coltish grace in her movement. She was a tall girl, just short of five-foot-eight, and after being teased about it she had retreated into a boyish behavior. She was just emerging from the awkward stage of youth into rounded womanhood and was confused by the changes it brought. If her mother had lived, she would have made the transition smoothly, but she had died of cholera fifteen months earlier. Thus, Julie had been isolated on the farm at the most critical time of her life.

An understanding father would have made the difference, but her own father had died when she was thirteen, and Jake Skinner, her stepfather, brought nothing but fear and loathing to her.

Even now she hurried downstairs, hoping to get into the buggy without an encounter with him, but she stopped short at the foot of the stairs, her lips suddenly tight as she saw him standing in the door waiting for her.

Jake Skinner had been attractive enough to capture the heart of Helen Wade only six months after the death of Julie's father. There had been a flashiness in his swarthy features, and there had been a gallant quality in the way he courted the widow, who was twenty years his senior. He had plenty of money, or so it seemed, but it was the end of the world for Julie when he swept her mother off her feet.

"Well, aren't you the little beauty now!"

Skinner had put on weight, the easy life and rich food padding his waist. His neck had thickened, and his bold eyes were now fixed on Julie in a way that had begun to make her feel odd.

"I'll have me the prettiest girl at the ball," he said, and stepping forward he put his thick hand on her bare shoulder. "We'll have us a time, won't we, Julie?"

The weight of his hand on her flesh was revolting to her, and there was something in his loose-lipped expression and the hungry light in his eyes that made her pull away abruptly. "I'm ready to go," she said shortly. Skinner had never paid the slightest attention to her while her mother was alive, but for the last few months she had felt his eyes following her, and there was an attempt at intimacy in his speech. And the clumsy caresses he passed off as being fatherly affection had gone beyond that.

She tried to squeeze by him, but he moved so slightly from the opening that their bodies touched, and he quickly put his heavy arms around her. When she raised her head to protest, he suddenly kissed her, ignoring her efforts to pull free.

When she managed to free herself, her heart was beating furio
Her voice quivered with rage and fear as she said, "Don't—don't do
that!"

He laughed, throwing his head back, then taking her arm he said
with a smirk on his full lips, "You'll get used to it, Julie. I been watching you." He kept a firm grip on her arm, and as he helped her into
the buggy he added, "You're a woman now, not a kid. We'll talk about
it."

The trip from the farm to Fort Smith took four hours, and although
Julie pressed herself against the outer edge of the seat, Skinner
sprawled loosely, letting his leg rest against hers. There was something so suggestive in his manner that it was with real relief that Julie
got out of the buggy in front of the town hall in the center of Fort
Smith. The town itself was a dusty jumble of unpaved streets and low
wooden buildings. It was perched on the border of the Indian Nations.
Some of the worst outlaws in the world used it as a convenient source
of information and supplies, disappearing into the trackless plains and
mountains of the Nations when the law breathed too heavily on them.

A new pavilion had been erected. Raw lumber reeking of pine sap
formed the structure, and the elite of Fort Smith had come to cele-
brate with a ball. It was dark enough for the myriad lanterns to be lit
as Julie saw her best friend, Lorene Dickerson. "I'll be around to get
the first dance, Julie!" her stepfather said with a broad grin, then left
to put up the buggy.

"Julie! You look so pretty!" Lorene said as she hurried up to hug
her. She was a short, plump girl, two years older than Julie. Her father
was a local lawyer, and Lorene knew much more about Julie than
most. "Did you make that dress?" Julie allowed herself to breathe
freely. She was going to spend the night with Lorene, and she refused
to think about the trip home.

The two girls went inside the large hall and spent an hour getting
caught up on things. Julie kept glancing nervously toward the door,

ding to see her stepfather. "I don't want to dance, Lorene. I'm just
ng to watch."

"Why, you can't do that, Julie! There are so many new men here!"

When Julie remained steadfast, Lorene said, "Well, all right—oh,
I almost forgot, Julie, there's someone here you must meet."

"I don't really want to, Lorene," Julie protested, but she was pulled
into a large room containing a series of tables with bowls of punch
and some fancy foods.

"Oh, Mr. Stevens, here she is!" Lorene said, and she pushed Julie
in front of a tall man, adding, "I'm going to the dance, Julie. Meet you
there later."

Julie was nonplussed as the tall man smiled down at her. He had a
sunburned face and mild blue eyes. "You don't remember me, do you,
Julie?"

"No, I—I don't think so," she faltered. He looked vaguely familiar,
but she could not place him.

"Be strange if you did," he said. "Last time I saw you, you were two
years old. "I'm your cousin, Julie. You probably heard your mother
mention me—Thad Stevens."

"Oh! Your picture is in the album," Julie said, and she smiled up at
him.

"Stacy, come here a minute," Stevens called, and a pretty woman
with blonde hair and gray eyes came to stand beside him. "This is my
wife, and this is my cousin I told you about, Julie Wade."

"Hello, Julie," Mrs. Stevens said, and she put out her hand with an
easy gesture. "I'm glad to meet some of Thad's family."

"Well, not much family left for you to meet," Thad said ruefully.
"Julie's mother, my aunt, was about all the kin I had left. I didn't know
she'd passed away until I got here, Julie."

He was not a handsome man, but there was a warmth in his manner, and he seemed genuinely interested in his cousin. His wife got
them all seated and skillfully put the shy girl at ease.

Without realizing it, Julie let slip the misery of her circumst...
and she did not see the quick nods exchanged by the couple wh...
she looked out at the crowd. It was obvious to them that the girl w...
lonely and afraid.

"We'll only be in Fort Smith for a couple of days," Stevens said,
"but maybe we can have some good visits before we leave."

"That would be nice," Julie said, then she asked suddenly, "Mr. Stevens, your picture in the album . . ."

"Yes?"

"There's a man with you in it. Who is he?"

Stevens grinned and said, "Has to be Jim Reno, my half brother.
We had it made in Texas and sent a copy of it to your mother." He
laughed and added, "You ought to see that picture, Stacy! We were
both young punks, but we thought we could whip the army! Got all
dressed up as close as we could to what we thought Wild Bill Hickok
might wear, two six-guns apiece, furry chaps, and a mean look." He
laughed in delight at the thought. "We were really young and full of
beans!"

"I thought you looked very nice," Julie protested.

"I'd like to see the picture, Julie," Stacy said.

"Don't you give it to her!" Thad said with a mock frown. "That son-of-a-gun Jim nearly stole her from me! I'm still jealous of that cuss!"

"Really?" Julie asked.

"He's quite an attractive man, Julie," Stacy said.

"Some would say he's better-looking than me," Thad said with a
grin.

"Those with eyes," Stacy commented with a barbed wit.

"Where is he now?" Julie asked.

"Well, he was a peace officer in Kansas last year. Had some sort of
personal trouble. Jim would never talk much about his troubles. But I
got a letter from him just before we left—last week, wasn't it, Stacy?
He said he was headed for California." He turned to his wife and

d his fingers. "He said he'd be at Independence, Missouri, if I
ed to write him. I've got to do that tomorrow!"

He would have said more, but he broke off, for he had seen the
girl stiffen and her face grow tense. A heavy man with a swarthy
face came over and said, "Dancin' is about to commence, Julie.
Come on."

"I don't want to," Julie began, but the big man took her firmly by
the arm and pulled her off without a word to the Stevenses.

"That girl has problems, Thad," Stacy said quietly. "I was talking to
Lorene earlier, and from what I understand, Julie's stepfather is lower
than a snake. Took the mother for everything she had and broke her
heart. Now he's got designs on the daughter."

"Why, that's—that's obscene!" Thad sputtered. "He can't get by
with that!"

"Why not?" Stacy asked, and the fire in her eyes belied her even
tone. "Lorene said that Skinner made Julie's mother sign all the property over to him, but Julie's name is still on the paper. Lorene thinks
that he'll force her to sign the papers over to him—or he'll make her
marry him to get control of the place."

Thad said at once, "I'll look into it."

"You know how these things are, Thad. You start interfering into
family matters and you can get shot for it."

Stevens said grimly, "I *am* her family, Stacy. I'll see what can be
done."

"We're leaving day after tomorrow. What can you do in two days?"

Frustration scored the cheeks of Stevens, and he shook his head.
"I ought to do *something.*"

He did try, but when he and Stacy saw Julie the following day,
there was nothing to say to her except good-bye. They left for home
feeling that they had seen the beginning of a tragedy, but they were
powerless to do anything.

Julie tried to get her stepfather to allow her to stay with Lorene for a longer visit, but he ignored her request, and on the second day their return, what Julie feared most happened.

She was turning down the covers on her bed when a heavy knoc sounded. Fear gripped her at once, and she said, "What is it?"

"Open the door!"

"I'm—I'm ready to go to bed," she faltered. Jake had been drinking steadily, and at the evening meal there had been a strange expression on his heavy face that frightened her.

He struck the door hard and said, "Open the door or I'll break it down! You hear me, Julie?"

She looked around for some escape, then, finding none, she turned the key and stepped back as he entered. His face was flushed, and he advanced toward her with burning eyes.

"Time we understood each other," he said thickly. She could smell the liquor on his breath, and she retreated until she felt the wall at her back. He laughed at her, a coarse sound that raked at her nerves. "I been purty patient with you, Julie, waitin' for you to grow up. But I'm tired of waitin'!"

"What—what do you mean?"

Skinner put his hands out, took her by the shoulders, and pulled her to him. He was a powerful brute, and she was as helpless in his grasp as a bird. "Aw, you ain't all *that* innocent," he said, grinning. "You've grown up to be a good-lookin' woman, Julie, and you need a man."

"No—please, let me go!" she pleaded, but he only pulled her closer.

"Shore, that's what you need—and I'm the man for you. Like I say, I've been patient for a long spell, but now it's time for a little action." He ran his eyes down her slim body encased in the light robe and licked his lips, adding, "Why, ain't no need to be trembling, girl! I'm talking marriage to you."

"Marriage!" She couldn't believe it! "But you're my stepfather!"

"No kin at all," he said. "I guess you don't maybe love me now, but I've got ways of making women care for me. I ain't had no complaints!"

h all her strength she jerked herself loose, and her eyes were
with fear and anger as she said, "You get out of here! You leave
alone!"

He threw his head back and laughed. "Go on, I like a lot of spunk
in a woman—more you fight, the better I like it!"

"I'll never marry you, Jake Skinner!" she cried out. "I'll run away!"

"Go on," he said, and his grin didn't change. "You're in my charge
till you're eighteen. Reckon I can have you brought back just as often
as you run off." Then he stopped laughing and said in a voice totally
devoid of mercy, "I'll have you, Julie, get that straight. You can't leave
this place, and I'm your pa in the sight of the law. You can't get away,
and I'm tellin' you flat, you might as well get used to the idea of having me for a husband!"

Then he smiled again and said, "Oh, I won't bother you none
tonight. But you better get your mind made up. We'll be married in a
month."

He laughed at her pale face and left the room, slamming the door
behind him.

Trembling and weak, Julie collapsed on the bed, biting her lip to
keep back the tears. For over an hour she lay there, her mind flutter-
ing like a wounded bird in a cage, but could think of no escape. She
knew that Skinner would do as he said, and she realized as well that
her chances of getting help, legally or otherwise, were nonexistent.
Skinner was a violent man, generally feared for his fits of rage. She
knew that wives—and daughters—had little recourse against the will
of a husband.

She lay so long on the bed, her mind racked with confused
thoughts, that the oil in her lamp burned down, and finally she got up
to refill it. Then she sat down and her hand fell on the worn Bible that
her mother had used for many years. Aimlessly she opened it. The
pages were thin as tissue from endless reading, and when she let it
drop open on her desk, she noticed a verse was underlined—by her

mother, she knew at once. A thin, spidery line of black ink
these words:

"Get thee out of thy country, and from thy kindred, and from
father's house, unto a land that I will show thee."

Julie had given little thought to religion and had read little of the
Bible. As she sat there, however, in a silence so intense that the loud-
est sound was the guttering out of the lamp, she was filled with a sudden purpose. Her jaw set firmly, and she nodded to herself. Blowing
out the lamp, she went to bed, but she did not sleep, for her mind was
putting together a plan. Just as dawn cast a red glow through her window, she said softly, "God, I don't know how to pray like Mama did.
I've never paid you much attention. All I can do now is ask you—get
me out of this mess I'm in!"

She let her stepfather get out of the house before she went downstairs, then she saddled her mare and rode across the freshly plowed
fields, taking a winding course toward the north. In less than an hour
she dismounted in front of a two-room log cabin and called out, "Jackson! Leah! You up yet?"

The door opened and a small black man came out with a wide grin
on his thin face. "Miz Julie! Whut in de world you doin' here so early?"
He came over and took the reins from her hands, and after tying the
horse to a post of the porch he said, "Come on in. Leah fixin' breakfast."

He was very thin and stooped, but he hopped about like a cricket
as he hustled before her, speaking to the large woman cooking at a
stone hearth. "Leah, here's Miz Julie. Put some mo' aigs in dat pan!"

Leah was clearly a mulatto, her yellow skin much lighter than Jackson's. She was larger than the man as well, and she looked sharply at
the girl who sat down in one of the two cane-bottomed chairs in the
cabin. "Whut's the matter, honey?" she asked at once. She pulled the
frying pan out of the glowing coals and came to take Julie's chin in
one hand, forcing the girl to lift her head.

Jackson and Leah had been slaves of Julie's father. After the war,

en them land, and they had worked it, but had also done
the work around the home place. Their loyalty to the family
en deep, and it had been a source of deep grief to them both
n Julie's mother had married Skinner.

They had practically raised Julie, and now they exchanged troubled glances over the girl's head, and Leah asked again, "Whut's the
trouble, Julie?"

Slowly Julie looked up at Leah, then at Jackson, and she said
slowly, "I've got to run away."

"Run away!" Jackson said in stunned wonder. "Whut fo' you hafter
do a thing like dat?"

"Skinner is after me." She saw Leah nod, and her mouth went tight.

"I seed it comin'," Leah said heavily. "He a bad man."

Jackson looked at Julie, then at Leah. His voice trembled when he
finally spoke. "White trash! I cut his gizzard out!"

"Hesh up, Jackson," Leah said. "You ain't gonna do no sech fool
thing."

"Will you help me?" Julie asked. "I can't trust anybody else."

"How you gonna do it?" Leah asked. "He gonna find you if you run
off."

"I'll have to fool him, Leah. There's one thing he doesn't know—
I've got some money." She took a heavy bag out of her pocket and
held it up. "It's gold pieces my daddy saved. Mama kept them and
gave them to me before she died. She told me not to let Jake know
about it."

"Pore leetle thing!" Leah clucked mournfully. "She grieved herself
to death 'cause she married that man. And she seen whut he wuz
afore they'd been married a week!"

"How you gonna get away, Miz Julie?" Jackson asked.

"I've got to get a long way off," Julie said. "If I just go east to the
next state, he'll find me. I've got to go west." She held up the bag and
said, "This is enough to get to California—and that's where I'm going!"

"Lawd!" Jackson breathed quietly. "You can't go way out to dat pr

"Be hard, child," Leah said with a nod.

"I know it will, but I'm going. Will you help me?"

Leah and Jackson exchanged glances and they seemed to read one another's mind. "You don't think I'se gwine to let my baby go all dat way without me, does you?"

"But—"

Jackson patted her head. "We done already decided to leave dis place, Miz Julie. It ain't lak it used to be when yo' daddy was here."

"We wuz goin' to Louisiana," Leah added. "But now we gwine to California!"

Julie tried to protest, but not very hard. The thought of making her way to the coast alone had frightened her, but with Jackson and Leah it seemed possible.

Finally they convinced her that they actually wanted to go, mostly by saying that they'd heard that the color of a person's skin didn't matter so much out there. Then she said eagerly, "All right, here's what we'll do. You sell this place as soon as you can, and let it out that you're going to move to Louisiana. Then you leave—but you go to Fayetteville."

"Why we go there?" Jackson asked.

"Because I've got a friend there, and I'm going to pretend to go see her. When I get there, you be ready. You get on that coach and we just keep right on going all the way."

"All the way to California?" Leah asked doubtfully.

"No—but all the way to Independence, Missouri. That's where all the wagon trains going to California leave from. We'll buy a wagon and join a wagon train."

By the time Julie had left the cabin and ridden back to the home place, she knew exactly what she must do.

The most difficult thing was waiting for Jackson and Leah to sell their place and leave, but that went faster than any of them had

ected. Skinner was always anxious to buy land adjoining the planta-
n, and he jumped at the chance, giving cash money to be sure the
ld people didn't back out.

He gloated to Julie after the papers were signed, "I been waitin' for
a chance to get that property for a long time! Now I got it!"

"You did real fine, Jake," Julie said. She had forced herself to
endure his heavy-handed caresses, even to appear to welcome them.
A less callous man would have seen through her in an instant, but the
colossal vanity of Skinner blinded him.

Now that Jackson and Leah were on their way, Julie drew her
breath and said, "I—I've been thinking about what you said, Jake—
about getting married."

"Yeah?"

"Well, I was a little bit scared when you first came at me."

"Sure," he said soothingly. "Natural thing for a girl. But you feel different now, don't you?"

"I—I *think* so Jake." Julie tried to look shy and added, "I'm almost
sure about it. The only thing is . . ."

"Yeah?"

"Well, I'd really like to talk to my friend, Martha Dutton, you know,
the girl from Fayetteville who visited here last summer. We were best
friends until her family moved away. I'd like to go see her and talk,
you know? A girl needs to find out some things about marriage."

"Reckon I can teach you all you need to know." He grinned, and
she forced herself to endure a kiss.

"Yes, but I'll need help with my dress and my clothes and all.
Please, Jake," she said softly, and moved closer to him. "Just this one
little thing—please!"

He stood there plainly torn by the need for a decision, then finally
he asked, "How long you plan to stay?"

Julie's heart lurched, and she said with a smile, "Oh, just a little
while, whatever you say, Jake."

"A week be enough?"

"Oh, that's fine!"

"All right, I'll get you a ticket on Tuesday's stage."

Time crawled by for Julie, and she expected Skinner to call the trip off at any minute, but finally she was in the stage, looking down at him as he stood in the street.

"You got your return ticket, Julie?" he asked.

"Right here. I'll be back next Friday." She made herself smile and throw him a kiss. "It won't be too long—and then we'll be together!"

The stage lurched at the command of the driver, and she fell back against the seat, weak with tension.

The trip to Fayetteville took two days. The coach stopped at one roach-infested station for the night, but the next day she sighed with relief as Leah and Jackson appeared in the crowd at the stage station in Fayetteville.

As the stage rolled on northward toward Missouri, Leah leaned forward and said "Chile, we's got a long ways to go. I hope you is prayed up!"

Julie laughed, but there was a thread of seriousness in her voice as she answered, "I hope so too, Leah. I have the feeling we're going to need all the help we can get!"

Books in the Reno Western Saga

From Gilbert Morris, the author of the Reno Western Saga and the House of Winslow series, comes a new Civil War series. . . .

The Appomattox Saga

Gilbert Morris is the author of many best-selling books, including the popular House of Winslow series and the Reno Western Saga.

He spent ten years as a pastor before becoming professor of English at Ouachita Baptist University in Arkansas and earning a Ph.D. at the University of Arkansas. Morris has had more than twenty-five scholarly articles and two hundred poems published. Currently, he is writing full-time.

His family includes three grown children, and he and his wife live in Baton Rouge, Louisiana.